Carey Brock

Charity Helstone

A Tale

SALZWASSER VERLAG

Carey Brock

Charity Helstone

A Tale

Reprint of the original, first published in 1865.

1st Edition 2022 | ISBN: 978-3-75258-797-5

Verlag (Publisher): Salzwasser Verlag GmbH, Zeilweg 44, 60439 Frankfurt, Deutschland
Vertretungsberechtigt (Authorized to represent): E. Roepke, Zeilweg 44, 60439 Frankfurt, Deutschland
Druck (Print): Books on Demand GmbH, In de Tarpen 42, 22848 Norderstedt, Deutschland

CHARITY HELSTONE.

A Tale.

BY

MRS. CAREY BROCK,

LONDON. MDCCCLXV.

CHARITY HELSTONE.

CHAPTER I.

A STRANGE child was Charity Helstone, and somewhat a strange lady was Charity's godmother, who had had not a little to do with the early training and discipline of Charity's charaster. Not that Mrs. Dorothy Helstone, or, as she was generally called, 'Aunt Dorothy,' had ever endeavoured to train or discipline her strange little godchild. No! 'Aunt Dorothy' was one of those characters who never seem to attempt to do anything, yet who, by some happy chance or other, are perpetually succeeding in accomplishing things, which, attempted by any one else, would probably have proved signal failures.

A certain well-known miller in the village, who was about the most intelligent man in it, but, unfortunately, somewhat 'free' as he called it, both in his religious opinions and in his style of life, and, consequently, an object of very great solicitude to his clergyman, had actually given up his 'free opinions' and his evil habits for ever, and become one of the most regular attendants at church, and one of the most steady men in the neighbourhood, since Mrs. Dorothy Helstone had entered into friendship with him. No one knew how Mrs. Dorothy had set about the reformation. When he was questioned on the subject, he said he did not know himself. When she was questioned, she said precisely the same thing. All she had to tell about it was that, 'somehow, it went against her very heart to see any one breaking God's law like that, and so she told him.' And all he could tell was that, 'somehow, Mrs. Dorothy Helstone, she comed down to his cottage, and . . . well . . . she was that persuading in her talk, she won him over.'

And many another besides the miller had very much the same story to tell about Mrs. Dorothy. Young girls, who seemed careless of all besides their bonnets and their faces, had laid aside their follies and taken up their Bibles at Aunt Dorothy's entreaty. Young men, who turned a deaf ear to their Rector's warnings or their employers' threats, had been coaxed from the ale-house and drawn to the church by Aunt Dorothy's persuasions. And little children, whom the parish schoolmaster had declared past all bearing and beyond all mending, had, somehow or other, learned, under Aunt Dorothy's influence, to sit quietly on their stools, refrain from mischief, and apply their eyes and their understandings to their books and samplers.

That Mrs. Dorothy Helstone was a rich and rare blessing to the parish in which, for the last five-and-twenty years, she had been living, was an acknowledged fact. She herself seemed the person least aware of it; and yet, she herself sometimes allowed that it was so. When any one spoke to her of those over whom she had exercised such a strange and blessed influence, she would bend her head and say, 'The Lord be praised! It is all His doing. To Him be all the glory!' When any one asked her how it was that she always seemed to succeed where others failed, she always had the same answer. 'That's just what I don't understand,' she would say: 'I don't mean that I can't understand why I should succeed, for that seems to me quite natural. If I want a blessing, I ask for it, and I have it. It's the Lord's promise that it should be so, and I always find that He keeps His word. It seems to me, that if others don't get what they want, it's because they don't ask, or else, as the Bible says, "they ask amiss." But for my part, the experience of my life has all gone to prove that those who ask obtain; and it's a blessed experience—a very blessed experience. My life has been a happy one—thank God, a very happy one.'

Many in the village had heard Aunt Dorothy speak thus of her own experience and her own life; but no one had ever heard her say more than this concerning her past life. Where it had been spent, or in what its happiness had consisted, was unknown to all. Aunt Dorothy was a middle-aged lady when first she came to live in the village of Arlington, and that was five-and-twenty years ago. There were deep lines in her face then, and they were all wrinkles now. There was a firm, compressed look about the benevolent mouth, which told the thoughtful observer that it had not spent all its strength in smiling, though it was so skilful at that art. There was a grave, fixed expression in the deep-set eyes, which told tales of tears that had never been seen. There was a slight nervous tremor in the quiet voice, a peculiar manner of folding the hands together, which all betokened that Aunt Dorothy's life had not always flowed in the same quiet stream in which it had gone since she came first to Arlington.

Few remembered her first coming. To most of the inhabitants of the place it seemed as if Aunt Dorothy had always lived amongst them, and always been very much what she was now. But amongst the few who remembered her first coming was the Rector of the parish, and well did he also remember the words she had said to him on the very first evening he had called upon her. 'My life has been a very sad one,' she said, quietly; 'so sad, that I can never now speak of its trials without necessity. But I can thank God for every one of them. And my life is not yet over. God has work for me to do, I know; and I feel that He has been preparing me for it. I have come to settle here, because this place is full to me of early association, and early association gives strength and vigour to the shattered nerves; so does distance from the scenes in which we have suffered; and so, still more, does *work*—work for God: for all other work, to those who have drunk deeply of life's sorrowful cup, all other work is weariness of both spirit and flesh. If you will give me work to do for God, I will seek in His strength to do it.' These had been Mrs. Dorothy Helstone's words to the Rector on that first evening of their acquaintance, and during the five-and-twenty years which that acquaintance had now lasted, the whole of Mrs. Dorothy's life had been in accordance with them. At first the Rector supplied her with work, but for a very long time now work had seemed to supply itself. Mrs. Dorothy had grown to be as well-known a person as the Rector himself. He himself would call her his curate, whilst his good wife often thanked the special Providence which had sent a friend like Mrs. Dorothy into the village, to do all the work there which her own kind heart would have led her to do herself, had not the charge of eight little children in her own home rendered it impossible for her to be very active out of it.

It was to these eight little children that Mrs. Dorothy owed her title of 'Aunt Dorothy.' The Rector's children had been the first to bestow it upon her, and truly no veritable aunt could have better deserved the title at their hands. If their books were shabby and mamma had no time to mend them, they carried them up to the Ivy Cottage, and brought them home all neatly stitched and covered with nice brown calico by Aunt Dorothy's skilful fingers. If any amongst them were ill, and Aunt Dorothy came down to the Rectory and found the over-worked mother pale and worn with a disturbed night, the result would surely be that next night, when the little voice asked for water, it was Aunt Dorothy's hand that supplied it; whilst a kind voice told them that they must try and be patient, and not cry or disturb their dear mamma, who was sleeping in the next room. Wherever help was wanted, there was Aunt Dorothy; night or day, no one was ever afraid to knock at her cottage-door and solicit aid, be the person who knocked who they might, or the hour midday or midnight.

Doubtless it was to this fact that Aunt Dorothy owed the possession of her strange little godchild, Charity Helstone. For seven years ago, in the darkest hour of one of the darkest nights that the month of January could show, a loud knocking had been heard at Aunt Dorothy's door. Old Betsy, the one servant who had come to Arlington with Mrs. Dorothy, and had lived with her ever since, had been the first to hear it, and starting up, had thrown open the window and inquired 'who in the world was knocking there at that unearthly hour?'

To Betsy's surprise, the voice that answered was a familiar one, and no more formidable an one than that of good Mistress Bryce, who kept the village inn just round the corner: the nearest house it was, indeed, to Aunt Dorothy's cottage.

'It's I, Betsy,' was the answer. 'I, Martha

Bryce; and you must come up to my house quick as you can get your clothes on, for I believe there 's a young woman dying there: and though I 've sent for the doctor, it will be ever such a time before he can be down, and there 's no one in the house but Bryce and me and Hester, and we want help, if ever creatures did. So come as quick as you can, and let your good mistress come along with you. For, as my husband said, "Get Mrs. Dorothy, get Mrs. Dorothy; she 's a host in herself, and she 'll be sick-nurse, and doctor, and parson all in one."'

Now old Betsy was one of those people who are never known to be quiet except when other people would be in a fuss. Morning, noon, and night, old Betsy was always in a fuss, and a decided annoyance this was to her quiet mistress; but let something happen which would put most people into a fever, and Betsy was as composed as possible. Thus it was now. When Mrs. Bryce's sharp knocking first roused her she started up, and on hearing it repeated so rapidly she felt at once something serious was the matter, and opened her window with as composed a manner as though such nightly disturbances were the most usual occurrences in the world.

'I 'll come at once,' she said, on hearing what was wanted of her; 'but I 'll not disturb my mistress. She was up nearly all last night with the baby at the Rectory, and she 'll sleep in her bed this blessed night, as sure as my name 's Betsy; and don't you be routing her out of it by any more noise.'

And thus saying, old Betsy shut down the

window, and began to hurry on her clothes, saying to herself, as she did so—for talking to herself was one of Betsy's pet peculiarities—'I dare say the woman's no more dying than I am; these people always cry wolf before they're hurt: and as for my mistress, I believe they think her public property—something that belongs to the parish, and that they have a right to wake her up out of her sleep, or call her off from her meals, whenever they've a mind to do so. It's a good thing for her, God bless her! that she's got old Betsy to look after her, or I do believe there wouldn't be a bit of flesh left on her bones. But I'm not going to wake her out of her sleep to-night—anyhow, not till I see for myself whether there's any need to do so. The house is not so far off but that she can be fetched quickly enough if she's wanted.'

And thus saying, Betsy opened her bedroom door; and was preparing to descend the stairs very slowly and noiselessly, when, to her great annoyance, another door was opened opposite to hers, and another figure prepared to do the same. A very different figure from her own. The villagers used to say sometimes, that never was there a greater contrast than Mrs. Dorothy Helstone and her maid Betsy. And they said rightly. Not only were they different in appearance, for Mrs. Dorothy was tall and dignified in figure, with a calm, placid face, and deep-set, earnest blue eyes; but they were yet more different in manner. For if Betsy was never known to be still, Mrs. Dorothy never seemed to be agitated.

Her step was always soft, her voice always low. The only signs of outward agitation, even the watchful eye of her good friend the Rector had ever observed in her, were an occasional heightening of the colour in her pale cheeks, and a nervous movement of the hands, which she had a peculiar way of crossing on her lap, especially when deeply interested in anything. But these were trifling indications indeed, and passed, for the most part, unobserved. Most of the people who knew her would have declared that, happen what might, Mrs. Dorothy was always the same; ready to enter into all that was going on around her, with the same kindness of heart, willingness of hand, and reality of interest, but herself seeming as though nothing had power either to depress or exhilarate her.

Betsy, on seeing her mistress, began a string of regretful and reproachful exclamations, which Mrs. Dorothy cut short by warning her that there was no time, perhaps, to lose; and herself unfastening the front-door, and passing out into the dark street. A few minutes' walk, during which Betsy never ceased speaking, and her mistress did not utter one word, brought them to Bryce's house. Bryce was standing at the door himself, with a face that silenced even Betsy's tongue. He did not speak either, but pointed with his hand to the door at the top of the stairs, and Mrs. Dorothy and Betsy obeyed the signal.

Mrs. Dorothy expected, from the man's manner, to meet death within; but on opening the door, her eyes fell on a living face, yet with an unmistakeable look upon it that told her at once life would hold but short possession there. A very young woman lay evidently dying, and apparently unconscious, whilst good Mrs. Bryce stood beside the bed, wiping from the pale forehead the cold perspiration that was rapidly gathering there. At a little distance stood Hester Bryce, the innkeeper's only daughter, and in her arms a little new-born baby. No one spoke; but Mrs. Bryce turned her eyes from the dying woman to Mrs. Dorothy, as much as to say, that it was too late to think of doing anything now. 'She's just passing,' she said; and at the word Mrs. Dorothy drew near the bed, and kneeling down she prayed aloud, in a low, yet distinct voice.

Whether the woman had been conscious before, but had not cared to speak, or whether it was only now that she regained consciousness, they never knew; but as Mrs. Dorothy prayed, she turned her eyes, which from being now set in a face from which almost all the flesh and every shade of colour had departed, looked unearthly in their largeness, full on Mrs. Dorothy's face; and it was evident from the expression in them that she was perfectly sensible. Mrs. Dorothy rose from her knees and stood by the bedside. The young woman never took her eyes off her. Mrs. Dorothy spoke in a low voice, asked her if she knew how ill she was; if her mind was at at peace. There was no answer.

'Bring the baby, Hester,' said Mrs. Bryce; 'that may rouse her. She has never spoken since its birth,' she said, turning to Mrs. Dorothy; 'she just seemed passing away without care or thought of anything.' Mrs. Dorothy took the little thing, and laid it gently by the mother's side, and then the large eyes were removed from Mrs. Dorothy's face and fixed upon the child. But the expression in them changed, and was troubled, melancholy, instead of, as it had been, piteous and appealing.

'What is it?' she asked; 'a boy?'

'No,' said Mrs. Bryce, 'it's a little girl.'

'Thank God!' she said: 'oh, thank God!'

No one dared ask why; and even Mrs. Dorothy was doubtful what to say or do, when the poor woman again turned her eyes to her and said, 'Pray! pray again!' And Mrs. Dorothy prayed a few earnest words, that 'unfeigned repentance might be given for all the errors of a past life, with steadfast faith in the Lord Jesus, so that all sins might be done away by God's mercy, and pardon sealed in heaven.'

The eyes brightened whilst this prayer was being offered, and when Mrs. Dorothy again paused the woman said, with heightened colour, and a degree of strength and excitement in the voice which made them doubtful whether consciousness was not again leaving her,—

'Thank you, thank you! I like that prayer. They read it over my mother—my poor, poor mother! I never forgot it. I've looked it out in the Prayer-book since, and read about repenting of errors past, and getting a pardon. It's a long while since I've been to church; but I haven't lost my Bible nor my Prayer-book. They're safely at home, now. But when shall I be there again? And the baby! ah! let the baby have the books—the Bible and the Prayer-book.'

Then, with brightened colour and an eager voice, she fixed her eyes full on Mrs. Dorothy, and said, 'The Prayer-book has got the mark still at the Marriage Service. I know that service by heart. You'll find a line marked under that sentence, "Those whom God hath joined together let not man put asunder." Let the baby have the book. I knew I should die when this time should come. You'll find the sentence marked plain enough. And there's another sentence marked. It isn't marked there, but it's written on my heart—I wish I could write it on my baby's—"Those whom God hath set asunder let not man put together." Yes,' she repeated, '"those whom God had put asunder let not man join together."' They were the last words she uttered, or rather, the last connected sentence. She sank back, apparently exhausted with the effort, and all further attempts to rouse her were in vain.

Bending over her, Mrs. Dorothy caught some faintly muttered words about 'errors past,' and 'pardon;' but all was indistinct; and a few minutes later, Mrs. Dorothy, old Betsy, Mrs. Bryce, and her daughter Hester, stood round the bed on which lay a pale, dead young mother, and a little, living, sleeping infant. Whose property was it? What was to be done with it? No one knew aught of the mother, save that she had come there that night, and implored them to take her in 'for pity's sake.' There was no paper about her; no mark even on anything she wore, save the initials, 'C. H.,' to show what was her name. Mrs. Bryce said she had inquired her name, but the woman had refused to tell; and only said she should soon have none—and a good thing, too. She had become too ill to be questioned almost immediately after her arrival; and the only other question Mrs. Bryce had been able to induce her to answer was, when she had asked 'what would become of the child?' and she had replied, 'God would take care of it—certainly she had no one in this world whom she could send it to. But there was a God above, and she left it to Him.'

It was whilst Mrs. Bryce was saying this that old Betsy first observed how ill her mistress had become. Mrs. Dorothy, generally so calm, was shaking now from head to foot. She tried to compose herself, but allowed that she was ill, and made no objection when Betsy led her out of the room; and Mrs. Bryce following, made her lie down on the sofa in the parlour, and covered her with blankets, for her very teeth were chattering, and she was shivering all over.

But when the doctor shortly after arrived, and found the patient he had come five miles to see had passed beyond all human skill, and Mrs. Bryce wished Mrs. Dorothy to see him, she positively refused to do so, saying he could do her no good. And Betsy, anxious as she always was about her mistress, did not second Mrs. Bryce's request. 'It was a nervous attack,' she said; 'and would pass off. Her mistress had had them before, but not for a long time.' No; for it had been a long time since anything had so shaken Mrs. Dorothy's whole nervous system as had the scene which had just taken place. A trying, harrowing scene it would have been to any one; but to Mrs. Dorothy it seemed something personal, and old Betsy, though she said nothing, seemed quite to understand that it should be so. She attempted no word of comfort, ready as she generally was with her words; but, after having covered her up warmly on good Mrs. Bryce's best parlour sofa, she left her alone for some time, and would allow no one to go near the room; saying, in reply to Mrs. Bryce's repeated declaration, that 'it was a downright sin to leave any one by herself who had been as ill as Mrs. Dorothy;' that 'she knew her mistress better than they did.' Which was evidently true; for on Betsy's going to the room about an hour afterwards she found Mrs. Dorothy, looking paler and more worn than usual, certainly, but perfectly composed and quiet. Betsy never inquired how she felt, but merely announced that the kitchen kettle was boiling, and she would bring her some tea directly. And Mrs. Dorothy said 'Thank you, Betsy: but this is not the time to be thinking first of me. Where is that poor baby?'

'Hester has it, ma'am; and Mrs. Bryce has dressed it up all comfortable in the clothes the mother had ready in a parcel: there were plenty of them, and all of the very best. It 's plain the poor creature was of the better class.'

'I saw that from her appearance,' replied Mrs. Dorothy: 'her hands were too white to have ever known much work.'

'They were thin enough,' said Betsy. 'Did you observe, ma'am, how large the wedding-ring was? By-the-bye, I must speak to Mrs. Bryce about the ring being kept safe.'

'I have it here, Betsy,' said Mrs. Dorothy. 'I drew it from her finger when I found that it was falling from the cold hand, for which it had grown, as you see, so much too large. We will not talk now of it, or of her, but as soon as it is light let Mr. Saville be sent for. And now I will go to the room, Betsy; whatever remains to be done for that poor creature, it is for us to do it. And the child——'

'She left it to God, poor thing!' said Betsy.

'And has not God given it in charge to us?' said Mrs. Dorothy; 'and shall we not receive it from Him, and in His grace do our duty by it?'

Thus it was that Mrs. Dorothy Helstone came to adopt as her own a little nameless orphan.

The following Sunday a christening interrupted the course of the service, and old Betsy, with a baby in her arms—a sight never before seen—approached the font, followed by Mrs. Dorothy and the Rector's wife. They, with the Rector, were the sponsors, and on Mrs. Dorothy's being desired to name the child, she pronounced the words 'Charity Helstone.'

As she had said to Mrs. Saville the evening before, 'Helstone' might be a help to her in other days, and might make the title of 'Aunt Dorothy,' by which she should teach her to call her, come more natural; and 'H.' was one of the initial letters on the mother's linen. 'C. H.' was marked there, and 'C. H.' alone marked that grave where the young mother now lay, with the date of her death, and the words, 'His compassions fail not.'

'Let the other initial, then, be for Charity,' Mrs. Dorothy had said, 'and they would seek God's grace to train the child in such a way that her character and conduct might be in accordance with those virtues, the greatest of which was charity.' So the baby was named Charity, and by no other name did either 'Aunt Dorothy' or Betsy ever call her. 'Cherrie,' indeed, was her own abbreviation of it, and 'Cherrie' she was generally called by others. Even the Rector would sometimes be heard to adopt the more familiar epithet, and when taken to task for so doing by Mrs. Dorothy, he would excuse himself by saying that really, just at present, there was more of the cherry than of anything else about her, and the shorter seemed the more appropriate title. Which was true, for a more rosy, bright, tempting little morsel to behold, it would have been difficult to discover; whilst her character and conduct were such that she was a constant torment and trouble to every one: so impossible to teach, so untameable, so uncontrollable, so domineering, that it was difficult to connect her with her name—unless, indeed, it was to be by allowing that name to remind others of the charity which they needs must exercise in their dealings with her.

CHAPTER II.

'SEVEN years old to-day, Miss Charity!' said Betsy to her little charge, as she drew near her cot, evidently with the intention of 'getting her up,' as she called it. 'This is your birthday, Miss; and you'll like to be up before Aunt Dorothy comes out of her room, won't you?'

'No, I won't!' was the reply. 'I'll like to stop here till Aunt Dorothy comes in; and nobody's going to touch me but her on my birthday.'

'Oh, but, Miss,' expostulated Betsy, whose one idea of managing the child was by what she termed 'coming round her;' a system which she persisted in pursuing, though both Mrs. Dorothy's counsel and her own experience were for ever telling her that it was the very worst in the world,—'Oh, but, Miss, you know Aunt Dorothy's ill. She went to bed very ill last night, and I felt sure you'd like to be a very good girl this morning, and be up and dressed without any trouble at all—on your birthday, too, when you 're seven years old. Come, my dear, put on your shoes and stockings, and do be a good girl, just to please me: don't you wish to please me?"

'No, I don't!' exclaimed Charity, throwing at the same time the shoes and stockings which Betsy had presented to her to the other end of the room. 'No, indeed, I don't want to please you, for I hate you!'

'Miss Charity!' said Betsy, in extreme astonishment; for, though she was accustomed to such assurances with regard to Charity's feelings towards her, when those feelings were roused by anger, it was something quite new to hear such a pleasant declaration from her charge the first thing in the morning, before she had done anything whatever to displease her. 'What! hate me? old Betsy, who am so good to you!'

'Good to me!' exclaimed Charity; 'indeed you're not good to me. You 're wicked, that 's what you are; and it 's right to hate you, for we ought to hate liars; and you 're a liar.'

'Me a liar?' exclaimed Betsy. 'You wicked, wicked child! I 'll tell your aunt, Miss Charity, that I will, the very moment she comes out of her room. Nice news for me to have to tell her, the very first thing, on your birthday! But I shall tell her, and what will she say then?'

'She 'll say it 's true,' replied the child. 'Aunt Dorothy doesn't tell lies; if she did, I wouldn't love her. But you do, Betsy: you 're a liar, and you shan't dress me to-day. I never mean to let you dress me again, and I wish you 'd go away. I won't get up with you—there! I won't get up till Aunt Dorothy comes.'

This being Charity's resolution, old Betsy knew perfectly well that, child as she was, she would adhere to it; therefore, leaving the shoes and stockings where Charity had thrown them, at the further end of the room, she went down-stairs to fetch the hot water to carry to her mistress. Whilst the water was pouring from the copper into the can, Betsy stood beside it with the most troubled of faces, talking to herself according to her usual fashion,—

'Well, if ever there was such a child! Ah! we little know what's in store for us. I did think my poor dear mistress would have had peace for the rest of her days. I did believe this village, where she'd found such a quiet haven after stormy days, would have been a peaceful resting-place for the rest of her life; but now the house is upside down with this child, and we're all up on end with her from morning to night. Ah! this very day it was, seven years ago, that Martha Bryce came knocking us all out of our beds, and we went down the street, little thinking what was going to happen; and came back with a baby; and since then, what with one thing and another, we've had more trouble than we'd had in all the eighteen years that had gone before. What with the Irish nurse my mistress got for the baby, and that worried my life out before the child could speak or walk; and what with the trouble the child has given me since I got Mrs. Dorothy to get rid of the creature and let me take care of her myself, it's been something awful. My mistress is always saying the child came to us from heaven. I can't say I see much signs of it at present. I'm sure the kingdom of heaven isn't of such as she, or it's a different place, indeed, from what we're accustomed to think of it.'

And thus saying, the can being full, and it never being Betsy's custom to waste a moment, even under the most painful of circumstances, she set off to her mistress's room and opened the window-shutters, feeling the most sincere regret at having to begin the day with a fresh account of Charity's misdemeanours.

'It's Miss Charity's birthday, Betsy,' said Mrs. Dorothy: 'we must make it a happy day for her, if we can.'

'Yes, ma'am, if we can,' replied Betsy; 'but there doesn't seem much chance of it. Miss Charity's in one of her tantrums, ma'am. I don't know when I've seen her so bad; she won't get up——'

'Won't get up, Betsy! and why not?'

'She says, ma'am, I'm a liar!—her very word, ma'am! Where she learns such I can't think, considering how very careful you've been over her ever since she could speak, and never allowing her to mix with any common children, but keeping her constantly under your own eye. It's my opinion, ma'am, she must have imbibed some of the ways and principles of that Irishwoman we had for a wet-nurse. It is, indeed.'

Mrs. Dorothy, concerned as she was at this fresh trouble between Betsy and Charity, could scarcely help smiling at the pertinacity with which Betsy would constantly refer Charity's evil ways and doings to the wet-nurse, who had been for nearly two years the object of her faithful maid's deepest aversion.

'Poor Kate O'Donnell!' said Mrs. Dorothy, gently, 'I'm afraid she has a good deal laid to her charge in your opinion, Betsy. But, surely, we need none of us feel any difficulty in accounting either for our own wrong actions or those of others; at least, not if we know anything of our own hearts. We can find evil enough there—can we not?—which we are quite aware in our own consciences was imbibed from no nurse whatever, but originated entirely with ourselves.'

'Well, ma'am, that's true, and no denying of it,' replied Betsy: 'yet surely, ma'am, there's something about Miss Charity unlike other children—leastways it's to be hoped there is, for the sake of them as have large families. Just think now, ma'am, if all the children at the Rectory were like ours. I don't believe there'd be a scrap of their mother left—no, I don't!'

'I'm afraid, Betsy, Miss Charity is a sad worry to you,' said Mrs. Dorothy.

'The most worry she gives me, ma'am, is in thinking of the trouble she gives you. If it was only for myself I wouldn't so much mind; but I can't bear to be for ever troubling you, ma'am, with tales of her naughtiness, and so I told her this morning. I told her I could not bear to have to come and complain of her the first thing in the morning—on her birthday, too.'

'But what was it all about, Betsy?'

'That's just what I can't say, ma'am: not a word can I get out of her but that I'm a liar, and she won't have anything to say to me, and does not mean to get up till you go to her, ma'am!'

'Well, then, Betsy, the only thing is just to leave her alone till I'm ready to go to her, and no doubt she will soon tell me what is the matter.'

Which proved to be the case, for no sooner had her godmother opened the door of the little room adjoining Betsy's, where Charity slept, than the child started up; and no sooner had Mrs. Dorothy approached near enough to the bed to allow of her doing so, than she threw her arms round her neck, exclaiming,—

'Oh, Aunt Dorothy, kiss me on my birthday! I'm not going to be naughty, indeed I'm not. Only I won't let Betsy dress me, because she told me a lie last night; and I hate people who are liars. She often tells lies, Aunt Dorothy, and last night she told me a great big one. I only found it out when I came to bed, and I made up my mind I wouldn't speak to Betsy all to-day,—no, and not for a long time. I *did*, Aunt Dorothy; indeed I did!'

'I dare say you did, Charity,' replied Mrs. Dorothy: 'little girls often make up their minds to do a great many things which are neither wise nor right.'

'But it's right to hate liars!' said Charity.

'That is a very ugly word, Charity,' replied Mrs. Dorothy.

'It 's in the Bible,' said Charity, 'and you made me learn it one day, Aunt Dorothy, and told me how it said there that the liars would never go into heaven. I wish you 'd make Betsy learn it, too.'

'Betsy never tells me untruths,' said Mrs. Dorothy.

'No, I know she doesn't; but she tells them to me, and that 's quite as bad. You know, Aunt Dorothy, you couldn't say it wasn't a lie that day she took me to have my tooth out when you were ill, and she told me the man wss going to put something in my mouth that would take all the pain away, and wouldn't hurt. I wouldn't have minded the pain a bit, or even cried, if she 'd told me what was coming; but I wouldn't be cheated like that, and *that* was a lie.'

'That was a long time ago, Charity,' said Mrs. Dorothy, 'and you have been very loving to Betsy since then.'

'Yes, till last night, when she told me another lie. I 'll tell you about it, Aunt Dorothy, and then you shall say whether it wasn't even worse than the other. You know my doll that Edward gave me, and I wouldn't let any one but myself touch, because he gave it me . . . well, Betsy broke it.'

'Broke your doll, Charity?'

'Yes, and never told me. I found it out, Aunt Dorothy, and I'll tell you how. Last night, when I went to read with you, I put my doll to bed, just as I always do; and don't you remember, Aunt Dorothy, when we were reading, we heard a noise in my bedroom?'

Mrs. Dorothy did remember, and said so.

'That was when Betsy broke my doll. I know it was. I asked her, when she was putting me to bed, what made that noise, and she said she was hanging the bell on the shutter and she let it fall; but she never told me it fell into my doll's cradle and broke it.'

'My dear Charity,' said Mrs Dorothy, 'who told you that it did so?'

'No one told me, Aunt Dorothy; I found it out: I always find out lies, and I always shall. And Betsy asked you to let her go out in the evening, after I was in bed; and she went to Mrs. Ellis's and bought that other doll that was so like mine—don't you remember, Aunt Dorothy, I didn't know which to choose when Edward took me to the shop? Betsy bought that doll, and put it into the cradle instead of mine, and she rumpled up the hair to make it look as if it was not quite new; and this morning when I woke I took it in my bed, and only that I found it out, I should have kissed it just as if it had been my own darling doll that Edward gave me a week ago. And then, if I had found out afterwards that it wasn't my doll . . . Aunt Dorothy, it was a shame, and it was a lie—now wasn't it?'

'Betsy did not mean it to be either a shame or a lie, Charity,' said Mrs. Dorothy: 'she thought it would make you very unhappy to know that your new doll had been broken, and as she knew that there was another almost exactly like it at Mrs. Ellis's, she hoped to replace it without your having the pain of knowing that yours was broken—if, indeed, all you suppose is correct.'

'Oh, it's all true, Aunt Dorothy! The moment I found out it wasn't my doll I knew all about it, and why Betsy looked so strange when I asked her what made that noise while we were reading, and why she had begged you to let her go out for half-an-hour, though it was raining so hard. It was a shame.'

'Betsy did it in kindness to you.'

'Then I don't think it *was* kindness, Aunt Dorothy. I hate being cheated. I never will be cheated. If Betsy had told me she'd broken my doll . . . well, of course I'd have been very sorry; but if I'd seen she was sorry too, I'd have tried not even to cry to vex her more when it wasn't her fault—of course I would; but to go and tell me a lie, and perhaps let me always go on loving that doll because it was the very doll that Edward gave me, when he had never given it to me at all, and it wasn't even the same doll that I had promised him always to keep while he was away in his ship—oh, it *was* a lie!'

Aunt Dorothy could only say again that Betsy had not meant it as such.

'Well, Aunt Dorothy, you can't say it was *true*. *You* wouldn't have done it—now would you?'

Charity's large blue eyes were fixed full on Mrs. Dorothy's face, and her godmother knew that there was no avoiding a question so put.

'No, Charity,' she said, 'I would not; but

Betsy does not see the thing in the same way as you do. She is afraid of vexing you, and also, Charity, of putting you into one of your passions, which disturb the whole house, and often make me very ill. You know, Charity, I was very ill last night, and it has not been very pleasant for me to be troubled as I have been this morning, especially when it is your birthday, and I thought we were going to have a happy day.'

'I couldn't help it, Aunt Dorothy; no, I couldn't bear for Betsy to be helping me to dress, when I knew how she'd been cheating me.'

'Charity,' said Mrs. Dorothy gravely, 'you shall begin to dress yourself to-day. You are seven years old, and it is quite time, and I will stay here with you; but we will not talk any more about Betsy or the broken doll, only, when we go into my room to say our prayer, I will give you the text which I had chosen for your birthday.'

Mrs. Dorothy was so grave that Charity attempted no reply, but dressed herself so quietly and skilfully that Mrs. Dorothy would have wondered to see her, had she not known that it seemed only necessary to tell Charity what to do, and she herself would find ways and means of doing it. She followed Mrs. Dorothy into her room, and knelt quietly by her side while she offered an earnest birthday prayer for the orphan godchild whom God had entrusted to her care, and she remained perfectly quiet until Aunt Dorothy said, 'Here is a birthday text for you from your godmother,—"Charity suffereth long, and is kind." Ah! when will that be said of *my* little Charity?'

Then, throwing her arms round her godmother's neck, the child hugged and kissed her, exclaiming as she did so,—

'Aunt Dorothy, I will try and be patient, and be kind to Betsy, and I'll go and pick up the doll.'

'Pick up what doll, Charity?'

'The doll Betsy bought, and tried to cheat me with. I threw it out of the window, Aunt Dorothy, into the yard, that she might see it when she went to feed the chickens, and know that it wasn't any use to try and cheat me. But I know I was in a great passion, and if *you* wish it, Aunt Dorothy, I'll go and pick it up.'

'No, Charity, I will go myself; and you shall stay here, and ask yourself whether you think this has been a good way for a little girl to begin her birthday—a little girl whose name is Charity, and whose godmother gave her that name in the hope that her character and conduct might be worthy of it.'

On reaching the bottom of the stairs Mrs. Dorothy was greeted by old Betsy, who, standing at the open back-door, was gazing with uplifted hands into the yard. 'There, ma'am, you can see for yourself the sort of child we've got to deal with! Just look there!' And looking where Betsy pointed, Mrs. Dorothy saw the shattered and scattered remains of a wax-doll. 'She must have dashed it out of the window, ma'am; and got out of bed to do it, too!

though it is freezing cold. No; there never was such a child! there doesn't seem to be any good in her.'

'I beg your pardon, Betsy,' said Mrs. Dorothy, gravely. 'Charity, like the rest of us, has her good points as well as her bad ones. And if she has shown some very wrong feelings this morning, as she certainly has, I can see right ones at work, even in the very temper she has displayed about this unfortunate doll.'

Betsy shrugged her shoulders in a way that said, as plainly as any words could, that her mistress was infatuated about the child. Mrs. Dorothy remarked the action, and replied to what she knew was passing in her servant's mind,—'No, Betsy, I do not spoil Charity; neither am I blind to her faults. Perhaps I see them even more plainly than you do; perhaps they grieve me even more than they grieve you. The child is passionate to a degree, and has no self-control whatever. Poor lamb! she is young yet, and we learn our lessons slowly in this life; but she has a very loving heart, and a keen sense of truth. If she had not been so fond of her little companion and playfellow, she would not have valued his parting present as she did; and it is the truthfulness of her character that makes her resent so keenly anything like pretence or deceit. You know, Betsy, this has always been the great difficulty between you and Charity: you try to deceive the child, and she cannot bear deceit. She has never been able to bear it, and she never will.

I only wish, Betsy, you would cease ever to think of trying to use it with her. To say nothing of its being wrong, it is unwise—most unwise.'

Mrs. Dorothy was not pleased, and Betsy saw it. She did not answer a single word; but she fetched a broom, and was just about to sweep up the remains of the doll, when Charity rushed up to her, and trying to snatch the broom from her hand exclaimed,—'I'm going to pick it up myself, Betsy, every bit of it. I won't let you do it. Aunt Dorothy says it was wrong to throw it out of window, and I know it was. I did it in a passion, and it's wicked to go in passions. But it was because you told me a lie, Betsy, and I can't bear lies. If you'd never tell me any more lies I wouldn't get into such passions. I know I wouldn't. But I'm sorry I vexed Aunt Dorothy on my birthday, and I'm sorry I called you bad names.'

'Never mind that now, Miss Charity,' said Betsy, only too glad to see any prospect of sunshine again through the clouds; 'never mind that now, Miss Charity. And don't you be going out in the cold after that unhappy doll. I'll pick it up, and we'll have a nice breakfast after all. There's a cake in the oven, Miss Charity—a beautiful plum-cake I made myself yesterday, because it would be your birthday to-day.'

'What do I care about cakes, Betsy?' exclaimed Charity; 'I'll pick up that doll myself.' And running into the yard before any one could stop her, she swept together the pieces with her little hands, and putting them all into her pinafore, ran into the parlour, where her aunt had already gone. 'There's the broken doll, Aunt Dorothy; and I'm sorry I broke it. I'll try to be a better girl; I will, indeed, because I know it makes you unhappy; and I love you very, very much!' And throwing her arms round Mrs. Dorothy's neck, she hugged and kissed her until her godmother was fairly out of breath.

CHAPTER III.

EIGHT more years have passed, and again we meet Charity Helstone in the very spot where last we left her, in the same old-fashioned parlour in Aunt Dorothy's cottage, and with the same Aunt Dorothy sitting, now as then, in her carved arm-chair in the chimney-corner. Tears, too, are in Aunt Dorothy's eyes now, as they were then; and evidently Charity, with increasing years, has not outgrown all her troubles; for the expression of her face is as sad now as it was on that day eight years ago, when, after destroying Betsy's newly-purchased doll, she knelt by her aunt in the parlour, with many protestations of regret for the past, and promises of amendment for the future. How many times had not such confessions and such resolutions been made during the course of the eight years that had passed over Charity since we parted from her; then a rosy, laughing, giddy child of seven, to meet her again now, a tall girl, in her fifteenth year!

We left her in great trouble, but we seem to find her in still greater; for her face is disfigured with crying, which, judging from its traces, must have been her chief occupation during the night that has just passed: whilst Aunt Dorothy looks more pale and worn herself than even eight years of time would seem altogether to account for; and the good maid Betsy, standing in the hall, looks yet more distressed now than she did then. For the sight on which she is gazing is a much more painful one to Betsy's loving eyes than even the sight that morning had been of the shattered doll, with which she had so skilfully plotted to deceive her little charge; and which well-laid plan Charity had so speedily overthrown and punished.

Far rather would Betsy be now spending her sighs on the same or similar sights than on the pile of boxes heaped up this morning in the tidy hall, evidently waiting to be carried away from the house. Betsy seemed but little altered during the years that had worked so great a change in Charity. There was the same bright sparkle in the round black eyes; the same settled red colour in the well-dried cheeks, which Charity used laughingly to tell her were just like well-preserved apples; the same tidy figure, in neat black gown and print apron; and the same old way of talking to herself when there was no one else to whom she could talk.

'I wish to goodness he'd come then!' she said, opening the front-door to look down the street, and then shutting it hastily again as the rush of cold wind blew in. 'I wish he'd come, if he is to come, and fetch the things right away. And I wish it was half-past nine o'clock, and they'd done their talk in the parlour, and the child was fairly off. When once a tooth is to come out . . . well, the sooner it's out the better. My mistress thinks she's doing wisely in sending her to school. It's my opinion she'd have done better to keep her at home. She's a bit too high-spirited, I own; but that's a fault that mends itself. It was only yesterday, when the miller was in here with the bill, and Miss Charity she wouldn't go out of the kitchen for my bidding, though she knew she was forbidden to stay in it, because she happened to hear him telling me of the accident his little Bessie had had with the mill-wing knocking her over; she would stop and hear all about it, until her aunt came to look for her herself: but after she'd gone, when I made an excuse like to the miller for her being so high-spirited, and said it wasn't a bit of good for me to speak to her, for she was one of those who would have her way; well, he only laughed, and said "she was a mighty fine young lady to look at; and we'd good reason to be proud of her, for it was every one that said what a pretty creature she was, and so clever to talk to, and so good to the poor. If she was a bit self-willed, why, that would right itself with time. She would be like his young colt, that was standing so quietly outside then, with the sacks across her back; the time was, and not so very long ago either, when there wasn't any way at all of doing anything with her, for the play and spirit she 'd got in her, but one was just obliged to let her have out her run: but now, why, bless you! she 'd come to know the hand that held her, and the work she was wanted to do, and there wasn't a better than she in all the country—no, nor as good an one; for she was all the more valuable for the go she 'd got in her by nature. Now she was a bit trained and taught, he 'd warrant her against any of the slow-paced things that were to be seen about here, that had no sense or life in them." Those were his words, and I repeated them to my mistress, word for word, last night; for Miller Brown is one of her great favourites: she often says he 's as good and sensible a man as there is in the parish, and I hoped it might make an impression like on her to hear what he thought about our young lady; but it seemed to make no difference at all. I waited to tell her till I went to put out her candle, which I know is just the best time for saying a word to my mistress that maybe she 'll think over: but all the answer she made was, "Miller Brown's colt wanted a hand to teach her and train her to the work she had to do. But for the training and teaching she has had, Betsy, she would not now be of the use she is to him." I longed to say more, but my mistress just said, "Now, good-night, Betsy, for I am very weary, and my mind is full," and so I had to come away. But it's my opinion, that between the trouble Mrs. Dorothy takes herself, and all the child learns up at the Rectory, we need not have sent her away from home just yet. As for me, I know my mistress thinks I'm the great cause of all the child does wrong. and that, so far as Miss Charity's concerned, I'm nothing but an old fool. And I believe she's not far wrong; for she's just the plague of my life at home. And yet it breaks my heart to stand here staring at these boxes, and think they're going from here, and she going along with them. And here's the man to fetch them!' And, admitting the porter into the house, Betsy turned the force of her words and feelings upon him, and gave him so many injunctions as to where he was to take the boxes, and how he was to carry them, and which might be turned upside down, and which might not on any account whatever, that the poor man was glad to get over his work as speedily as possible, and set off with his truck down the frosty street.

Betsy watched him till he had turned the corner, and then, retreating into the kitchen, sat down by the fire—a thing she had never, perhaps, been seen to do before five o'clock in the afternoon at earliest, when every cup and pan had been put into its proper place, and nothing was to be seen about but Betsy's tidy little workbox on the well-scrubbed deal-table—and shed the first tears that had fallen for years. For Betsy was not given to crying. Her joys and sorrows alike found their vent in words, not tears. But she cried now, long and sadly, and made no attempt to do anything else whilst waiting for the Rectory carriage, that was to come at half-past nine to take her young lady away to school.

But while poor Betsy was thinking so much of

Charity, Charity was thinking very little of poor Betsy. All her thoughts were engrossed with her Aunt Dorothy, as, sitting on her accustomed place on a stool at her feet, she laid her head on her aunt's knee, and announced her intention of being miserable at school.

'Then, Charity,' said Mrs. Dorothy, 'I shall be miserable, too: I can never be happy unless I feel that you are so also.'

'But how can any one be happy at school?' exclaimed Charity, raising her head and looking at her aunt, with the fire of her bright eyes shining through the tears that were still in them; 'how can any one be happy shut up in a school-room, deprived of liberty, cooped up like a bird in a cage? Oh, how often I've pitied those poor girls at Miss Somer's here, walking two-and-two along the streets, like the convicts we saw that day we went to Portsmouth! And Miss Somer's girls are better off than I shall be, for they *do* get into the fields and see the blue sky and breathe the fresh air, even though it is after the fashion of prisoners; but I, shut up in a horrid town, perambulating through nasty streets, with some girl as a companion that I shall be sure to hate, just because she's forced upon me; and obliged, I dare say, to keep my mouth shut, unless I wish to open it to talk in a strange tongue, which I shall hate, because I'm ordered to do it. I shall never have a word to say if I'm made to say it, and have to put my thoughts into a foreign grammar and dictionary before I can utter them! Aunt Dorothy, how *can* I be happy?'

'Charity, my child,'' said Mrs. Dorothy, 'you can be anything you choose to be—anything you make up your mind that you will be. Yours is a decided character; you have a strong will.'

'Yes, I know I have,' said Charity, in her ingenuous way. 'I often wish I hadn't, for I'm sure it's given trouble enough to me, and everybody else. But one can't make one's self happy by willing it.'

'Can't one, Charity?' said Aunt Dorothy. 'I should have thought it was one of the very things that one could do.'

'Aunt Dorothy!' exclaimed Charity; 'why, are you not always saying that happiness is just what people can't secure for themselves? Did you not say only last night, when we were coming home from church'—and Charity's tone was lower and more reverent as she spoke—'did you not say only then, Aunt Dorothy, that you liked Mr. Saville's sermon so much, because it showed so plainly that people could not make themselves happy?'

'Ah, Charity!' replied Mrs. Dorothy, 'we were speaking then of a higher happiness—even of that blessed peace which none can ever taste until they find it in Jesus, and without the possession of which there must always—always be a blank in the heart; since God, when He created the heart, made a place in it for that peace of conscience which man lost when he sinned, and can never feel again until he repents and believes. Ah, yes! there is no true happiness without this peace. But we were not speaking just now of this highest happiness, but of being happy in the common acceptation of that much-abused word: for instance, you are happy at home, Charity; if you were asked, you would say very readily that you are happy here with me and our good Betsy, and in the village, and with your young friends at the Rectory?'

'Happy, Aunt Dorothy! yes, indeed I am happy; happy, happy! I never wish to be happier. That is just why I am so miserable at the thought of going away;' and Charity burst into tears.

'And yet,' said Aunt Dorothy, passing her thin hands caressingly over the young head; 'yet my child, my darling child and my godchild, knows nothing of the true happiness which Jesus gives; the day has not come yet for her to feel the want of it: but it will surely come, for it comes to all, sooner or later, and often it comes very early to those who have heads to think and hearts to feel as you do, Charity—the day when there is a deep gulf in the soul; a gulf so deep, that only Jesus, the Infinite Jesus, can fill it: but that day has not come yet for you, Charity. God grant that, when it does, you may at all events have learned from your godmother where to seek for refuge and relief—where to find peace and happiness: yes! such happiness as can compensate for all earthly sorrow, even the bitterest, and make the most barren heart to blossom and bud, and the most broken voice to sing again with a new song of rejoicing. But till my child needs this happiness I am afraid she will not seek it. I was not speaking of such joy or peace, but only of that cheerful contentment which has been yours, Charity, at home; and which, if you so choose, can be yours also at school.'

'At school, Aunt Dorothy! in prison, with a lot of strange companions whom I shall be sure to hate, because they will be new!—and I hate any thing new—and with a gaoler of a governess over me, whom I have never seen but once, instead of my dear old aunt, whom I have loved all my life!' And there were such kisses pressed on her godmother's hands as well-nigh overcame Mrs. Dorothy's resolute composure.

'The school need not be a prison, Charity, or the girls hateful, or the governess a gaoler. They will only be so if you make them so. We make our circumstances; circumstances do not make us: at least, not if we have any strength of character or any real principle. And surely, Charity, you would not wish me to torment myself with the thought that you, who are capable of so much effort, are resolved now not to make any for my sake, out of regard for me—my wishes for you—my plans for your good?'

'Aunt Dorothy,' said Charity, 'what can I do?'

'Only, Charity, make up your mind to what *must* be; set your will, so to speak, against your will; resolve that you will subdue circumstances, not that circumstances shall subdue you. I would add, Charity, *pray* that it may be so: but you do not yet feel your need of prayer; and a character like yours will never truly pray until it does. You do not care to ask for what you do not feel you want. You told me that last night, when I spoke to you about continuing to pray at school.'

'I said I would always say my prayers, Aunt Dorothy; even if the other girls who sleep with me don't say theirs, I will.'

'Because I wish it, Charity; because you know it would make me yet more unhappy about you if you did not. God grant, that ere long there may be another and a better motive. But until the higher motive is given, it is well to act by the lower; and I have this one comfort about you, Charity, that I believe what you promise that you will perform. You have given me trouble, Charity, often; for you have been headstrong, self-willed, even disobedient: but thank God, thank God, you have never yet deceived me. I am not conscious that you have ever told me a falsehood.'

'No, Aunt Dorothy!' exclaimed Charity, vehemently: 'I never have; I hate lies! I will never tell a lie—no never, so long as I live—not if it were to save my life!'

'Hush, Charity!' said Mrs. Dorothy, gently: 'none can say what they may do. Say that you trust you never may—that you hope you never may.'

'No, Aunt Dorothy! I will say that I never will, that I know I never shall. For it is just what I hate most. One can't help doing other wrong things. It's so hard to do always what one's told, and to go only where one's allowed to go, and not to answer again when one's scolded, especially when it's as unjust as it can be that one should be scolded at all; but it's so mean to tell a lie. I can't think how any one can be so mean. I would rather—yes, I would a great deal rather, be going away to school as I am now, than have told a lie that day about our going to Towton, as Ellen did. I can't think now how she could tell such a lie; I wonder it didn't choke her. I told her so yesterday, and Edward said I was quite right to be so angry with her, and that he didn't mind girls, or boys either, being high-spirited, or self-willed, but that he hated people who told lies: they were always cowards, and he hated cowards.'

'Edward is a great oracle in your eyes, Charity,' said Mrs. Dorothy.

'Which is more than he is in yours, Aunt Dorothy,' replied Charity, quickly. 'I don't think you like him at all since he has been home this time from sea, or think at all well of him.'

Mrs. Dorothy smiled, in spite of her present sadness, at the warmth with which Charity spoke. 'I think, Charity,' she said, 'in your crusade against untruth, you sometimes forget its near relationship to exaggeration, which you certainly do not hold in the same abhorrence.'

'Oh, one can't help what you call exaggerating, Aunt Dorothy, especially when one speaks fast, and of something that's very much on one's mind. Besides, I really do think you don't like Edward as you used to do, or believe there's any good in him.'

'Then,' said Aunt Dorothy, 'you think quite wrongly, my child, as you very often do: for I love Edward very much; he is my godson, my dear godson; and much as I love all the Savilles, I must always love him more than any of the others. And I think, too, there is a great deal of good in him—a great deal, which often makes me thank God and take courage. Edward is affectionate, truthful, brave.'

'Just what I like so much,' interrupted Charity.

'And just what I like so much too, Charity,' continued Mrs. Dorothy. 'But to be affectionate, truthful, and brave, "is not *every* thing."'

'No; and you mean that Edward is proud, and conceited, and likes his own way, and is obstinate, and self-willed—very like me, Aunt Dorothy,' again interrupted Charity.

'And therefore, Charity,' said Mrs. Dorothy, 'not always the best companion for you, or certainly the best adviser. But look, here is this very Edward!' And Charity jumped up from her place at her aunt's feet, just in time to receive a fine youth some two or three years older than herself, who burst into the house, leaving the front-door wide open behind him, and the marks of a muddy pair of boots all along Betsy's newly-swept passage.

Such an entrance made a sudden change in every one's feelings and thoughts. Betsy ceased her meditations by the kitchen fire, and came out into the passage to shut the front-door, declaring as she did so, that 'she believed it was just because Master Edward was at home that her mistress had been so bad with the rheumatism: he left that door open every time he came through it, and that was on an average three or four times a-day. She didn't wonder Mrs. Dorothy said there was no keeping Miss Charity regular at her lessons, with him bursting in and out, whether he was asked to come or not, and not minding a word any one said to him!' And then Betsy retreated again into the kitchen to fetch a damp duster, and wipe off the stains the dirty boots had left on the bright-patterned floor-cloth.

Meanwhile, Edward himself, 'bursting,' as Betsy appropriately styled his manner of entrance, into the little parlour, and falling over the footstool which Charity had just vacated, almost into Mrs. Dorothy's lap, in his eagerness, greeted his godmother with a hearty kiss.

'You have nearly thrown Aunt Dorothy out of her chair, Edward,' said Charity.

'Well, it's your fault if I have, Cherrie,' he replied, 'for leaving these horrid stumbling-blocks in one's way. I am sure you lay a snare for a fellow's feet, if ever any one did; for I never come into this house but I fall over some of your footstools. I suppose it's because you're always getting into some fresh disgrace or other that I always find you on the penitential stool. Well, when we get you back from this fine-lady school, no doubt you'll have grown too wise to get into disgrace any more, and too old to sit on a stool at Aunt Dorothy's feet—eh, Cherrie?'

'I'm afraid I shall never be too wise to get into trouble, Edward,' Charity replied, with a very forced smile, 'and I'm sure I shall never be too old to sit at Aunt Dorothy's feet. I wish you had not come to take away the little time I have for sitting there now.'

'Well, that's polite, I must say; and affectionate,

too—isn't it, Aunt Dorothy? considering that she 's going away for six months in about five minutes, and that I shall have gone away for nearly as many years before she comes back. I don't think she need grudge me five minutes of her company—do you, Aunt Dorothy? Anyhow, Cherrie, you 'll have to put up with it, and to say good-bye to Aunt Dorothy, and come along with me, for my father is waiting for you round the corner by Bryce's house; the streets are so slippery he was afraid to drive up here, so he sent me to fetch you. And he told me to tell you, Aunt Dorothy, he would come and see you after we got back from the station. Now make haste, Cherrie, and get ready, or you 'll be late for the train.'

'Put on your things, my child,' said Mrs. Dorothy. 'Give them to her, Edward—there they are on that chair—her jacket and hat.'

'Come on then, Cherrie,' said Edward; and helping her into the warm cloth jacket, which old Betsy's care had placed right in front of the fire, with a gentleness which seemed somewhat inconsistent with some of his former proceedings, he held the hat in his hand and looked out of the window whilst Charity gave her godmother a long farewell kiss. Edward's presence, however, seemed an effectual hindrance to any last word she might have wished to say, for she did not speak a word, but hurried away into the passage to look for Betsy, who, however, was nowhere to be seen. Edward gave her such a shout as might have summoned her, not only from the most distant corner of the house, but from the furthest end of the long street; but there was no response. 'Oh, come along, Cherrie, do!' he exclaimed, 'or we're safe to be late for the train. There's no use calling her any more. She's gone to hide herself out of sight, as they say donkeys do when they know they're going to die—not,' he added, 'that Betsy is such a donkey after all, if she has made off somewhere because she can't stay here to see you go, Cherrie. But do make haste; my father particularly told me to make you come at once.'

'Well, I'm coming, Edward, only I must say one word more to Aunt Dorothy. I won't be a moment, if you'll stop here—do wait here, just one moment.' And rushing back into the little parlour, where she found her godmother sitting with her face resting on both her hands, Charity threw herself on her knees before her, pulled the hands down from the tearful face, and covered them with passionate kisses, exclaiming as she did so,—

'Oh, Aunt Dorothy, I am so sorry I've been such a wicked girl. I am so sorry I ever went to Towton, or ever did anything to vex you. I love you—love you—love you—and I'll never vex you again in all my life. I'm glad to go to school since you wish it, and I'll be happy there to please you, and work so hard. I'll be the very best girl in all the school. You shall see if I'm not. Oh, Aunt Dorothy, say that you love me and forgive me!'

But Mrs. Dorothy could say nothing, only press her lips fervently on the child's head, and whisper,—

'Go, Charity, go! and God bless you, my poor, dear child!'

'Cherrie, are you coming?' shouted Edward, and at the sound of his approaching step Charity bounded to her feet, threw her arms round her godmother, and was half-way down the street, with Edward at her side, before she well knew where she was.

Edward drew her arm in his, and hastened on without speaking either, till they had turned the corner by Bryce's house, and could see the carriage winding its way slowly up the steep hill in front of them.

Then he slackened his pace and said,—'We're in plenty of time, Cherrie. My father's driving himself, and he sees us; but he doesn't seem in any hurry. I say, Cherrie,' he added, 'I can't help feeling it's partly my fault that you're going away.'

'How your fault, Edward? Aunt Dorothy has been saying for months that she saw the time was coming when she must send me to school.'

'Well, but I don't think it would have come so soon if we hadn't gone to Towton that day. How angry Mrs. Dorothy was, to be sure!'

'I think, Edward, she was more unhappy than angry.'

'Well, unhappy, then. Do you mean, Cherrie, that she'd actually forbidden you to go?'

'She said,' replied Charity, 'when Betsy asked her in the morning, and told her I particularly wished to see horsemanship because I had such a love for horses, that it was no place for me, and she wondered how Betsy could propose such a thing. You know I told you so at the time, Edward. I told you just what she had said.'

'Yes; and I believe it was all my fault. It was I persuaded you, saying it was a very different thing to go to a Circus with me, your elder brother, to take care of you, or to go with a servant like Betsy. It was every bit my fault.'

'No it wasn't, Edward. If it was any one's fault except mine, it was more Ellen's.'

'Ellen's!' said Edward; 'why, I am sure Nell did her best to keep us all from going! Poor Nell! why we pretty near forced her to go with us. I am sure she did her best to keep us back.'

'Yes,' said Charity, 'just in that way that always makes me more determined to do a thing: first preaching up about its being wrong and wicked, and we should be unhappy afterwards, in that stupid, weak way of hers—if she really thought it was so wrong and wicked, why did she come with us afterwards?—and then saying we ought to be afraid of going, as if I would keep back from anything just from fear! I tell you what, Edward, when I keep from doing wrong things, it won't be because I'm afraid of doing them. If I'm a good girl at school, as I mean to be, it won't be because I'm afraid, as Ellen is, of being a wicked one.'

'Poor Nell!' said Edward; 'you're not partial to her.'

'No,' said Charity, 'I'm not, because she's such a coward. And then people praise her, and she's considered a pattern! I've laughed many times to hear that poor deluded Miss Danvers talk of the difference between her and me. You'd have laughed too, Edward, if you'd been there. She used to take up Ellen's conduct-book on a Saturday evening and say, "Now just see the difference, Miss Helstone, between your marks and Ellen's." And then she would tell your mother she was afraid I did not improve at all; but Miss Ellen was all she could wish—all Miss Danvers could wish, indeed, because she has not sense to see, nor a heart to care for anything beyond the surface; and so long as the outside of the platter is clean, she won't take the trouble even to look underneath to see what that may be like. If the sepulchre is only white outside, what does she, or the like of her, care for the dead men's bones within?'

'You are hard upon poor Nell,' said Edward, who, fond as he was of Charity, did not quite like to hear his sister thus dealt with.

'No, I'm not,' said Charity; 'I was scarcely thinking of Ellen. I'm hard on Miss Danvers, if you like, and on those who are like her, which I think is the greater part of the world.'

'You don't see much of the world here, Cherrie, to be able to form so decided a judgment,' replied Edward. 'I don't suppose you've come across more than some half-hundred of people during the course of your long life in this large village of ours.'

'How you do take one up, Edward!' said Charity, pettishly. 'I believe the people one knows are a pretty fair sample of those one doesn't know. Isn't it said that the heart of man answereth to man, just as the face answers to itself in the water?'

'I did not think you were as well read in your Bible, Cherrie, as you seem to be. That is your second quotation from it during this short walk.'

'Well, what if it is?' exclaimed Cherrie. Then, after a moment's pause, during which Edward was thinking within himself that Cherrie's departure from home seemed to be effecting some most undesirable change in her usually bright temper, she added,—'I tell you what, Edward; I believe it's pretty much with books as it is with people,—there are not many that speak the truth, or make things out as they really are. And I believe the Bible is the one book that does speak the truth, just as Aunt Dorothy is the one person that does.'

'Which is very complimentary to everybody else,' replied Edward. 'You're a strange girl, Cherrie!'

'Am I?' replied Cherrie: 'well, so people seem to think; though I'm sure I can't see what people see strange in me, unless it is that I *do* speak the truth.'

'Well,' said Edward, 'we haven't time to discuss the question now, Cherrie; for look, my father's waiting for us at the top of the hill, and he'll be wondering what we two can always find to talk about.'

'No, he wont!' said Charity, 'I should think he knew by this time that you and I had always plenty to say to each other. You 're about the only person I *do* care to talk to, Edward—I mean, to have long chats with—except Aunt Dorothy and the miller.'

'Well,' said Edward, and his light, cheerful manner barely concealed an undertone of deep sadness; 'well, Cherrie, the miller—poor old fellow!—will have you all to himself when you come home in six months' time. I shall be far enough away then, and by the time I come back, some years hence, I must expect to find you and everything else changed.'

'Then,' said Charity, 'you expect wrong. I can't say what other things or other people may do, but as far as I am concerned, Edward, I shall never change. When I like people once, I like them always. If I didn't, then I should never have really liked them at all.'

But just at that moment the young people reached the top of the hill, and after receiving a somewhat mild reprimand from the good Rector, on keeping him waiting as usual, they set off at a brisk pace for the station.

CHAPTER IV.

ON the evening of that same day, a group of girls might have been seen standing round a wide fire-place in a long school-room, warming their hands in turn; and as they did so, chatting together at a speed which seems peculiar to school-girls' tongues.

A most diverse group they were, as is usually the case,—some tall, some short; some fair, some dark; some with grave, earnest faces, which told that the young brain was already engaged in its own busy work, and the young heart had its own feelings hidden away out of sight. Others, and perhaps these were the greater number, with that listless indifference of countenance which said that, although for the moment they were roused to interest in the subject under discussion, the interest would pass away with the moment. One name was frequently repeated, the name of 'Charity Helstone,' as the girls discussed, as school-girls will, the appearance, manners, dress, and voice of the new companion who had that day joined them, and speculated concerning what her antecedents might have been, and what her capabilities would prove to be.

'Such a name!' exclaimed one girl; 'how could any people in their senses give a child such a name as Charity! One would think she had been found on a door-step, or taken out of a hospital; and I'm sure she looks as miserable as if she hadn't a friend or a penny in the world.'

'And as proud as if she had a fortune at command, and had been accustomed to be monarch of all she surveyed,' replied another. 'I can't say much for your discernment, Ellinor, if you think this girl looks like a charity-child, whatever her name may be. For my part I think she looks more like a queen.'

The greater number of the girls agreed with this latter opinion, and Ellinor Temple replied, in somewhat a discomfited manner, that she 'had not said that she looked humble, only that she looked miserable—as if she had not a friend in the world.'

'Or perhaps,' added a third speaker, 'as if she had some very dear friend whom it had made her very unhappy to leave: may not that be it?'

The voice that asked this question was so low and gentle, that it might have been thought it would have had small chance of making itself heard amidst the buzz of loud and eager talkers, especially as the speaker stood behind the other girls, at a little distance from the fire, round which most of them were crowding. Yet, at the sound of Helen Anstruther's gentle voice the girls stopped their loud talking for an instant, as if anything Helen said ought surely to be listened to, and one of them replied,—

'I dare say she has, poor thing! and perhaps she has never been to school before. I know I was wretched enough the first day I came. But it's very different now, when one has old friends to return to as well as to leave. I'm sure I wouldn't be hard on the poor girl, though she does look so miserable. She isn't meeting old friends in her companions, as the rest of us are.'

'Well, then, let us try to make her feel that she is going to make new ones,' replied Helen, gaily. 'She will be back in a few minutes. Shall we clear a place for her by the fire? It must have been cold work travelling by the night train this weather. She lives, no doubt, at some distance, to arrive so late.'

Several of the girls moved back from the fire at Helen's words, and as they did so Ellinor Temple pushed forward a little girl, who was really almost too small to be seen amongst such a crowd of larger ones, saying, in her rapid way,—

'Why! fancy your stopping up till these hours, little Alice! Miss Mowbray must have forgotten you in her anxiety about the new girl's not getting lost or frost-bitten before she arrived, or she would never have left you up till nine o'clock. And you must be frozen yourself out there, with everybody between you and the fire.'

'No I'm not, Ellinor,' replied the child. 'I've been sitting on Helen's lap, and she has rubbed my hands till they're quite warm. I tried to get by the fire, only there was no room for me; but Helen said she'd warm my hands by rubbing them, and that was better for my chilblains. And Miss Mowbray told me I was to sit up till the new girl came, that she might see us all together when she arrived. And here she is coming—isn't she, Helen?'

'Yes, dear,' said Helen; 'and you are opening your little sleepy eyes to stare at her. I do pity a new girl arriving amongst so many strangers. It is such trying work.'

Certainly, Charity Helstone looked as if *she* found it so, for as she entered the room with Miss Mowbray she scarcely raised her eyes. Had her old friend the miller seen her then, he would not have known her again, and Edward would not have been quite certain whether to laugh or cry at the demure face which Charity presented to her companions, and the low voice with which she replied to Miss Mowbray, and said, in answer to her question, 'whether she would like to come down to the parlour with her now, or remain in the school-room till the supper-bell rang,' that 'she thought she would rather stay in the school-room, if she might.'

'Then,' said Miss Mowbray, 'I will introduce you to Helen Anstruther, who is the eldest of our party now, and leave her to introduce you to your other new companions.'

Helen Anstruther came forward, and Charity shook hands with her, with an evident effort at sociability, and thanked the girls when they asked, as Miss Mowbray left the room, 'if she had not found the journey very cold,' and made room for her by the fire. But Charity had never been accustomed to strangers; she scarcely knew, indeed, what it was to see a face or hear a voice with which she had not been familiar from childhood; and a strange inability to speak now took possession of her, which was really shyness, though it looked to most of the girls more like pride or coldness. A most uncomfortable five minutes followed; when the silence was broken by Ellinor Temple's saying that 'this time Miss Mowbray surely had forgotten little Alice, for she was certain she never meant her to sit up for supper.'

'No,' said Helen Anstruther; 'it is my fault. Miss Mowbray told me she was to go to bed after Miss Helstone had arrived. Come, Alice dear, make haste and wish good night; there will be time still for me to go up with you. Miss Mowbray said supper would not be ready for a quarter of an hour.'

The child went round the little circle, wishing good night to one after another, until she came to Charity, when she stopped doubtfully, and looked at Helen, as if asking her instructions as to what she ought to do.

'Will you not wish Miss Helstone good night, too?' said Helen; and the little girl held out her hand.

'Will you not give me a kiss, too?' said Charity; and the child put up her face at once. It was a sweet little face, with bright blue eyes and rosy lips, and at sight of it the first warm feeling that Charity's heart had known that dreary day passed across it.

'You must not call me Miss Helstone,' she said; 'my name is Charity, but they call me Cherrie: you must call me Cherrie, too.'

'What a funny name!' exclaimed the child. 'Isn't it a funny name, Helen?—like a cherry!' and she laughed merrily.

Helen looked rather grave, and several of the elder girls made her reproving signs. But to their surprise Charity laughed too, and gave the child another kiss, saying,—

'Yes, it is a funny name; and you are a good little thing to say what you think about it. Now mind you don't forget it, and always call me by it.'

'Yes, I will,' said the child, quickly; 'it's a very pretty name, and I like it. Don't you, Helen?'

'I think Miss Helstone will think you a very funny little girl, Alice,' said Helen. 'Now come to bed, or you'll have to go without me.'

'Oh! I won't do that,' said Alice, quickly, 'because I'm afraid to go along the passage.' And she put her hand in Helen's, to be led away; looking back, however, when she came to the door, with the most wakeful of blue eyes, and saying, in the most roguish of voices,—'Good night, everybody! Good night, Cherrie!'

'What a dear little thing!' said Charity; 'and what a pretty child! How old is she?'

'Only six,' said Ellinor: 'and she's been sadly spoiled. Helen Anstruther does the best she can for her, but there's no taming her spirits.'

'So much the better, I should think,' said Charity. 'I suppose Miss Anstruther is her sister?'

'Oh, no!' replied Ellinor. 'The child's name is Rhodes—Alice Rhodes; and she's an only child—a niece of Miss Mowbray's. Her father is a planter in the West Indies, and he's a widower. The mother died when this little creature was born, and she's been running wild among the sugar-canes and the negroes till now, when he has sent her over to Miss Mowbray to be educated. Miss Mowbray never takes such little things as she is; but the child's mother was her only sister, and she is her godmother, and so she has made an exception in favour of her, and that is how we come to have the queer little creature amongst all of us big girls. She's a terrible nuisance to every one but Helen Anstruther, who seems as fond of her as though she were her own sister; though why she should be I can't make out.'

'I should think,' said Charity, shortly, 'it was not difficult to be fond of such a dear little soul as that, with those eyes, and that rosy mouth, and that sweet little voice.'

Ellinor laughed, and two or three of the girls joined in the laugh. 'Wait a little,' she said, 'till you find the blue eyes peering into everything they have no business to see, and the rosy mouth and sweet voice uttering all sorts of impertinences; and then, perhaps, Miss Helstone, you 'll change your mind about little Miss Alice.'

But just at this moment the return of Helen Anstruther interrupted the conversation, and a large bell in the hall making itself heard almost immediately afterwards, the girls went down together to supper, Helen showing Charity the way to the long dining-room.

To her great regret, Charity discovered that Ellinor Temple, for whom she had at once formed a dislike, was to share her room, and not Helen Anstruther, as she had hoped it might be. Ellinor was inclined to be very conversational as they were undressing, but Charity had relapsed into more than her former reserve and silence, and the conversation being all on one side soon fell to the ground. It did not end, however, before Ellinor had given Charity certain pieces of information which she had heard and understood, though without appearing to pay much attention to them. From her Charity learned that Helen Anstruther was considered the good girl of the school—that she was high in favour with Miss Mowbray—that Miss Mowbray was awfully strict and particular, but very just, and kind enough when everything went right—that the German governess was a 'cheat' and a 'humbug,' and she did not know how Miss Mowbray could put up with her—that old Mrs. Mowbray was the most cross, disagreeable old lady, it was possible to see, and hard upon every one except little Alice Rhodes, whom she spoiled outrageously, and that it was quite absurd to see the amount of respect which Miss Mowbray expected the girls should pay to her old mother—that the lessons were very hard, and the masters, most of them, very cross; and that the only nice lessons were the music and dancing when they went to classes, and saw something of the world outside. From all Ellinor said, Charity saw plainly that she could scarcely have met with a companion less congenial to her taste, and she longed ardently for her own little bedroom at home, and for the companionship of her dear Aunt Dorothy.

Ellinor Temple went to rest without reading, after a few hurried instants of kneeling by her bedside, whilst Charity could not help wondering whether she could possibly have had time to repeat the Lord's Prayer. Charity took her little Bible from her travelling bag and read the usual chapter—a happier feeling coming over her as she did so, and remembered that Aunt Dorothy would read the same chapter that same evening. Then she knelt reverently, and repeated the prayers which from childhood she had been used to say.

Ellinor marked it all; and the next day informed the girls in the school-room that she believed the new girl would turn out to be as religious as Helen Anstruther herself. Some one repeated the remark to Helen, and a thankful feeling rose in Helen's heart as she heard that there was to be now some one besides herself in the school who felt the value of prayer, and loved to read the words of her God. Helen felt drawn to Charity at once, and longed for some opportunity of entering into more intimate conversation with her; but Charity remained quiet and silent, and did not appear desirous of making friends with any one.

At length, however, the opportunity seemed to present itself. Helen had been sent one morning by Miss Mowbray to desire Charity to go and speak to her in the half-hour between breakfast and lessons. Charity was not in the school-room; and on seeking her in her own room, Helen found her, with her Bible open before her, reading. She delivered Miss Mowbray's message, then could not refrain from adding, as she cast her eyes on the open Bible, 'It is a great help and comfort—is it not?—especially when one is away from all one's own, and has nowhere else to go to.' Charity looked at her with her large, truthful eyes, and said, quietly,—'I dare say it is to you; I can't say I find it so.'

Helen looked astonished.

'But you love your Bible?' she said; 'you read it every day?'

'No,' said Charity, 'I do not love it. I read it because I promised Aunt Dorothy I would; otherwise I shouldn't read it.' And passing quietly by Helen she ran down the stairs to Miss Mowbray's sitting-room.

CHAPTER V.

SOME months had passed away, and Charity Helstone was fully settled at school, and as happy there as she had made up her mind she would be. Miss Mowbray was all that Mrs. Dorothy had supposed her to be when she intrusted her godchild to her charge; and several of the girls, Helen Anstruther especially, loved her dearly. But it was not Charity's way to love, either very frequently or very quickly, or, indeed, to attach herself to any one, unless there were some peculiar attraction to draw her either in the way of mind, person, or circumstance. A peculiarly lovely face would attract her attention at once, even at church, so that it was with difficulty that she could withdraw her eyes from it; whilst her busy mind would be wondering who such a face could belong to, and imagining the home, the friends, the circumstances connected with it. Or a very superior mind had power to attract her, and she would listen for hours to conversation which excited and interested her, and feel drawn to one who had such power to rouse and warm the soul of another. Whilst early association excercised its influence over her as strongly as it does over most of us, and she loved Betsy and the miller, and Mr. and Mrs. Saville, and the rest of the family at the Rectory—all of them, indeed, except Edward, whom she loved because she loved him—not so much for anything in themselves, or for anything they had ever been to her, but because she had known them all her life, and their faces, voices, and ways, were bound up with every early habit and action of her own life—so bound up, that they could never be separated from it.

But Miss Mowbray neither fascinated her by her beauty nor attracted her by her brilliancy, nor was she in any way connected with her early associations. She was only, therefore, in Charity's eyes, a kind, clever, excellent governess, whom she had met for the first time in her life a few months since, and from whom she would part very willingly a few months hence. Helen Anstruther's devotion seemed to her somewhat absurd, as Helen had not been very long at school, and therefore so strong an affection seemed strange to Charity. But it was no business of hers, and she made no remark upon it. Indeed, Charity made very few remarks about anything, and the girls, who had had Miss Mowbray's authority for imagining that their new companion would prove a merry, high-spirited girl, were all of them greatly surprised, and some of them not a little disappointed, as month after month passed, and little progress was made either towards familiarity or friendship with Charity Helstone.

The Midsummer holidays drew near, and Charity was almost as much a stranger at school as she had been on her first arrival there, and none of the girls seemed able to make her out. Miss Mowbray herself could not tell what to make of her quiet ways, and steady attention to her studies, and careful observance of every rule of the school; for she had been prepared by Mr. Saville, who had come up to London to make the necessary arrangements for placing Charity with her, for a very different charge and a very different conduct.

Mr. Saville had described her as possessing a singularly unbroken spirit, and as having been, unhappily, but too little accustomed to anything like either discipline or regularity; but the oldest and best-trained of her pupils did not pay more scrupulous attention to rules and regulations than did Charity Helstone, and that from the very first. Mr. Saville had pronounced her to be impulsive, self-willed, and passionate, but Miss Mowbray found her calm, most willing to listen to all that was told her, and apparently caring too little about everything to excite herself about anything. Mr. Saville had also declared that she was most warm-hearted and affectionate, but she appeared indifferent to every one except the child Alice, who, from the first day, seemed to have excited an interest in her, which was daily increasing and strengthening.

That first night, when at length Ellinor Temple's

voice had ceased, and Charity laid her tired head on her pillow, and the events of the long day passed uninvited across her mind, the only one of the many new faces she had seen which had stamped its image on her mind was the laughing, dimpled countenance of little Alice Rhodes, and the only voice that had repeated its echoes on her tired ear was the merry tone of the saucy child, as she looked back from the door and wished her good night. And next morning, when she awoke to the unpleasant consciousness that she must go down-stairs and meet a number of strange faces, to whom she was nothing and who were just nothing to her, it was with a feeling of satisfaction that she recollected little Alice's sweet face, and recalled the clear, truthful tones of the child's voice — a poor little thing, too, who had no mother, and whose father was many long miles away; an untamed, joyous little creature, who must feel like an imprisoned bird in that dull school. Charity's heart, cold as it felt to everything else, warmed to the little Creole, and it was in her defence that she first showed the girls of Miss Mowbray's school, as Ellinor Temple afterwards expressed it, 'the real sort of stuff she was made of.'

But this was not until after the Midsummer holidays had come and gone. Very pleasant holidays had they been, yet was Charity not unwilling to return to school, and the advantages she was enjoying there, albeit she felt the same dislike to Ellinor which that talkative young lady had from the first inspired in her mind.

It was on a pleasant afternoon, a few weeks after Charity Helstone's return to school, that the girls were all assembled, as usual, in the school-room after dinner, amusing themselves as best they liked in the half-hour before lessons. Helen Anstruther writing, some few working, others reading, but the greater part chatting and doing nothing. Little Alice was standing close to the open window by Charity's side, who was reading quietly and taking little notice of what was going on, either within or without the room, until she, as well as the other girls, were suddenly aroused by little Alice's calling out, with all the strength her small lungs were capable of exerting, 'Stop thief! stop thief!' As Alice's eyes were turned towards the garden over which the window looked, every one else turned their eyes in the same direction also; but no one was to be seen there but Fraulein, the German governess, who was the object of general dislike to the greater number of them. She, too, heard Alice's cry, and laying down the basket which she was filling with gooseberries, she was evidently about to inquire into the cause of such an unusual alarm, when little Alice called out again, louder than before, 'Stop thief!'

'Miss Alice Rhodes!' exclaimed the poor little German woman, speaking in the worst possible English in her excitement, 'Miss Alice Rhodes! if any one have stolen you anything you may complain to Miss Mowbray; but you are not to call out 'Stop thief!' like that, for all the neighbourhood to think we are a set of thiefs.'

'I'm speaking to you, Fraulein!' exclaimed the saucy child, as gravely as possible.

'To me, Miss Alice Rhodes! what dare you mean by that?'

'Yes, Fraulein, to you. I say "Stop thief!" to you, for stealing Miss Mowbray's gooseberries.'

'Miss Alice Rhodes, you pay for this!' exclaimed the angry governess, drawing nearer to the window and raising her voice at each step, until Miss Mowbray herself, disturbed by the noise, came into the school-room to inquire into the cause of it. She was answered by a shower of words from poor Fraulein, who, entering the school-room through the open window at the same moment as Miss Mowbray came into it by the door, poured forth her complaints against little Alice Rhodes. 'She was the most wicked, the most impertinent of children—she had been so spoiled, there was no bounds now to her insolence—she would not stay in that house to be insulted by every badly-behaved child that came into it—she had accused her of stealing—she had called her a thief!'

Miss Mowbray looked at Alice, who stood by Charity's side, the heightened colour in her cheeks and the extreme quiet of her manner showing that she felt a little fear as to what the result of her conduct might be, though a certain twinkling in her blue eyes showed that she was amused as well as uneasy. But she attempted no denial of Fraulein's accusation, and Miss Mowbray, turning to Helen Anstruther, said,—'Helen, what is all this about?'

'Really, ma'am,' said Helen, who, like the others, had risen from her desk when Miss Mowbray came into the room, 'really I don't know. I was writing over here, when I heard Alice calling out "Stop thief!" but I thought she was playing, talking to the bees or the birds, until I heard Fraulein answering her. I had not an idea till then that she was speaking to Fraulein.'

'Nor was she, probably,' said Miss Mowbray quietly, and with a sign of her hand silencing the excited governess, who was about to pour forth a fresh volley of words. 'Who saw what happened?' she asked. 'What was the child playing at?'

A hope of escaping punishment had arisen in little Alice's mind, when she saw the view which Miss Mowbray was inclined to take of the matter; but it died out again, as Charity came forward and said,—

'I saw the whole, ma'am; but Alice was not playing at anything.'

'Then what was she doing?' asked Miss Mowbray.

'She was watching Fraulein gathering the gooseberries,' replied Charity.

'Well!' exclaimed Fraulein, this time resolved to make her voice heard, 'and Miss Mowbray, did she not ask me, in the presence of all the young ladies, to gather the gooseberries? Did she not say once, when we arose from the table—"Fraulein, will you do me the favour to gather me a basket of the ripest gooseberries?" I ask, Did she not?'

She stopped to draw breath, and Charity continued, as quietly as though she had not been interrupted,—

'Alice was here, ma'am, in the window with me, and she had just asked me whether I had heard you desire Fraulein to eat three gooseberries for every one she put in the basket?'

'Which was an exceedingly impertinent remark,' said Miss Mowbray, 'and one which you ought to have known you should not have encouraged the child to make.'

'I thought,' said Charity, her quick temper rising at the reproof, the first she had received since she came to school, 'I thought, ma'am, that it was a very true one.'

And little Alice, gathering courage from Charity's example, burst forth vehemently,—'You know, Aunt Mary, you told me the other day, when I was in the garden, that I mustn't touch your fruit without your leave. You know you said you would call it stealing.' And the excited child burst out crying.

'We will talk of this elsewhere,' said Miss Mowbray. 'Helen, take Alice to her room until I can attend to her. Fraulein, will you speak with me in my study?' And she left the room, the little German lady following her; not, however, without casting a withering glance at Charity.

'She won't forget the good turn you've done her,' exclaimed one or two of the girls; 'she'll find some way of paying you off.'

'Will she?' said Charity, quietly: 'I'm sure she's quite welcome.' And resuming her book, she continued her reading in the window-seat.

The girls were right. Fraulein did not forget the turn Charity had done her, and from that day she sought in every possible way to annoy her. But Charity Helstone seemed quite beyond the reach of annoyance. She had wrapped herself round in such an impenetrable case of quiet indifference, that all Fraulein's efforts failed to take the smallest effect. Her exercises were always wrong, her compositions never gave satisfaction. Charity corrected the exercises and rewrote the compositions with the most unfailing good-humour, or rather, with the most perfect absence of ill-humour. The other girls hated Fraulein, and were constantly getting into trouble for insubordination or impertinence towards her. But Charity, whom she seemed steadily to seek to provoke, was unprovokable. Ellinor Temple had asked her one day 'whether she did not think Fraulein the most provoking person on earth,' and Charity had quietly replied, 'she really had not thought about it . . . yes, she did seem very disagreeable; but, so far as she was concerned, it was all one to her: she did not care about it.'

Ellinor repeated these words to her companions, adding,—'Do you know, I don't think she cares for anything.'

'No, that she doesn't,' replied another girl. 'I think she 's the most haughty, selfish, disagreeable girl in the world. She 's been here more than six months, and we don't know her a bit better than we did the day she came. I can't make her out, and I wish she were gone.'

To which there was a general assent from every one but Helen Anstruther, to whom Ellinor Temple consequently addressed herself, asking her 'whether she liked her, whether she understood her better than they did?'

'No, indeed,' said Helen, 'I do not understand her at all; but I'm sure she has a great deal in her. I don't think any one ever had such eyes who had not a heart as well: perhaps, when she knows us all better, she may warm towards us. Miss Mowbray thinks she is painfully shy.'

'Shy!' replied Ellinor, 'when she stands up as she does before Miss Mowbray to say her lessons, and speaks out as she does sometimes! Just see how she comes into a room, or walks up the aisle in church!'

'I think,' said Helen, 'she's proud as well as shy, and that when people are both very proud and very shy it gives them just that manner she has. Miss Mowbray was saying the other day, that what makes some people seem so strange, and prevents one's being able to make them out, as we call it, is just from their having different qualities in their character, which are opposite to one another, and act independently of each other perhaps at the very same time.'

'Oh,' said Ellinor, 'you use such fine words, Helen, there's no understanding what you mean!'

Helen laughed. 'I didn't mean to use fine words, Ellinor; I only repeated what Miss Mowbray said to me. It seemed very clear, and it helped me to understand Charity better than I did before. I think her shyness keeps her back from making friends with us, and her pride makes her determined that we shall not think her shy, and gives her that haughty manner.'

'Oh,' said one of the girls, 'that's just like you, Helen; covering up everybody's faults with some excuse or other! For my part, I think her shyness is just ill-temper, and nothing else; and as for her pride, it ought to be taken out of her; and Fraulein says she never means to rest till she has found some way of taking it down.'

'I think,' said Helen, the colour rising in her cheek, 'that Fraulein ought to be ashamed of herself for saying so. I'm sure, if Miss Mowbray knew how she behaved to Miss Helstone, she would be very seriously angry.'

'Well,' said one of the girls, 'you'd better tell her, since you're so intimate with her.'

'I'm not at all sure,' Helen replied, quickly, 'that I ought not to do so.' And she left the room.

'She's an odd compound herself,' said Ellinor, as the door closed. 'See how angry she is now! and how angry she always gets when Fraulein goes on trying to provoke Charity Helstone! and yet, if you were to teaze her, or do anything to annoy her, she would be as meek as a lamb. Did you see how she flushed up about Charity?'

'Because she thinks it a shame for Fraulein to teaze her as she does,' exclaimed little Alice Rhodes, who, having been punished for her impertinence to the German governess, was quite willing now to put her word in. 'Helen is good and kind, and she thinks it very wicked to be as cruel to any one as Fraulein is to Miss Helstone. Helen was ready to cry yesterday about it, and when I asked her if it did not make her very angry, she said, "Yes, she couldn't help being angry when she saw any one unkindly treated." And she said, too, that she thought such things ought to make one angry, only that one must remember the verse in the Bible that said, "Be ye angry, and sin not." That's what Helen said, and I think she's very good and kind, and Fraulein's very cruel and wicked.'

At that moment Fraulein, entering the room, caught the sound of her own name, and hastily inquired 'who was talking of her, and what they were saying?' No one liked to bring little Alice into fresh trouble with the irritable little lady, and some one of the girls tried to turn off the matter by saying that 'it was nothing; they had only said that Fraulein did not like Miss Helstone.'

'Like Miss Helstone!' exclaimed Fraulein. 'No, indeed! she should very much wish to know who would like Miss Helstone—a proud, disagreeable girl like that, who cares no more for what you do nor say, than if she were a rock in the sea that just let the waves dash over it, and then look just like the same it did before—quite unmoved—as much as to say to the waves, "You give yourselves a great deal of trouble, but you hurt not me once;" that provoked her more than anything—to find fault and reprove, and no notice taken—no, not more than to lay a little cane on the back of the rhinoceros. That was just like Miss Helstone; no more moving her than the rock in the sea—no more making her feel than the rhinoceros. She never saw such pride—and for what? Who was she, that she should give herself such airs? Fraulein did not know, and she did not believe any one knew. For she had asked Miss Mowbray who Miss Helstone was, and she could not tell her. There was some secret, she saw that. Miss Mowbray did not like that question. She asked who Miss Helstone's parents were, and she could get no answer. Miss Mowbray tried to turn off the question, but Fraulein would not be turned off. She put it again, and then Miss Mowbray draw herself up, and look grand, and say she does not see that it concerns any one to inquire into the family affairs of the young ladies. That was quite enough; she could see very well there was something better kept secret; she doubt very much whether any one know, in that school, who are Miss Charity's parents: perhaps Miss Charity, proud as she is, may not know that one thing herself.'

But at that moment a general consternation fell on every one; for, standing in the doorway, was Charity herself. That she had heard Fraulein's last words was evident enough from the ashy paleness of her countenance; but what impression it had made upon her it would have been impossible to say. She uttered no word, but stood for a second or two in the open doorway, pale as death; no colour remaining even in her lips, but as motionless as the rock to which Fraulein had compared her. For an instant she seemed doubtful whether to enter the room or not. Then, coming steadily forward with a firm step, she approached the book-case, ran her eye along the shelves till she found the book she wanted, took it down, and left the room with it.

No one spoke till she was out of sight and hearing; then every one began to reproach the other. Fraulein accused Ellinor, and Ellinor upbraided little Alice; and Fraulein went into a passion, and Alice sobbed; and there was a general commotion in the school-room, which was only subdued by the dressing-bell ringing for tea, and every one's feeling the necessity of recovering self-control before they should again meet Miss Mowbray, and yet more, Charity Helstone.

Meanwhile, Charity herself went quietly to her room; her knees were trembling in a strange way, and she felt as if the weather had changed suddenly back to winter from the bright summer day it had been before, she felt so cold as she opened her desk and sat down to write. But there was no time to lose. It wanted but ten minutes to tea-time; and if her letter was not put into the plate before tea it would not go by that day's post. There was not a moment to spare. She wrote as hurriedly as she could, but in her own clear, decided writing:—

'My dear Aunt Dorothy,

'Who were my parents—my father and my

mother? how were they connected with you? You remember my asking you to tell me all about them once, when we were coming home from the churchyard, and your saying you could not then, but you would some day. I saw it made you unhappy to be asked, and I thought it was because you loved my mother so very much that it grieved you to talk of her, and I did not like to grieve you. But now, Aunt Dorothy, I must know all—everything—by return of post.

'Your loving godchild,

'CHARITY.'

She was about to sign herself 'godchild and niece,' as usual, but something prevented her adding the latter epithet, and she omitted the 'Helstone.' Then, sealing and stamping her letter with a firm hand, though a very pale face, she ran down-stairs just as the bell for tea rang, and put it into the plate on the hall-table as she passed into the dining-room. Miss Mowbray was crossing the hall at the moment, and remarked, as they all sat down to tea,—

'I thought, Charity, you told me you were not going to write letters to-day; you said you were too busy preparing your composition for M. Perrot, and were looking for a book to help you, not a quarter of an hour ago?' Charity looked up, and saw that Fraulein's eyes were fixed upon her. A slight flush passed over her face, but she replied very quietly,—

'Yes; but I changed my mind afterwards, and wrote to my aunt.'

CHAPTER VI.

MRS. DOROTHY was seated in her arm-chair by the window the next afternoon, and Mr. Saville was sitting with her. It was a lovely day, and the window was open. Mrs. Dorothy loved to hear the birds sing and feel the fresh breezes blow in upon her. It all reminded her so much of Charity, who was so fond of sunshine and summer, and the free, happy, out-door life they brought with them. She and Mr. Saville had been talking of Charity, and Mrs. Dorothy was consequently in her most cheerful spirits; for to talk of Charity was, to her, just what talking of those we love best to those who love them also, and appreciate our love for them, is to most of us—life and strength. And the news from Charity continued so good—there had been such a charming letter from her only two days ago—such a pleasant account of her from Miss Mowbray the very day before, that Mrs. Dorothy had much to tell Mr. Saville about their common godchild, when their conversation was interrupted by the unexpected sound of the postman's knock.

It was evidently as unexpected to Betsy in the kitchen as it was to her mistress in the parlour; for though Mr. Saville had gone himself to open the door on Mrs. Dorothy's exclaiming, with evident anxiety, 'A letter to-day! I trust the child isn't ill—that there's nothing the matter!' Betsy had reached the door before him; and it was from her hands that Mr. Saville received the note Charity had penned so hurriedly the day before. 'From our young lady, sir,' she said; in the quiet way in which Betsy was never known to speak, save when there was some agitating feeling at work within, which she was conscious must be kept down by external force. 'From our young lady, sir; and we heard on Monday—and she seldom writes more than once a-week!'

'Well, Betsy, she writes herself,' said the Rector, 'so she is not ill. She has some question to ask, no doubt; but your mistress will tell us.' And he carried the letter into the parlour.

Yes, indeed, Charity had a question to ask. And how was that question to be answered? Mrs. Dorothy put the letter into Mr. Saville's hands, and they both sat for long, anxiously discussing the matter; not, however, without Betsy's impatience having brought her into the parlour to inquire if Miss Charity was ill. 'No, not ill—quite well,' Mrs. Dorothy said; and that was a relief to Betsy.

She saw that there was trouble from her mistress's face and voice, but that did not much surprise her. Betsy's only surprise had been that the trouble had not come before. She was fully prepared to hear now that there had been some outbreak with the music master, or the French master, since her return, and that, perhaps, Miss Charity was to be dismissed from school; and Betsy returned to her work with the comfortable feeling, that if this were the case they would at least have the satisfaction of having their darling back again with them.

Meanwhile Mrs. Dorothy and Mr. Saville considered and reconsidered what answer must be sent to Charity 'by return of post.'

'I wish we had taken your advice,' said Mr. Saville, 'and told her the whole truth before she left. I feel very much to blame for having prevented your doing so.'

'There is no use in lamenting the past,' said Mrs. Dorothy, softly. 'You gave me such advice as seemed best to you, and it was my own decision to adopt it; though I have always found that with Charity simple truth, however painful, is what she can best endure.'

'I wonder,' said Mr. Saville, 'that she has not mooted this question long before, and insisted on discovering the truth.'

'She would have done so,' replied Mrs. Dorothy, 'had her mind ever been disturbed about it. But it never has been. Charity, you know, has such a truthful nature. She is not at all a child to suspect evil, or imagine things different from what they appear to be.'

'No,' said Mr. Saville; 'we have often remarked how very simple she was. It seemed almost strange to see so much simplicity combined with such extreme discernment and quickness of perception.'

'I think,' said Mrs. Dorothy, 'it arises from the truthfulness of her character. She is so true herself, that she does not imagine anything or anybody not to be what they seem. Though, let her trust in a person be once shaken, I think nothing will restore it. And then, she is not the least inquisitive.'

'Which is also strange,' said Mr. Saville, 'considering how very thoughtful she is. Besides, on a subject so nearly concerning herself, poor child! extreme interest could scarcely be considered as curiosity.'

'No,' replied Mrs Dorothy; 'and she was very anxious. She used frequently to make remarks, as I have told you, which showed that her mind was at work on the subject, and that one evening to which she alludes in her letter, when we were on our way home from church, she asked me to tell her all about her mother. I was very much agitated at the time, and told her it must not be then—at some other time I would do so; and it was, you see, from regard to me, from fear of making me ill, that she said no more then, and she never again alluded to the subject.'

'She might have learned the truth from Betsy,' said Mr. Saville.

'Oh,' replied Mrs. Dorothy, 'you do not know

Charity. She is far too proud ever to inquire from Betsy anything I had not told her, especially anything concerning herself. Indeed, I doubt whether, anxious as she now is to discover the truth, she would seek, or perhaps even accept information, from any one but me—even from you, Mr. Saville.'

'Then,' he replied, 'it would, perhaps, be useless for me to propose, as I was just about to do, that I should go up to London myself this evening, and give her the information she requires more cautiously than, perhaps, it could be conveyed in a letter.'

Mrs. Dorothy leant her head on her hands, and thought—may be, prayed—silently and earnestly.

Then she said,—'No, thank you, dear, kind friend! I may be wrong, but I think it will be best to write. Charity has written to me. She will expect an answer from me. The simplest way of acting, I do believe, will always be the best way for that child. I will write, as she says, by return of post.'

'Then,' said Mr. Saville, 'I will leave you to do so. I think, as you say, that you understand our godchild best: indeed, experience has proved that it is so.'

He left her with the assurance, that if he could not help her with his advice, he would with his prayers; and Mrs. Dorothy rang the bell for Betsy.

'My writing-case, Betsy,' she said; 'I must write to Miss Charity by to-day's post.'

'Write to Miss Charity by to-day's post!' exclaimed Betsy. 'Why, ma'am, you wrote only yesterday, and it just kills you to write letters two days running! You won't have a bit of strength left in you to-night, ma'am—that you won't!'

'Perhaps not,' replied Mrs. Dorothy, with a faint smile; 'I think it very likely I shall not: but I must write to Miss Charity to-day.'

'Ma'am,' said Betsy, looking her mistress full in the face, with such an intensity of sympathy and interest in her countenance that it excluded the possibility of disrespect,—'Ma'am, there's trouble!'

'Only this,' said Mrs. Dorothy, giving her faithful old servant at once the confidence she deserved, 'only this, Betsy, which must have come sooner or later. Miss Charity has written to me, begging to know at once every particular concerning herself.'

'And you 're not a-going to tell her?' exclaimed Betsy, forgetting all dread of agitating her mistress in her excitement: 'you 're surely not a-going to tell her, ma'am?'

'Yes, I am,' said Mrs. Dorothy, gently. 'I think, Betsy, we both of us know, that when Miss Charity's mind is set on a thing, the only way of quieting her is to let her have it. How often have you not tried to convince me of this, Betsy, when I have refused to give Miss Charity something she was determined to have?'

'Yes,' said Betsy, 'I know I 've often begged that the child might have her way, because I knew she would go on clamouring till she 'd got it. But to satisfy her in this, ma'am, it goes against my very heart to think of it. Miss Charity 's so proud, ma'am. The young ladies at Huntley Tower, when they 're down here, though they be duke's daughters, and their papa, folks say, high in the Queen's council, don't hold their heads as high as she does—no, nor come into church with the same air. Miss Charity 's a deal prouder than any one of them, ma'am, and it 's my belief, that if any one wished to give her a deathblow like, one couldn't set about it better than by telling her she 's just nobody that we know of, that she hasn't got any name at all that we can be sure of. You 'll forgive old Betsy for speaking out so plain. God knows I don't mean to forget my place or show any disrespect to you, ma'am, but it goes through my heart like a dagger to think of the effect such a piece of news as this would have on a young lady like Miss Charity. It 's my belief, ma'am, she 'll be running away, or doing something desperate like that. I can't but speak my mind about it, for it would be like a fire in my bones if I did not.'

'You are quite right, Betsy, to say what you think,' said Mrs. Dorothy, and her voice was quite calm, though Betsy's excitement had set her whole frame trembling, and her hands were moving nervously in her lap. 'You love Miss Charity, I know, almost as much as I do myself. But I think, Betsy, I have generally been the best judge of what the child could and could not bear. You remember all you said when first I determined on sending her to school.'

'Well, yes, ma'am, that's true,' replied Betsy; 'I never did think she would have gone away to school, or behaved as she has done there. I thought that she'd have clamoured to stay at home till she'd driven you nearly wild, and that if she had been forced to go to school, for certain she would have run away as soon as she got there. Yes, I know I've been greatly mistaken in the way she would take that trouble.'

'And we must hope, Betsy, you will be mistaken again now,' said Mrs. Dorothy. 'Charity will suffer terribly, I believe; we must hope that it will not be in vain. But Miss Charity is not the character to be crushed by any sorrow, however great. She will rise to any necessity when she feels that it is a necessity. Any how, Betsy, we can but act according to what seems best. One comfort is—it is the greatest poor, weak mortals can know—that we have a Father in heaven who can overrule all for good: He sees the thoughts of our heart, and knows when we desire to do His will; and if we do err through the weakness of our judgment, there is no mistake so great that He cannot set it to rights again. So give me my desk, Betsy, and leave me quiet.'

Betsy arranged the writing-desk, and left the room without saying another word. But when she returned to the kitchen she began setting the tea-tray ready, polishing the bright tea-pot, rubbing the japanned tray, and dusting the shining cups with an energy which might have told any one who was at all experienced in Betsy's character that her thoughts were busy within, even if she had not indulged in a constant running strain of soliloquy. 'Well, the Lord be with my mistress,' she said, 'and teach her how to smooth the point of that arrow, so that it don't run too sharp into our dear child. It's my belief, that if there's one thing on earth that could make her flesh quiver, 'tis just the news she'll get to-morrow. I believe there isn't many that can feel for her as old Betsy can. My lady don't know what it is. She's had her trials, God knows, and they've been heavy enough; the Lord keep Miss Charity from knowing the like, as doubtless He will. For 'tisn't the Lord's way to give all trials to all people. He makes compensation like, as I've often thought. Rachel, she had her husband; and Leah, she had her children; and the Lord's ways are a deal fairer than they often seem to be just at first sight. Mrs. Dorothy, she had her trials pretty sharp, as no one knows better than I do. But this here blow that's going to fall on our poor child's head, she never felt the weight of *that*. She was brought up by her own parents, born in her own home, where she'd a right to be, and there was no one could have thrown a stone at her or her belongings. She don't know the shame or sorrow of belonging to no one; but I do: for wasn't I born in an almshouse and fed with the bread of charity? and didn't I find it bitter bread to eat, too? Ah, 'tis a many years agone now, but well do I remember how I'd sit in church, and look at the poor children that were free like, till I could have cried my heart out for envy; and many times did. Once I remember trying to open my mind on the subject to one of the ladies that came to visit us, when she asked me what made me look so unhappy. A kind lady she was, and a good, but *she* didn't know what it was to be a workhouse child. She told me I had good clothes to wear, and that I looked very different on Sundays from the little children that sat in the aisles. May be I did; I know I felt very different. 'Tisn't a bonnet on one's head, or a good gown and cape, that can make the heart warm inside; better a free heart under the veriest rag that could be laid across it, than good clothes outside and a feeling of desolation and shame within. No; my lady's as good a lady as ever breathed, and she's got as loving a heart towards her adopted child as though she were her own. But it's my opinion she doesn't, no, nor can't, feel for her in this particular trouble as I can. It's them that have been under that cloud that know the feel of it.'

Thus Betsy soliloquised during that summer afternoon, all the sunshine of which, bright as it had been before, had seemed to die out during the short time that elapsed between her answering her mistress's bell, and her return to the kitchen.

The clock struck six, and, punctual to the moment, Betsy carried the tea into the parlour: the letter lay upon the table, and Betsy took it into the hall and put it into the bag without any further word about it. She looked so downcast, however, as she arranged the tea-things, and set the hissing kettle on the fire before making Mrs. Dorothy's tea, that the old lady said,—'God has often been better to us than our fears, Betsy.'

'I trust He may be so now, ma'am,' replied

Betsy, 'for my heart's gone down that low about Miss Charity, I believe I haven't felt as I do now—no, not since the old days, near half a century ago, when I was in the workhouse, ma'am, and would watch my legs and arms to see if they were growing, and count up the months that must pass before I'd be big enough and strong enough to be allowed to work for myself, and have done for ever with the bread of charity, which used, so to speak, to grit against my teeth, and go nigh to choke me. It's my belief, ma'am, 'tis only those that have been obliged to eat of that food that know how hard it is of digestion.'

'Charity has *never* eaten that bread,' said Mrs. Dorothy, with the slightest possible shade of annoyance, mingled with the tones of her gentle voice; 'Charity has never eaten that bread, Betsy: she has been nourished with the food of affection from her cradle. No child was ever more truly, tenderly loved.'

'Well, then, and that's true, ma'am,' replied Betsy: 'no child, I know well enough—no, not the duke's little ladies at Huntley Tower, ever had more love or care. But there's a different feel in the love we've a right to and any other.'

'Betsy,' said Mrs. Dorothy, 'did you not tell me once, that the trial of your early years had been, through God's mercy, the blessing of your after life?'

'Yes, ma'am, and so it was; for I had that proud spirit that may be no other trial would have subdued, and it's just this that makes me feel so much for Miss Charity, as I said this afternoon. It will be her pride that will make her suffer, ma'am, as I know very well.'

'And cannot God do as much for her as He did for you, Betsy?' said Mrs. Dorothy, gravely. 'We will not talk any more about it, for it is of no use. But we will both think of Miss Charity, and we will both pray.'

'No need for my lady to tell me that,' said Betsy, as she returned to her kitchen, and sat down to her solitary supper; 'no need for my lady to tell me that. If ever one poor creature carried another to the Lord, I shall take Miss Charity to Him this blessed day. It's my firm belief now, that the Lord, who sees the end of the road from the very beginning—yes, and doesn't fail to mark out every little turn or winding, however small—it's my belief that He knew very well the day would come when this poor little foundling would be left desolate in Bryce's house, and that He was preparing me, in that dreary workhouse, for the charge He meant one day to give me. Many and many's the time I've said to myself, when that Irish nurse my mistress would get for the baby was finding fault with it, and calling it hard names,—"Ah, *your* heart, Kitty O'Donnell, was never taught to feel for the orphan bairn as mine has been." Many's the time, when I've been afraid the child would hear some word or see some look that might grieve her, I've thanked the Lord who let me know what the pain of such things was that I might feel for others, and do my best to shield them. Many 's the time I 've thought how wise the good God was to put us in those very circumstances in our youth which would turn out useful to us in after years. It 's like a wise master teaching the children the lessons that it 's best for them to learn. They seem hard at the time, and not a bit of use in them either; but wait till the day arrives when the knowledge of them comes to hand just at the right moment, and then we praise and bless the Lord who set us the task, and forced us to get it well by heart, whether we would or not. Ah, that bit of my life was dark enough when I was going through it! But the light of the Lord has shone on it many times since. And it 's shining on it now. How could I ever have borne the child on my heart as I do now, if I hadn't known all the pain and shame she 's going to bear? Pray for the child! no need to tell me to do that. My lady will pray herself, and she 'll put it in better words, no doubt, for she do pray most beautiful, as every one in the village who has ever heard her can say. But the Lord above, He doesn't look to scholarship. Words are just nothing at all to Him, nor persons neither. He just looks to the heart, and, thanks to His mercy, I can pour that out before Him this day. It 's filled up, every corner of it, with one thought—the thought of Miss Charity; and there wouldn't be any relief for me, if I couldn't lay it all at the Saviour's feet. But once there, it won't weigh as it does now. It oughtn't to weigh at all, if we set about things rightly, as Mr. Saville put before us plain enough last Sunday. 'If we had but faith to cast our burden on the Lord, and go on our way without it, that would be the way to be bravely lightened, no doubt. Somehow, I think my mistress has learned that secret, or she never could get rid of her troubles as she does. But that 's a point I haven't reached yet. My way is to cast the burden at the feet of the Lord, and get Him to look at it, and talk it over with Him; and the Lord, He 's so merciful and kind, that He lets even that do me good, and give me strength and comfort to feel the better for it afterwards: may be, one day He 'll give me the faith to feel free of it altogether, like Hannah. She went her way and did eat, we 're told, and her countenance was no more sad, though it was but a promise she had to stay her soul upon. Well, I can't feel quite like that as yet.' And Betsy cleared away the untasted meal, and heaved a heavy sigh.

That night when she went, as usual, to put out Mrs. Dorothy's candle and prepare the night-lamp, her mistress said to her,—

'Betsy, you remember that little poem you were always so fond of hearing Miss Charity repeat?'

'You mean, ma'am, "The Master has come over Jordan?" Yes, indeed, I remember. She had a many fine pieces she could say, but never one I liked as much as I did that. I often think I hear her sweet voice now, saying it to me of a Sunday evening, and telling, in her pretty way, of the mother's carrying the children—little Rachel, and Samuel, and John, and the baby Esther—over the hills of Judah, and along by the vine-rows green, for the Lord to look upon.'

'And you remember, Betsy,' said the old lady, 'that mother's answer to the father, when he strove to dissuade her from her purpose?'

'Yes, ma'am, I believe I could repeat the words, though 'tis some time now since they've come into my mind.' And Betsy repeated the verse.

> 'Nay, do not hinder me, Nathan;
> I feel such a burden of care,
> If I carry it to the Master
> Perhaps I shall leave it there.
> If He lay His hand on the children
> My heart will be lighter, I know;
> For a blessing for ever and ever
> Will follow them as they go.'

'I have been lying here thinking of those words, Betsy,' continued Mrs. Dorothy, cheerfully, 'and my own heart has grown lighter in doing so; that is why I would remind you of them, too. For remember, *we* need not say with that poor woman, "If I carry it to the Master, *perhaps* I shall leave it there." No, if we feel a burden of care, we may say boldly, "If I carry it to the Master, *I know* I shall leave it there." Our dear Lord is nearer to us, Betsy, than He was when He crossed the Jordan, and the people thronged to Him to be healed with a touch of His finger. Let us carry our dear child to the Lord, and lay her at His feet; she will be safe enough there.'

'The very words I would have said myself!' said Betsy, as she left her mistress's room and repaired to her own; 'only I can't put things in the same way. Sure enough, my lady's heart and mine are beating together. Our prayers will be set to the same key this night; only my lady, she gets up higher than I can, having more faith. Well, we can but do our best, according to the gift the good God gives. If I can't get up as high as she can . . . well, it will be all in the same tune; my poor voice shall accompany hers, though it be but in a low sort of bass, and, as I say, the God above, He accepts all: the rich and poor they meet together, and He who made them both, He hears them both.'

CHAPTER VII.

THE letters reached Miss Mowbray's house between seven and eight in the morning, but it was not usual with her to give them to the girls until after family prayers, when they all gathered round the breakfast table. They could be procured earlier, however, in any case of necessity. Charity remembered, that only a fortnight before Helen Anstruther had gone to Miss Mowbray's room one evening, to ask her whether she would allow her to have her letters next day as soon as the postman arrived, as she was expecting news of her brother's examination, and wished much to know whether he had passed before coming downstairs, and her request had been immediately granted. And this was no special favour to Helen; for Charity recollected also that, when she first came to school, one of the girls was anxious about a sister who was ill, and Miss Mowbray used to send her her letter from home every morning as soon as it arrived. She knew she had only to tell Miss Mowbray that she was anxious for a letter from her Aunt Dorothy, and she could receive it in private.

But she would not do so. She felt almost sure that her aunt would write, as she had so earnestly requested her to do, by return of post, and Charity resolved to abide and endure whatever the day's news might bring. She would neither dread it before it came, nor shrink from it when it arrived. A *sudden* blow, Charity knew, would sometimes take her off her equilibrium, and many an angry word, many a passionate tear, had she shed on the impulse of the moment, which her pride had led her afterwards bitterly to regret. But only let her be prepared for a thing, and there was nothing she could not meet. So she dressed as quietly as usual, and joined in conversation with Ellinor Temple with an ease and apparent interest which made that young lady remark afterwards, that 'really Charity Helstone was growing quite agreeable.' On coming into the dining-room, her eye fell on the pile of letters lying by the side of Miss Mowbray's plate, and at once she recognised amongst them the large, upright characters of her Aunt Dorothy's peculiar writing. But she felt rather than saw that Fraulein was watching her, and she passed to her place without any external sign of discomposure.

'Another letter from your aunt, my dear,' said Miss Mowbray, as she handed the letter to Charity, whose place was next to hers at the breakfast-table. 'I hope she is not ill. You heard from her yesterday, did you not? and she does not generally write more than once a-week.'

This remark attracted towards Charity the attention of one or two of the girls who were sitting at that end of the table, and were not engaged with letters of their own, and Charity's quick eyes did not fail to perceive that Ellinor Temple, who was one of them, turned crimson. She had made up her mind, on hearing Miss Mowbray's remark, that the letter which Charity had so suddenly despatched to her aunt two evenings before had been, as she had told Fraulein, to complain of the treatment she had received, and now this was doubtless the answer. She, therefore, waited with beating heart and flushed face whilst Charity broke the seal of her letter, and then replied to Miss Mowbray's repeated question, that her aunt seemed quite well. Ellinor remarked, also, that the letter was a long one; that Charity did not read it, though she made a sort of pretence of doing so,—indeed, Ellinor believed she had not turned over the first page. Nor had she. That preliminary page had told Charity that the tidings she might expect to learn concerning herself might be such as she had best read with no eyes upon her, and folding up the letter she put it into her pocket. Had she been alone that morning, she could not have eaten a morsel; but Ellinor Temple was sitting exactly opposite to her, so she ate her breakfast as usual. The Scripture-class followed. Once Miss Mowbray said, 'My dear Charity, I do not think you are attending,' but after that observation Charity answered every question with her usual correctness, and read every text and reference that came to her turn in her usual clear, decided voice.

Then followed the hour's recreation before morning lessons. Charity went to her room, and Ellinor, burning as she was with desire to follow her, did not dare to do so. To her surprise, a quarter of an hour later she saw Charity playing in the garden with little Alice Rhodes.

'Look!' she said to Fraulein, 'there she is, romping in the garden! There can't be any great news in her letter. Look at her running races with Alice, and tossing the child up in the air when she catches her! There can't be anything in her letter.'

'Not to trouble her, perhaps,' replied Fraulein. 'But suppose her old aunt, who, Miss Mowbray say, love her so much, like all old maids do love everything, dogs, or cats, or children, or whatever they fix their heart upon, without any reason; suppose the old lady, she writes to tell her she means not once to leave her longer in a place where she receives insult, that may not trouble Miss Helstone very much—that may make her run faster up and down the garden, perhaps, or toss the little Alice very high in the air, like she is doing at this moment; we grow very strong and active in the body when we hear something that we find pleasing to the mind. But when Miss Mowbray, she send for me to her study, and say in her grave voice, which always mean, "Now this is my last intention, and it is no use to argue against it; I have done the argument in my own mind, and I mean all what I say;"—when she say to me in that voice, "Fraulein, you insult my pupils, you may return to Germany," and I lose my good home and I have no place to go to, for the sake of Miss Charity Helstone, that may be no trouble to her indeed, but it may be one very large trouble to me.'

Poor Fraulein ! how it would have lightened her heart could she have known that a quarter of an hour before Charity had put on her hat, and run desperately downstairs to play and jump with little Alice, she had been standing in her bedroom, the door locked, and her aunt's letter in her hand, with such a wretchedly anxious face as, happily, few girls of Charity's age are ever seen to wear. She read the first page again, and she meditated reading the letter through; but then she remembered, that in three quarters of an hour she must be at her Grecian History class; that if she failed there it would be the subject of general remark, for she stood first, and was sure of the prize. And after the history lesson she must go to her drawing, and she would not for worlds have an unsteady hand there, with Ellinor Temple sitting next to her and marking every stroke of her pencil. Then would come dinner, and after dinner the walk, when, for all she knew, Fraulein herself, or Ellinor, might be her companion. And after the walk, an hour's arithmetic and an hour's French before tea. And after tea, reading and working, and then supper and prayers, and Ellinor Temple for her companion in her bedroom afterwards.

No; that day and the next would be all too busy for her to be able to read that letter. She would lock it up till Saturday. Then there would be a half-holiday, and on half-holidays Charity was always many hours alone. It was one of her gravest offences with many of the girls, now that the weather was warm enough to allow of her sitting in her bedroom, that she generally spent all her holiday hours there. Ellinor Temple never attempted to join her, and Charity felt she must wait for this leisure time if she would read that letter, and get over it, as she felt sure she could if she had only time. She could not always quiet emotion or restrain passion at the moment, as past experience had taught her; though even this, with Pride for her master, was a lesson she had acquired wonderfully since she had been at school. But give her time, let her but be prepared, and there was nothing to which she could not make up her mind. As she had said to Betsy on the occasion of the tooth-drawing, years and years ago,—'They didn't tell me what was coming, but gave a great pull, and of course I called out; but if they had told me what they were going to do, do you think I'd have cried? No!'

So the letter was locked up, and Charity was as active and diligent in all her lessons as ever. Only Miss Mowbray remarked at dinner on the second day that she looked ill. And one or two of the girls said that certainly Charity Helstone was, as Ellinor had said, 'growing more sociable; she had talked more during the last two days than she generally did in a month.' Even Fraulein, after watching her narrowly, came to the pleasant conclusion that she was not likely to get into any trouble on Miss Helstone's account, and by Saturday afternoon she had ceased to think much about it.

On that day it rained heavily—one steady downpour; so, to Charity's relief, there was no talk of going out, and she could retire to her bedroom immediately after dinner, with almost the certainty of being able to remain undisturbed there till tea.

No one took any notice of her doing so, for it was her usual custom; but as she left the room she heard, with satisfaction, Ellinor Temple consent to play a game of battledore with another girl in the hall, and little Alice Rhodes present a petition to Helen Anstruther to 'be allowed to stop with her all the afternoon,' which was favourably received. Therefore Charity went to her room, locked her door, and sat down to her letter in perfect quiet. She read it once. She read it twice. She read it three times. At first the words seemed all to dance before her eyes, and to have no meaning at all in them. The idea of her not being really Aunt Dorothy's niece had never entered her mind. The Rectory children called her 'Aunt' without any right to do so, save that of affection and early habit. Charity had never thought it strange of them, or implying any idea of untruth. Every one knew that Mrs. Dorothy was *not* their aunt, and that they only termed her so because they did not know what else to call her: probably they had caught it up from Charity herself, from associating so much with one who *was*, as she believed, Aunt Dorothy's own true, real niece, and had a right to call her 'Aunt,' in which she allowed her little companions to join. But that she should not be her niece at all, not have more right to the title than Ellen Saville had—not have, indeed, any right to it at all!—the first feeling that came into Charity's mind as she realized this first, and comparatively very small portion of her trouble, was that it was a 'shame—a wicked, wicked shame!' And had she given vent to her feelings, she could at that moment have found it in her heart to apply to Mrs. Dorothy some such epithets as she had occasionally, in times of passion, applied to Betsy. For Charity's was a character in which, when once passion was strongly roused, it raised its voice so loudly as for the time to silence every other. Love, gratitude, respect, fled before her present indignant resentment; and instead of recognising all that had been done for her, Charity felt as though she had been cruelly ill-treated.

What could she do? what should she do? This was the first question that obtained any definite attention in her mind. To remain at school seemed impossible. Doubtless Miss Mowbray, and many others, were acquainted with her humiliating circumstances, though she herself had been kept in such cruel ignorance of them. Fraulein evidently knew all about her, or she would not have dared to insult her. Perhaps Miss Danvers had known also, and that was one reason why she had always sought to exalt Ellen Saville and depreciate her. Perhaps even the Rectory children knew; and if so, how ridiculous she must often have appeared in their eyes when, in her childhood's days, she had boasted of things as belonging to her, to which it now appeared she had never had the smallest right!

And then there flashed across her mind the remembrance of one day in particular, when she and Ellen, who were never very good friends at the best of times, had had one of their most desperate quarrels. Charity had been amusing herself in the attic, where all sorts of relics of past days—family pictures too faded to appear on the walls, and old books too shabby to be placed on the bookshelves—were stored away; and in so doing, she had come upon an old book entitled 'Family Records,' drawn up by some defunct member of the Helstone family, and containing an account of various Helstones of ancient times, who had distinguished themselves in various ways; together with a genealogy, taken from the Heralds' Office, which traced the family back to very early days, and proved that it was one of the best and oldest that could be gloried in.

The attic was ever Charity's favourite place of resort, for its contents were all old; and in this lay one great charm. And they were for the most part extremely undefined, and in this lay another; for she could invest them with any ideas and facts which her fertile imagination chose to invent; and often she would come down from her hiding-place, with her little brain so full of the romantic stories she had been connecting with the venerable old lady with a high cap and ruffles, or the young maiden standing on the top of a flight of marble steps, that she would find it utterly impossible to commit to memory the dates of the most remarkable battles in English history, or the simplest rules of syntax in English grammar. But that morning on which she discovered the old book of 'Family Records' had been a most delightful one. To read of heroes, not of her own imagining, but of heroes who had existed in her own family, and whose blood was actually at that moment flowing in her veins, brightened the sparkle in her bright eyes, raised the colour in her rosy cheeks, and quickened the pulses in her ardent little frame. The book was prefaced with the words,—

> 'I cannot but remember such things were,
> That were most precious to me.'

And, child as she still was, Charity could fully enter into the feeling that was in Shakespeare's mind when he wrote them.

Full of her 'Family Records,' Charity came downstairs at the call of the breakfast-bell with a radiant face; happily, Betsy was the first person with whom she came into collision—or perhaps we should rather say, unhappily; for had she poured out her mind on the subject to Mrs. Dorothy, her godmother might have earlier seen the mistake she was making in bringing up the child in a belief concerning herself which was incorrect, and might have discovered earlier that to breathe in a false atmosphere can never be healthy for the moral lungs of any one created with a thirst for truth.

But Betsy was waiting at the bottom of the stairs, knowing from experience that, after Charity had been spending a couple of hours in the dusty old attic, amongst the old books and boxes, she would be in no condition to present herself at Mrs. Dorothy's breakfast-table. And while Betsy obliged her to brush her hair and wash her hands, Charity, in the fulness of her heart, informed her of the *trouvaille* she had made in these 'Family Records' of the Helstone family, and said she longed to ask Aunt Dorothy all about them.

'My dear,' said Betsy, at once realising the difficulty Mrs. Dorothy would be in when she found Charity thus laying claim to bygone ancestors who had never belonged to her, 'my dear, you must not mention that book to your aunt.'

'And why not?' asked Charity.

Betsy thought about for a reason, and was not long in finding one. 'My dear,' she said, 'do you remember how ill your aunt was not a month ago, when she fainted, and had that shivering fit, and we thought she was going to die?'

'Of course I do!' replied Charity, impatiently; 'but what has that got to do with it?'

'Shall I tell you what made her so ill?' said Betsy. 'It was only because, in turning over an old desk, she came upon a paper that had been written years ago, and she couldn't stand the sight of it. That old paper brought on one of my mistress's attacks. She used to have them often in years gone by, Miss Charity; and many 's the time I 've thought she 'd die in one of them. But she rarely has them now—sometimes, not for years. It seems there 's but one thing now that can bring them upon her, and that is when the past comes up suddenly again without her being prepared like to meet it.'

'Well, but,' said Charity, whose quickness of perception often baffled poor Betsy's powers of persuasion, 'well, but, Betsy, I suppose that paper was something Aunt Dorothy had written herself, or that somebody had written to her. She couldn't mind hearing about the people in that book. They died ages ago. Aunt Dorothy never knew one of them. And she can't care much about them, or the book either, to have left it all this time up in the attic with all the rubbish; amongst those pictures of people she says she never saw, which were left to her mother by an old bachelor cousin, who died before she was born. I don't believe she knows the book is there.'

Betsy was puzzled; for she could never have brought herself to utter a deliberate falsehood, however she might fail in perceiving that her equivocations were really such.

'Miss Charity,' she said, after an instant's hesitation, 'it 's my belief, that if you say a word to your aunt about that book, the consequence will be that she 'll be more upset, may be, than she was that day. So if you go talking about it when I 've warned you not, remember it will be your fault if you make your aunt as ill as she was the other night. You know how she was then.'

Yes, Charity did know; for she had never expected her godmother to live through the fainting-fit, which had alarmed even Betsy, though she had kept saying she had seen her mistress in as bad, and worse. Charity did not in the least see how the mention of that old book could possibly produce the same effect on Mrs. Dorothy, or, indeed, any effect at all; but Betsy was so positive that she dared not run any risk on the matter, and, therefore, by a violent effort of self-control, sat through breakfast without mentioning the matter.

But no sooner did she find herself in the Rectory school-room with Ellen Saville, than out of the abundance of her heart her mouth began to talk, and whilst the two girls were getting their books ready, and waiting for Miss Danvers to join them, Charity gave Ellen such a grand account of former Helstones, and questioned her so closely concerning former Savilles, that the poor girl's brain, which always found enough to do to meet whatever fact might be at the moment before it, was fairly bewildered. She could only tell Charity that she knew nothing about any other Savilles, except her grandpapa, who was a gentleman-farmer in Yorkshire, and died five years ago; but she would ask mamma, and tell her in the afternoon.

Accordingly in the afternoon, when they met again for their lessons, Charity recommenced the subject; and it was on hearing that Mrs. Saville had replied to Ellen's question by saying that she was too much occupied then to attend to it, but that Mr. Saville had said Charity had much better be minding her lessons and her duties than meddling in these matters, that the quarrel had arisen; Charity having triumphed over Ellen till Ellen cried, and the noise having brought Edward to set them both to rights, Charity remembered that he had turned off the subject laughingly, and gone away repeating the lines,—

'When Adam delved, and Eve span,
Where was then the gentleman?'

At the time she had thought he applied it to his own case, and she had felt true pity for those who could not carry their acquaintance with their own family beyond their grandfather. But now, as memory recalled that scene, she felt sure that Edward knew all about her birth, and she reflected how ridiculous she must have made herself in his eyes on that, and many other occasions. Yes, what must Edward think of her? How differently, indeed, she now felt towards him! a wide gulf seemed suddenly to have opened between them. Hitherto she had considered herself as his sister, and more than his sister; for Ellen, with her want of mind and her narrow feelings, would never, Charity had often thought to herself, been the near and dear companion to him which she had ever been, and as she had imagined, until to-day, ever would be. But now a sudden separation seemed made between her and Edward. He was amongst those who owned a name and a home; she had neither. The bread she ate was the bread of charity; the clothes she wore were the clothes of charity. It was a dreadful, hateful position; she could not remain in it. The irons were even now entering into her soul, and she felt that she must shake them off: but how to do so?

Long did Charity remain, her head bent over her desk, her hot brow pressed between her hands, whilst her tearless eyes ached and burned in their sockets, as she turned over and over again in her mind what she could do. To live all her life in idle independence at Mrs. Dorothy's, and on her godmother's death inherit the property which had belonged to her, was a course which others might have chalked out for her, but which she herself would never stoop to accept. Rather would she beg her daily bread, for in so doing she would have but one evil to endure—that of humiliation; whilst in living upon Mrs. Dorothy's charity she would be breathing air as false as it was humbling. She was not Miss Charity Helstone; she was not Mrs. Dorothy's only surviving relation, or the heir to her property. She was an unfortunate foundling, belonging to no one in particular, but born to the poverty, shame, and sorrow, which, because they were her own, the only heritage which she could possess, she would far rather endure than be dependent upon any one, however kind or generous.

The tea-bell roused Charity from her three-hours' reflections, and the sight of her own livid face, as she smoothed her hair at the glass, reminded her how great an effort she must needs make, if the misery she had suffered during those hours in her solitary room was not to pass to the knowledge of those without.

CHAPTER VIII.

CHARITY'S answer to Mrs. Dorothy's letter was so vague, that neither her aunt nor Mr. Saville had known what to make of it. One thing, however, soon became clear, and this was consolation enough to satisfy Betsy's anxieties, at all events. Charity had no intention of running away from school to hide herself in some unknown corner of the world. On the contrary, whilst not alluding to the letter beyond acknowledging it, and thanking Mrs. Dorothy for complying at once with her request, Charity continued to write on the subject of her various studies with greater interest than ever; whilst Miss Mowbray's letters confirmed the impression that she was working zealously, and making very rapid progress. 'There was everything in her conduct to give satisfaction. She was the favourite pupil with all the masters, who were constantly upholding her as an example of industry and perseverance to her companions: the only thing Miss Mowbray had to regret was, that she was not as great a favourite with these same companions;

but doubtless it was her nature to be reticent and reserved, though it was not the character which Mr. Saville had led her to expect she should find in her.' Nor was it, Mrs. Dorothy remarked to Mr. Saville, Charity's natural character. Ardent, enthusiastic, and unreserved at home, why should she have become so altered at school? Mr. Saville could only reply, that he thought shyness at first had led to Charity's making this impression—shyness, and being utterly unaccustomed to strangers. He would not have added any further reason, but Mrs. Dorothy herself remarked,—'Yes, she was always very shy with strangers; but I dare say she would have grown sociable in time, if it had not been for my letter. I believe that may be weighing on her mind all this while, though she will not allow us to see that it is so—from pride, perhaps. Charity is so very proud, or else she fears making me unhappy.'

'Well,' replied Mr. Saville, 'Christmas will soon be here now, and then we shall have her at home again, and be able to judge for ourselves. It is a comfort, as you say, that your good Betsy's fears have not been fulfilled, and that the effect of this news upon Charity's mind should evidently have been to lead her to devote herself more diligently than ever to the duty before her.'

Yes, Charity was indeed more devoted than ever to her studies; for the motive now influencing her exertions was far stronger than that which had inspired her before. And do not we all work in proportion to the propelling power within? Hitherto,

Charity had studied to please her Aunt Dorothy, and because she had promised to do her best, and longed for the approving smile and the words of commendation which would be her reward when she should return for the Christmas vacation to her happy little home. But now, day and night, she was urged forward with the one desire that had taken possession of her energetic mind and strong will—the desire of becoming learned enough, and accomplished enough, to earn her own living as a governess—yes, and *such* a governess that it should be no charity, no favour, on the part of any parents to engage her services for their children; the benefit should be on their side; and those through whom she should receive the means of existence should feel, whilst rendering them to her, that they were far more indebted to her for what they received than she could be for what they gave.

With this motive at work within, Charity studied diligently, and carefully kept aloof from making friends; and the efforts of her will prevented her heart from feeling the trouble as it would otherwise have done. Her time and mind were too fully occupied to allow of her being miserable. And she had a power within her which, until now, she never knew that she possessed—the power of resolutely turning from that which it pained her to see; of pushing, as it were, the painful subjects down into the depths of her mind, somewhere out of present sight, and covering them over with a crust of activity and occupation, which kept them in their place. Happy she was not, for there is no happiness without freedom, and there could be no freedom in a heart thus loaded and restrained; and at times one or other of the imprisoned thoughts within would force its way through the outward barrier, and for some moments—occasionally even for some hours—there would be hard work for Charity before she could get her heart to rights again. But in the end she always came off victorious, and no one who had seen her at Miss Mowbray's dinner-table, or in her place amongst the other girls at class, would have imagined that one short hour before, perhaps, the face which was so still now had been hidden between the hands in bitter weeping; and the voice which answered so calmly, forcing its way up from the heart in deep sobs.

But as time went on the work grew easier. It became a habit with Charity to answer questions with apparent interest, which she had really scarcely heard, and could not have repeated five minutes afterwards. She could play now quite merrily with little Alice; not wildly, as when the trouble was fresh, but cheerfully running races with her as formerly; even telling her stories: but all mechanically. There was no heart in anything she did; as how can there ever be, when between the inner life and the outward world there is a bitter secret? Charity was studious, diligent, respectful to her superiors, kind to those around her; but she was not herself, and all felt that there was something wanting.

The one thought that made itself most troublesome, was the thought of the approaching Christmas holidays. Charity was fully resolved not to return to Arlington; but how to broach the subject with Mrs. Dorothy she did not quite see. For she knew how much her godmother would take this resolve to heart, and she dreaded the effect which such an agitating piece of news might have upon her. Yet, go back to Arlington she could not, and would not. Some of Miss Mowbray's pupils, whose parents were in India, were to remain at school, and she would stay with them, and sedulously carry on her studies. But she would neither go back to Arlington to occupy the false position she had formerly held there, nor would she go back to have the truth disclosed and bear the humiliation that would follow.

Some months had passed since Charity's letter to Mrs. Dorothy had been written and answered, when a day came, a memorable day, which was to work a greater fermentation in Charity's mind than had been made even by the arrival of that letter, and the reflections of the long hours spent over it on the Saturday following.

One of Charity's chief interests at school—perhaps, indeed, her greatest pleasure—was going to church, and listening to Mr. Morton's sermons. Not that she cared at all more for heavenly things now than she had done six months ago, when Mrs. Dorothy had said truly that the day had not come for Charity to need religion, and that until it did she feared she would not seek it. The very reality of her character made her care but little for the mere form of anything, and often when her godmother had grieved over the absence of all semblance of piety had she taken comfort from the thought, that in a heart like Charity's the semblance would never show itself unless the substance were beneath. Charity had sent Mrs. Dorothy flowing descriptions of Mr. Morton's sermons ever since she had been at school, generally concluding, however, with the same words,—'As I say, dear Aunt Dorothy, you would delight in him because he is so good, and I delight in him because he is so clever.'

The day came, however, when one of Mr. Morton's sermons fell on Charity's heart as none other had ever done before; and that, *not* because it was so clever that her attention was arrested and her mind riveted by his usual power of reasoning and charm of expression, for it was a singularly simple sermon, addressed to little children, and for their sakes clothed in simplest words. But the subject of the sermon—the very text, as he gave it out in his peculiarly deep voice, which, in the fervour of its tone, had struck Charity the first day she heard it as unlike any other she had ever heard before—the very text as it fell upon her ear did not pass thence, as usual, only into the brain, but went beyond—down, down into the heart:—'Leave thy fatherless children; I will preserve them alive."

The sermon was in favour of the large foundling hospital close at hand, and it was addressed partly to those whose help was sought for these little ones, partly to the little ones themselves, who sat around the Communion rails. Charity had often seen them there before, a little company of white-capped, white-tippeted maidens, but till now she had never associated their feelings with her own; but as the words of that sermon sounded in her ears a sort of sacred sisterhood seemed to form itself within her heart, and a very blessed sisterhood it would be if all that Mr. Morton said to them and of them were indeed true. For he represented their situation, not as one of peculiar misery, but of peculiar blessing and of special promise, would they but believe the promise and avail themselves of the blessing. 'True it is,' he told them, 'that in this life the desolation of orphanhood is great; so great, that when the prophet was in sore distress at the sight of Jerusalem's miseries—in such distress, that his heart was turned within him and his eyes ran down with water, he could find no more significant expression to serve as a type of the people of Zion in their affliction than that "they were orphans and fatherless." Yet, attached to the desolation is the great blessing, the sorrow and the joy, the darkness and the light, side by side. For these fatherless ones are those who are especially entreated to find mercy in God. Others have earthly fathers to watch over them and protect them in houses made with clay. "A father of the fatherless is God in His holy habitation." The cause of the fatherless is His cause, which He has bound Himself to protect, and plead for Himself. He is their keeper; they have but to cry to Him, and He has given His own word that He will surely hear their cry. And if they have God for a father, what else can they need? All the fulness of their affection may be given to Him, and He will receive it and value it, for the heart of His children is what He seeks to possess. All the service of their lives may be given to Him, and He will receive it at their hands. They might have—many amongst them had—no name on earth to call their own, but this would be but for a very short time if they were the children of God. He would Himself write a new name for them above, and soon, in the glory of knowing and possessing that name, the passing sorrow or shame of earth would vanish like a cloud, and be no more remembered.

'All the many secret sorrows, the private troubles, and infirmities, and weaknesses, which a parent's ear alone seems formed to hear, and which those who are parentless can breathe to no other—all these things can be told to the tender Father above: for, like as a father pitieth his children, so does He pity them that fear Him; like as a mother comforteth, so does He comfort, and yet more tenderly; for a mother may forget, and experience has proved that there is a point in human weakness and despair so low, that the day may come when a woman shall not have compassion on the son of her womb: but the Father of Lights knows no variableness or shadow of turning. That which is of flesh, however firm, *may* fail, or faint; but the "Father which is in heaven" changeth not—"the same yesterday, and to-day, and for ever."

'And several proofs from holy scripture are there to prove the tender care which God provides for fatherless children. We have a striking instance of this in the history of Lot, whose father Haran had died before his grandfather Terah, in the land of his nativity; how completely was that loss provided for by the conduct of Abraham, who carried Lot with him into Canaan, rescued him by his own exertions, and at the risk of his own life, when he was carried captive from the city where his self-will had led him to dwell, and finally obtained his deliverance from the destruction which overwhelmed the other inhabitants of that sinful city! Was it not because God remembered Abraham that Lot was saved? and was it not the God of Abraham who inspired this fatherly feeling and conduct in His servant's heart towards the fatherless Lot?

'Those amongst God's servants who stood highest in His favour, and were privileged to draw closest to His person, seemed to learn directly from Himself that special care for the fatherless which He Himself feels, and would have every faithful follower of His to feel likewise. Moses we find pleading the cause of the daughters of Zelophehad, whose father had died in the wilderness, and obtaining from the Lord a very ready hearing and answer. One of the few kings of Israel who "did that which was right in the sight of the Lord," the young king Joash, who was privileged to repair the temple of the Lord, was orphaned in his youth; but God raised up the friends needful to protect his early years, and prepare him for the work which He intended him to perform.

'Esther had neither father nor mother—moreover, she was beautiful, and the very circumstances of her career were full of danger and temptation; yet was she not one of the fatherless children, who, being left to God, found in Him all the support, all the guidance, all the strength she needed. Was there not enough in the simple story of that captive maiden's life to raise the most drooping heart, and to prove to the understanding of every orphan child there present that they need not let their hands hang down, or their hearts fail them, because they have not fathers or mothers, or friends or fortunes, like others,—no, all they have to do is to turn to Him, the sunshine of whose love is extended over all, but rests with special brightness where the clouds of earth have gathered thickest, that it may make the greater display of its power by dispersing them all. The golden sceptre of God's favour, so willingly extended to every suppliant who ventures in faith to draw near His throne, will, as it were, ever be extended, with a smile of special sweetness, to the desolate and the orphaned. All the fulness of His mercy and protection is promised to the fatherless.'

Such words fell on Charity's soul that day with strange power. It seemed as though Mr. Morton must have read her heart, and must have known some of the thoughts that of late had been weighing so heavily there. At the close of the sermon he stood up to speak, and Charity felt as though he was going to speak to her. But it was only to say that confirmation classes would be held after the Christmas holidays—that those who desired to become catechumens were to meet him in the church to-morrow morning.

No sooner had the girls left the church than the sermon seemed to pass from the minds of almost every one amongst them. Helen Anstruther, indeed, was grave and thoughtful, as she generally was; but evidently the sermon had made but little impression even on her, for on one of the other girls saying that she had quite forgotten they were going to have a charity sermon, and asking her if she had remembered, she had replied,—

'Oh, yes! I recollected it very well, for I felt so sorry last Sunday when it was given out. It's very wrong, I know, for charity sermons must be preached, to get money for good objects; but I always feel so sorry when Mr. Morton has to preach one. He does preach such beautiful sermons; but, somehow, he never seems to preach half as well when he is tied down to any particular subject. To-day, for instance, he was not a bit like himself—was he?' she added, appealing to Charity, who, Helen had long since remarked, paid much greater attention to Mr. Morton's sermons than most of the girls did.

The colour mounted to Charity's face. 'I'm sure I don't know,' she said: 'I thought the sermon a very good one.'

Her manner was so peculiar, that Helen and the other girls were struck by it. Helen's kind heart led her at once to regret the remark she had made, without at the moment remembering the strong suspicion that existed in the school concerning Charity, for she feared her inadvertent words had given pain; and asking Charity to let her be her companion in the homeward walk, she sought to pay her every attention, for which Charity felt anything but grateful.

Fraulein and Ellinor Temple, between whom a curious friendship had lately arisen, had also remarked the peculiarity of Charity's manner, the heightened colour and the cold, restrained reply, and it all went to confirm their impressions, and, it must be confessed, their wishes. Not having felt any inconvenient results from their former insolent treatment of Charity, as at one time they feared might have been the case, and being strengthened in their dislike of her by the cool indifference with which she treated them, it afforded the spiteful little governess and the silly girl whom she had lately selected as her special favourite, and who, in consequence, was never now heard to say a single word against Fraulein, but was, on the contrary, always ready to fight her battles,—it afforded these two real satisfaction to suppose that their suspicions were correct, and Charity was doubtless some unfortunate foundling, rescued from poverty and shame by the mistaken kindness of good Mrs. Dorothy Helstone.

As Helen and Charity followed Miss Mowbray and her mother down the street which led from the church to their house, Fraulein took Ellinor's arm and followed them; and as they did so, Charity distinctly heard Fraulein say,—'Miss Ellinor Temple, my dear, we have not made no mistake once; you see how red our young lady grows. It is no wonder that young lady has no manners, and cannot behave herself like other polite young ladies. You have one proverb here in England; Miss Mowbray say one day there is great vulgarity in it, but I think there is likewise the truth,—"What is bred in the bone, that come out in the flesh." I think we can see the truth of that without needing to go one hundred mile off.'

Every word of this speech Helen distinctly heard, and she was afraid to look at Charity, who, she felt sure, must have heard also; indeed, Helen thought that Fraulein must surely have intended her to do so. And Charity had heard and understood, but at that moment Mr. Morton's words were so present to her mind that it seemed to have no power to entertain any other ideas.

It was the usual custom at Miss Mowbray's school for the girls to write out as much of the sermon as they could remember, and Charity's notes were generally very superior to any of the others; but that afternoon she went to Miss Mowbray's room, and asked permission to be exempted from writing the morning's sermon—her head ached, and she did not feel well. Permission was granted at once, and Charity was leaving the room, when Miss Mowbray recalled her to speak to her of the confirmation classes which Mr. Morton had announced. Annie Danvers was going to be confirmed, and one or two of the others. Miss Mowbray had written to Mrs.

Dorothy on the subject, and her answer had been that she left it with Charity, to do exactly as she wished. 'The names were to be given to Mr. Morton, and she would like to know what Charity felt about it in the course of the day.'

'Must I decide to-day?' Charity timidly asked.

'You heard what Mr. Morton said, my dear,' Miss Mowbray replied; 'he said the names were to be given in to-morrow: but I did not imagine the idea would take you by surprise. I thought you would have heard from your aunt on the subject. I wrote to her more than a fortnight ago, and as I tell you, she wrote me word that she had left it entirely with you. I felt sure she would have written to you herself; and really, my dear, you are so very quiet and reserved with me, that I thought you would prefer my leaving this matter entirely to your aunt.'

'Aunt Dorothy did write to me, ma'am, and I had decided on not attending the classes; but I think——'

'You would like to change your mind, my dear?' said Miss Mowbray, encouragingly.

'I thought,' said Charity—'it has only been to-day that I have thought so—that perhaps I might like to go with the others. Aunt Dorothy says we are not obliged to be confirmed because we attend the classes, if, after all, we do not wish to be.'

'Your aunt is quite right, my dear. Mr. Morton says that many a young person comes forward as a candidate for confirmation just because they have reached the age appointed, but without the least understanding the meaning of that service or the preparation of heart and life which it requires; and he would far rather see such draw back than come forward, if, at the close of his confirmation classes, the teaching they have received from him has led them to see how unfit they are for taking such solemn vows upon themselves. He told me only last week, that often young persons who had come boldly forward as candidates for confirmation have, at the closing of the classes, declared themselves utterly unfit to be confirmed, and that to bring them to the knowledge of this he has considered more than a sufficient result of his labour in instructing them: so that you can give in your name with a perfect feeling of liberty.'

Charity next inquired whether Miss Mowbray would give the names to Mr. Morton; and on being informed that the catechumens must all meet in the church on the following day, when Mr. Morton, after a short address, would himself take their names, she seemed again to hesitate. But after a moment's thought she repeated her words—'I think I shall like to go with the others,' and left the room.

'Poor child!' said Miss Mowbray to herself, as the door closed upon her; 'it certainly is a mistake to bring up children in a rank that does not belong to them. My dear friend Mr. Saville is a good man, and doubtless, from all he says, his friend Mrs. Dorothy Helstone must be a very good woman. It seems strange that such good people should be allowed to make the mistakes they often do; and, certainly, I do think this has been a great mistake. The child is full of feeling, and energy too. I believe there is material in her to make a very fine character, but she is just crushed and kept down by her own false position. I told Mr. Saville that I feared it might be so. Had Mrs. Helstone placed this little foundling, whoever she may be, in the hospital Mr. Morton preached about to-day, instead of bringing her up as her own child, I believe it would have been a much wiser plan, and much more for the child's happiness, too. It's all very well for Mr. Saville to delude himself with the belief that the child is perfectly happy, and has never, as he told me, seemed to have an uncomfortable or doubtful thought about herself. No one who had watched her face, as I did in church this morning, but must have seen what she was feeling and suffering. Not one of the little orphans at his feet felt the force of his words as powerfully as that poor child did, sitting by my side in her pretty hat and pelisse. All Mr. Saville and Mrs. Dorothy Helstone can say will never make me believe that the poor child does not know that she is a foundling; yes, and feel it, too!'

CHAPTER IX.

MR. MORTON'S address to the girls—for there were only girls present, and in that large district a vast number of these were assembled on the following morning as candidates for the approaching confirmation—Mr. Morton's address was very short, and yet more simple than his sermon had been on the previous day. He remembered, that though the number of young creatures before him included many from the highest walks of life, yet was it for the most part composed of the poor and the uneducated, and his words were such as all could understand.

Beginning with the question, 'What mean ye by this service?' he strove to set before them, first, what the Church certainly did *not* mean by it; namely, that any should enter upon it who had no meaning whatever in doing so. Then, in a few earnest words, he carried them back to the days of their baptism, and the solemn vow which had then been made for them; a vow so short, that it required but a very small effort to commit it to memory, as he had begged each one of them to do before coming there that morning, and would take but a very few moments to repeat by rote; yet a vow so 'exceeding broad' in the largeness of its comprehension, that it seemed, in those few words, to include all that was needful in the Christian life—to embrace at one view every effort, every difficulty, every struggle connected with a godly walk.

In the day of their baptism, their godfathers and godmothers had pronounced the vow by which, in their name, they 'renounced the devil and all his works; the vain pomp and glory of this world, with all covetous desires of the same; and the carnal desires of the flesh.' They were met together that day to consider whether they could declare themselves of the number of those who were fit to take upon themselves the renewing of that solemn promise and vow made for them in the unconscious day of their baptism, and to undertake to ratify and confirm it in their own persons, binding themselves henceforth to believe *and to do* all those things which had been undertaken for them. They were then desired to turn to the first sentence in the service for the Order of Confirmation, and there remark what the Church required of those who came forward to receive the benefit of this service. None were to be confirmed but such as could say the Creed, the Lord's Prayer, the Ten Commandments, and the other short answers contained in the Catechism; but this was only the opening condition, and very easily carried out. The closing condition was of a very different character, and could never be performed by mere natural power or desire: for it required that none should come save those who were ready to promise that, by the grace of God, they would *evermore* endeavour faithfully to observe such things as they would in confirmation assent unto.

He therefore brought this solemn subject before them now, and begged them to give it their most serious consideration during the approaching holidays. The Confirmation classes would begin immediately after the vacation and continue for some weeks, and very thankful should he be if he could hope that on their conclusion not one then present would come forward for confirmation with a lie in their mouth, either of their own wilful resolving, or of the great enemy's subtle deluding. Far, rather, would he see the number now before him reduced to a mere handful, and know that every heart amongst them was sincere, than feel that amongst that army of professing soldiers of Christ, who were ready now to 'confess the faith of Christ crucified, and promise to fight under His banner against sin, the world, and the devil,' a large number would be found who, instead of continuing His faithful soldiers unto their lives' end, would speedily desert their colours, and betray His cause. And why? Because, in enlisting in His service, they had no higher motive than the mere excitement of the moment—the wish to be like others and do like others; perhaps, even, for he had lived to see how very low and unworthy a motive some minds could entertain—perhaps, even inspired only by the desire of joining in the same scene of interest and excitement, and wearing the same costume, as their young companions.

Such were not the soldiers whom Christ or the Church invited to take His cause upon them. There was stern service to be rendered in the Christian field: none could enter into the conflict thus plainly set before them, and meet such enemies as the world, the flesh, and the devil, without enduring such sharp struggles as would speedily test the reality of their motives. Now all could promise; but the question was,—'In a short time hence, who would have performed their promise?' If it has been undertaken now in sincerity; if faith, however feeble, has brought them to the resolve, and truth, however trembling, has uttered it, the grace of God in the heart prompts the desire, and that same grace will be granted to perform it. The young soldier will go from strength to strength; though he may sometimes faint, yet will power ever be given unto him to pursue. God loves the day of small things, therefore none should despise them. Sincerity, reality, were all that he would insist upon. If the motive were but sincere, if the feeling of desire for confirmation were but real, that was all that was needed; for the faintest feeling of faith, the smallest ray of truth, was of God. It was like the early light stealing into a darkened chamber; none could create that light: but through God's mercy, though the light itself can neither be created or extinguished, yet can its reception be helped forward; and this is just what the Church seeks to do for her children in her many blessed services, unclosing many a barred shutter, and introducing the light of God's truth.

A few solemn words were added on the nature of a vow in God's sight. The truth was strongly brought before those young minds, that although but little is said in holy writ concerning the necessity or the advisability of making vows—though the very greatest freedom of conscience is allowed, and would almost appear to be advised in this matter—yet is very much said, and strongly said too, on the necessity of keeping every vow ever made before the great God of heaven and earth, whether it has been made in the fervour of gratitude, in the impulse of feeling, in the fear of death, or in the agony of distress. Better, the wise man tells us, is it not to vow, than not to pay that which one has vowed; for God hath no pleasure in fools, and that which has once been vowed He will surely require. It may be no sin to forbear to vow; but Scripture shows us very plainly that it is an undoubted sin not to keep and perform that which has gone out from the lips, or even to be slack in paying that which has been promised with the mouth. When the children of earth vow, the God of heaven hears and remembers; nor can they with impunity break the oath with which they have bound their soul, or afterwards decline to do according to all that has proceeded out of their mouth. Jacob was careful to go up to Bethel to raise an altar unto God, and pay there the vow which he had vowed in the day of his distress. Jephthah felt, that having opened his mouth unto the Lord, he must not go back, however great the sacrifice might be. The wealthy place in which David found himself, did not prevent his remembering the vows he had made unto his God when he was passing through fire and water, and men were riding over his head: his mouth had spoken them, and his lips had uttered them, and he went into God's house to pay them. The Lord's benefits being upon him, he took the cup of salvation and paid his vows unto the Lord, in the presence of all His people; and he gives it as one of the leading features in the character of him who should be found worthy to abide in the tabernacle of the Lord, and dwell in His holy hill, that though he sweareth to his own hurt, He "changeth not.'

Thus, with simple, yet solemn words of exhortation and warning, did the good clergyman that morning set before his young hearers the importance of that service into which they sought to enter; and then, with a few words of blessing, he went into the vestry, and himself received the name of each young girl, as one by one they followed him there to give it. It seemed but the work of a moment, and when Charity's turn came, she had regained the courage which at first she feared would altogether fail her, and went forward to the interview with a stranger more bravely than she had expected to do.

Her name was asked and given—'Charity Helstone.' But before proceeding to the next question, and asking how old she was, which the girls who had returned from the vestry had assured her was the only other question the clergyman put to each, Mr. Morton made a most decided pause. A look of increased thoughtfulness was apparent even in his deeply thoughtful face. He glanced at the name on the list before him, then looked at Charity,—'Helstone!' he said; 'your name is Helstone?'

The warm blood rushed into Charity's face, and crimsoned it to the very temples; accustomed as she was to the name, her right to it naturally escaped her thoughts, unless some circumstance brought it forward. This was the case now, and as the clergyman, who attributed her manner solely to the timidity which he saw was natural to her, repeated the words, yet more kindly than before, but evidently with some meaning in doing so, 'You say your name is Helstone?' she trembled with emotion, and had some difficulty in commanding her voice sufficiently to say, 'I cannot tell; I do not know: they call me Charity Helstone.'

There was a mystery about it Mr. Morton saw at once. A deeper feeling than timidity had brought that smarting blood into the burning cheeks, and caused the young voice to tremble with deep emotion. He greatly regretted the pain he had so unintentionally occasioned, but he felt that any words of his now would probably increase rather than soften it; the opportunity for tenderness and sympathy would be better afforded later in their intercourse. He looked again at the name, still wet on his paper, so that Charity might be relieved by having his eyes removed from her, and said, 'Charity is a lovely name to own. I sometimes ask my young people to select some portion of Holy Scripture for their special study; you could scarcely have a greener spot of pasture to feed your young soul upon than the lovely explanation and amplification of your own name in the 13th chapter of the First Epistle of St. Paul to the Corinthians.' And shaking hands kindly with Charity he took leave of her.

She had certainly been twice as long in the vestry as any of the other girls—a circumstance which Ellinor Temple had not failed to remark, and which greatly excited her curiosity, ready as it always was to be excited on the smallest possible occasion.

No sooner had Charity returned home than she went into the garden, to be out of the way of all eyes in general, and Ellinor Temple's eyes in particular, and there she meditated on the short but strange interview that had taken place between herself and Mr. Morton. She remembered the expression of his face, the tone of his voice, and she felt sure that the name of Helstone was familiar to him; but where he had heard it, or what he knew concerning it, how gladly would Charity have known! and yet, how impossible would it be for her ever to inquire!

It was a pity that Charity could not have been at that moment in Mr. Morton's drawing-room, when this part of the mystery of her life would have been very simply explained. On his return to his own home, Mr. Morton's first inquiry to his wife was 'whether she remembered young Mrs. Helstone, in whom they had both been so deeply interested so many long years ago?'

'Remember her!' replied Mrs. Morton; 'of course I remember her, and all connected with her, as well as if it had happened yesterday. Oh, Arthur, have you heard anything more of her, or of him?'

Mr. Morton answered very quietly, yet in a tone, the gravity of which bespoke quite as deep an interest in the matter as did his wife's eager excitement. 'I think,' he said, 'I have just parted with her child: indeed, I do not think so, for I feel quite sure.'

'Oh, Arthur! how do you know? how did you find it out? Is she one of our catechumens? Tell me everything, for I have longed to know whether, if the child lived, what would become of it. How marvellous it is how things come to light after so long a time! Do tell me all about it!'

'There is very little to tell,' he replied; 'nothing, indeed: though one day I earnestly hope we may discover more; for, like you, I have often longed to know what could have been the end of that poor young creature. But all I now know is merely this, that amongst the catechumens to-day, who, as usual, came to me one by one in the vestry, was a young girl whose appearance struck me the very first moment I saw her. I felt sure I had seen her somewhere before, though where I could not remember in the least,—her face and figure were perfectly familiar to me.'

'A poor girl, of course?' interrupted Mrs. Morton.

'Indeed, no,' he replied; 'just the contrary; a lady in every respect; as aristocratic a looking girl as you could see anywhere; very tall and slight, with singularly fair hair, and a remarkable pair of large blue eyes with black lashes—the sort of face which must strike one's attention even amongst such a number, and with one's mind as occupied as mine was to-day. It was a peculiar countenance altogether; yet what riveted my attention was its being so strangely familiar. I felt quite bewildered till she gave me her name, "Helstone," and then at once I was transported back all those years to that little parlour in Duke Street, and again I saw before me that lovely young woman, whose appearance we used to say contrasted so strangely with the wretched lodging in which we found her. It is the very same face—that lovely oval with delicate features; the eyes, the hair, the figure—I could see no difference; and had I remembered that it was to Mrs. Helstone that my mind had been thus recalled before the child gave me her name, I should have felt certain it was her daughter that stood before me, even without this additional proof. It certainly is a disadvantage to be so shortsighted,' he added; 'for, otherwise, I must have remarked that face even amongst such a crowded troop as Miss Mowbray's young ladies.'

'Whom you say you never can tell one from another, dressed as they are nearly all alike,' replied his wife. 'Well, I am sure I should have remarked any one who resembled Mrs. Helstone if I sat within sight of Miss Mowbray's pews. I have never seen any one whom I thought as pretty as she was; and oh, what interest we took in her! Do you remember how miserable I was when she went away so suddenly, and how much I thought of her when our child was born, knowing that hers must have been born just at the same time?'

'Which it was,' said Mr. Morton. '"Sixteen next January," she said.'

'And her name?' asked Mrs. Morton.

'Charity,' he replied; 'and to me that is so strange.'

'How much I should like to know!' exclaimed Mrs. Morton. 'Arthur, we *must* know. We must see her—have her here. You say she is quite a lady in appearance; but of course she must be that, or she would not be at Miss Mowbray's, she is so very particular.'

'The most fastidious could not but be satisfied with Miss Helstone,' Mr. Morton replied, 'so far as appearance, manner, and voice go; which are, of course, all I have to judge from. She seems perfectly unconscious of her own extreme beauty, and has a very lovely, modest manner. What distresses me is, that I am afraid I showed plainly the surprise I felt at the sound of her name, and this seemed to distress her. She could, indeed, scarcely command her voice sufficiently to reply to me.

'Poor child!' said Mrs. Morton; 'perhaps there is some sad end to the story, even more sad than all we knew. I wonder whether the husband ever found his wife, and whether they are still alive, or what became of him? We must find out all we can, Arthur. I should so like to see the child, and be kind to her. Can we not ask her here?'

'I am thinking of it,' he said: 'I believe I am as interested in her as you can be; but this is not a thing one can enter into without caution.'

'Of which you have so much, and I so little,' said his wife.

'Just so,' he replied. 'I dare say you would like to send for this pretty young creature on the spot, and set her down amongst our own young ones, and perhaps have her father appearing here again a little later in the drama. I think, that till we know what has become of him, or what she has to do with him, we had better be careful. Mr. Helstone was not exactly the man you would like to introduce into your family circle, even out of sympathy for his lovely daughter; for his daughter I am convinced this sweet-looking girl is.'

'Oh, no!' exclaimed his wife; 'I trust we shall never see him again, for he was a wretched man.'

'As wretched as could be *then*,' said Mr. Morton; 'but he may be very different now. Sixteen years is a long time ago, and God may have done great things since then. Certainly, whoever has had the bringing up of this young lady must have been most careful to do so well. It is a very mysterious business, and we cannot take any steps in the matter until I have made further inquiries. In a thing of this kind it would certainly not be wise to follow the impulses of one's heart.'

Meanwhile, Charity returned from the garden, and went into her bedroom to prepare for tea. Ellinor Temple had taken off her things, and hurried to the school-room to talk over the events of the afternoon, the most important of which, in her mind, appeared to be the unaccountable length of time which Mr. Morton had detained Charity. Why should he have kept her at least twice as long as any of the other girls?

This question being, in Ellinor's opinion, worthy of deeper consideration than any other that had been brought before her mind by anything she had heard that day, she sought out Fraulein, in order to receive the benefit of her assistance; and the two retired into the window-seat, to employ part of the holiday given for the occasion in discussing it.

Charity, quite unconscious of the interest she was exciting below, was thankful to have her room to herself, for the dressing-bell had summoned her from the quiet of the garden, and she shrank from the half-hour of school-room chat before tea. She had thought and thought over Mr. Morton's words and manner, but she could come to no conclusion concerning them, so she had dismissed the subject from her mind with the resolve that she would think no more about it. There were other things she *must* think of, and this would but distract her attention; the sermon yesterday—the short address to-day, every word of which had taken root in her mind, until Mr. Morton's words to herself had temporarily dislodged them by the excitement they had occasioned there.

But now she must think—there was a feeling within which compelled her to do so; and, leaning her head against the table, she asked herself again and again whether she was one of those who dared to take upon herself these vows. Certainly, were she obliged to do so now, she should at once withdraw. But there were several weeks before her, and during that time it was possible—Mr. Morton had said so—that some great change might be effected. Charity earnestly desired that this might be the case with her, for, during the last few months, she had grown weary of her life; she, too, who had once been so happy, so lighthearted, with nothing to depress her, and everything to encourage her.

Now, one feeling had taken possession of her whole mind—that she was a foundling, with no one belonging to her whom she had any *right* to look to for help, counsel, protection, and, above all, love! unless, indeed, it were this great Father in heaven, who might be, Mr. Morton had said, as much her Father as the Father of any one else.

She raised her eyes to the sky, then looking so blue and bright overhead, and she thought how happy it must be to be somewhere up there, away from all the troubles of life. But it all seemed very dreamy and unreal, and, taught as she had been from her infancy in all the truths of the Gospel, she seemed that day to know as little about them as though she had never heard of them. There was a longing, a desire in her heart—a longing for rest, a desire for happiness; but how to find either one or the other she did not seem to know.

Mr. Morton had said, that the way to the heavenly Father they all knew; it was through the Lord Jesus Christ. These words were only a repetition of what she had heard over and over again ever since she had been a baby. The way to God was through the Son. He was 'the way,' 'the door.' Charity could have proved that great truth out of her own head, with chapter and verse, as readily as the best taught of Mr. Morton's own Sunday scholars. But to her this 'door,' that led into the presence of the Father, was closed. The 'way' was there, she did not doubt, but her feet had not been led to walk in it.

Her eyes fell on the Bible she had laid down on entering the room, and, remembering Mr. Morton's words, she took it up and turned to the chapter he had spoken of, the 13th chapter of the First Epistle to the Corinthians. Charity had learned the chapter as a child with her godmother, and Mrs. Dorothy was in the habit of frequently alluding to it in reference to her name, but it had never made much impression on her. Nor did it do so now; she read it through, but, notwithstanding Mr. Morton's words, the pasture did not seem very green or tempting, and, with a heavy sigh from her heavy heart, she closed the book, and began to brush her hair in readiness for tea: the thought that dwelt principally upon her mind was, 'What could Mr. Morton's manner have meant?' And that night Charity never closed her eyes, but was perpetually asking herself the same question, to which her imagination could supply no satisfactory answer.

But the impression Mr. Morton's sermon had made was far too real and deep to allow this thought long to remain the most prominent one. Her mind fully aroused to perceive and feel what it must be to be the child of the great Father of the fatherless, her one desire became to be able to claim Him as *her* Father; to be able to look on heaven as *her* inheritance; to be able to take to herself the glorious new name of which Mr. Morton had spoken. But as this desire increased in intensity there arose also a feeling of utter helplessness, of entire inability to reach this great Father in heaven. Who was she, a sinful, passionate, wilful, ignorant child, that she should dare to approach the great God in heaven, and call Him 'Father?' She tried to pray, but now the very truthfulness of her character seemed in arms against her, rising up as it were to stop the words which did not come from the heart, and prevent their finding utterance.

Often and often did poor Charity rise from her bed during those nights, and carry her heavy heart up and down her room by the light of the pale, cold, unsympathising moon, while Ellinor slept soundly. Often and often during those wretched, sleepless hours, did Job's words escape from her lips—'Oh that I knew where I might find Him!'

This time her misery was too great to be altogether concealed, and many noticed, though none could account for, the change that had come over Charity Helstone. It was, of course, the more remarkable just at this time, when, in the prospect of a speedy sight of home, school-girls generally look their brightest and laugh their merriest. Plenty of merriment was there in Miss Mowbray's school-room during those days. More than once, even during lesson-time, were young heads to be seen bent closely together over the same desk, while young voices carried on earnest whispering talk, brought suddenly to an untimely end by Fraulein's sour exclamation, 'So, Miss Annie! so, Miss Alice! you talk once—you get one bad mark; of that you may make yourself easy!' But Charity's voice was silent, and Charity's countenance was clouded. And those who watched her made their own remarks, and drew their own conclusions, Fraulein's and Ellinor's minds being especially active on the subject. Little Alice asked Helen more than once what she thought *could* be the matter with Cherrie; and even Miss Mowbray grew so troubled at the cloud on the young brow, that one night, on Charity's coming to her for the accustomed good-night kiss she gently detained her, to ask in kind, winning tones, 'if she were quite well.' For one instant the lip trembled, but her natural proud reserve coming at once to her aid, Charity answered, in the coldest and most constrained of voices,—'Quite well, thank you, ma'am.'

For the moment Miss Mowbray felt annoyed, for

she was not accustomed to meet with such a chilling reply to a kind inquiry, but the feeling of annoyance quickly passed from that well-regulated mind, and gave way to one of most sincere pity for the child whose real and better self seemed wrapped in such an impenetrable icy covering. And in her prayers that night the little orphan was specially remembered, for clearly did Miss Mowbray see that a nature like Charity's would lay itself open to God alone, and that only under the constraining power of the Holy Spirit. Little did the kind lady then guess, that the sorrowful young face which presented itself so vividly to her mind's eye, was at that moment hidden in passionate weeping, the troubled mind beneath a very chaos of confusion, waiting for the Spirit of God to move upon the face of the waters, and the command that there should be light to go forth before its appearance could be otherwise than 'without form and void.'

One feeling, however, made itself clearly felt, and that was, that it was her duty to go home. Charity discarded, as wrong and sinful, the thought of asking leave to remain at school; she would go to Arlington, and there endure all that might be awaiting her. But she would not say a word on the hateful subject to Mrs. Dorothy. Nor did she. But no sooner had she returned home, than both Mrs. Dorothy and Betsy perceived that there was something at work within their darling's heart. The waters were troubled beneath, and that not slightly, though the child's strength of will was sufficient to check their rising. Mrs. Dorothy saw the change, felt it, and said nothing. Betsy saw it, and said a great deal, both to herself and to her mistress. 'She knew how it would be; she saw plain enough what was at work in her young lady's mind. Only that very blessed day, when the miller had asked her how her mistress was, and she had replied, quite innocent like, that her "*niece's*" coming had seemed to have done her a world of good, hadn't Miss Charity, who, as ill-luck would have it, was in the kitchen at the moment, turned such a fierce look on her as she uttered the word *niece!* for all the world with the same look in her eyes that she had had that day so many years agone, when she had said, "Betsy, you 're a liar!" To be sure, ma'am,' continued Betsy, 'I was that taken back, I was all of a tremble, and couldn't find my voice to say a civil good-day to the miller. Our young lady 's a-worriting and a-fretting her young life out of her; that 's as true as that my kettle be boiling.' And, upon this recollection, Betsy departed in all haste to make the tea.

But God is good, and Charity's fretting was not to be of long continuance; perhaps it was not likely it should be, when so many were praying that it might come speedily to an end. When two or three are agreed to ask the same thing in the dear Master's name, have we not His own promise that it shall be granted? and surely a more faithful 'two or three' were never united in one common desire than Mrs. Dorothy, old Betsy, and Mr. Saville, who had also remarked the change in his once light-hearted little godchild.

One Sunday, shortly before her return to school, the longed-for rest came to Charity, the 'due time' when the burden was to fall from her shoulders at the foot of the cross. That Sunday morning, when Mr. Saville gave out his text, the words fastened themselves with strange power on her mind,—'Blessed be the God and *Father* of our Lord Jesus Christ, which according to His abundant mercy hath begotten us again unto a lively hope by the resurrection of Jesus Christ from the dead, to an inheritance incorruptible and undefiled, and that fadeth not away, reserved in heaven for you, who are kept by the power of God through faith unto salvation.' And as Mr. Saville showed how sinners could alone approach God the Father, even through God the Son; how, *because* He was the Father of our Lord Jesus Christ, He must, according to His own word of promise, become the Father of all who come to Him in Jesus, the one appointed way;—as Mr. Saville showed all this, rays of light and hope darted into the mind of the earnest young listener. Her large blue eyes were riveted on her godfather's face as he quoted the words of the Lord Jesus Himself,—'No man cometh unto *the Father* but by me;' and after dwelling earnestly on the love of that Saviour, who had laid down His own sacred life to make atonement for the sins of the world, and thus reconcile lost sinners to their offended God, passed on to notice the blessings secured to man by the death and resurrection of Him who was 'the way:' among them the 'inheritance,' spoken of in this same blessed word of promise, as reserved in heaven for those who should become the children of God 'by faith in Christ Jesus.'

On her way home from church that day Charity did not speak one word. Mrs. Dorothy was not there, and Betsy could not help remarking that Charity left the church before she did, and seemed purposely to hurry homewards. Once locked into her own room, Charity poured forth her heart in a long tearful prayer, which in its full, fresh reality, was like the uprising of the tender herbs, stretching their green heads towards the sun, after the rain had fallen upon their parched dryness.

The few remaining days of the vacation passed, and Charity's heart was too full, and her ideas, as yet, too undeveloped, to allow of their being expressed even to dear Aunt Dorothy; so that, although her brow cleared into more than its former light, and her smile brightened into more than its old warmth, no word on the subject passed her lips. But she returned to school with her mind full of the confirmation classes, which were to commence immediately after the holidays, when she hoped she would receive all the teaching she required from dear, good Mr. Morton. Nor was she disappointed.

CHAPTER X.

TWO months later and Charity Helstone might have been seen once more in her bedroom at school, again employed in the very commonplace occupation of brushing her brown hair in readiness for tea; but with such an altered expression of countenance, that those who had seen her listening that last Sunday to Mr. Morton's sermon, or standing next day in the little vestry, could scarcely have believed that the same girl stood before them now.

And was it the same? for if the same, whence this great difference? It seemed the same, and yet not the same. And as it seemed, so indeed it was. For the soft brown hair, which now she brushed out in all its glossy thickness, and then, dividing into several curls, twisted around her finger and let fall in rings, each one of which seemed to catch the slanting light of the setting sun, and sparkle brightly in response, looked then as it did now; and so did the delicate, regular features of the small oval face:

but in the eyes, which were then so grave and sad, now dwelt a placid, peaceful light; and on the brow, then so unduly anxious for one so young, now rested a soft repose; whilst around the thoughtful mouth there played a satisfied smile of sweet content, as though it had been opened once to ask some mighty question which lay beneath, burdening the heart, and had received an answer which in itself solved all other questions, and left it at liberty, in future, to spend all its energy in words of love and happiness, without needing again to shape its sweet form into unhappy or restless utterances.

A great change had passed, indeed, over Charity Helstone, and she seemed conscious of it herself—conscious, and yet most unconscious. Her heart felt light within her, though at this moment there were thoughts passing through it which might have been a weight; but that underneath them all there was a knowledge which acted as a buoy in bearing them up, and keeping them from even touching, much less pressing upon, the springs of the heart's life—the knowledge that all things were working together for good in her young life. Even now she saw in part, and as God strengthened the eyesight of her faith she would see more and more of His gracious works with her and for her. She knew it would be so. Her mind rested on what she saw of God's dealings and discipline. It was very wonderful. It was as much, and more, than she could comprehend.

That there was more behind she knew, for she

saw glimpses of God's providential dealings yet on the horizon, and felt, though she could not see, that there was a beyond even to that; and that when she had reached that horizon, others would extend themselves yet further on, and so on and on, perhaps, through all eternity: for of God's understanding there is no searching out, no reaching to the limits of His wisdom or His mercy. Our happiness consists in enjoying to the full the present prospect, with just the knowledge that there is more beyond, but without straining our eyes to reach that which we see in the far distance, whilst we neglect the wonders which lie around our path now—wonders of grace and providence so marvellous and beautiful in their minutest details, that they who heed them see in each smallest event, each lightest word, a meaning, a beauty, and a teaching, which are just as much lost to others as are lost the colouring of the bright feathers of the butterfly that flies past, or the loveliness of the tiny flower at their feet, to those who walk along their road heedless of all around, or speculating, may be, on the prospect beyond, or the reachless stars above.

To such God is not the 'very present' God that He had become to our little Charity. Truly had Mr. Morton said that a very great change might, through God's grace, be wrought in many a young heart, between the day when he spoke the warning words and the day when the vow should be taken, the solemnity of which he sought to impress upon their minds. That such a change had been wrought in Charity, none who had seen her then, and who saw her now, could have doubted. For then the face was heavy with care, and now it actually shone with brightness; every movement told of a heart at rest, as she stood there with her pretty face and figure light and bright with gladness. An open book lay before her on the dressing-table, from which she was apparently learning, for her eyes wandered constantly from the glass to its pages, and her lips moved as if repeating the words they met there.

The first bell rang, and Charity closed the book and ran downstairs. There was yet half an hour before tea, and she might have remained longer in her room, but she wished to speak to Helen Anstruther and so went now. Helen was not there, however, and Charity would have returned to her room; for Ellinor Temple and her now constant companion, Fraulein, being, with little Alice Rhodes, the only other occupants of the school-room, there was not much temptation to remain. But at sight of her, little Alice threw down the playthings which she was amusing herself with in one window-seat, while Fraulein and Ellinor talked whisperingly in another, and running up to Charity she begged for a story.

Charity's quick eyes had seen the look which the two friends had fixed on her as she came in: something seemed to tell her that they had been speaking of her, and that was why they paused so suddenly upon her entrance, and gladly would she have returned to the solitude of her own room, since the rules of the school did not allow of her seeking Helen in hers, or of taking little Alice back with her, to tell her in peace the story she desired to hear. But just as she was disentangling little Alice's arms from her neck, and was about to say that she must let her go now, and she should have a story another day, the words she had just seen upon the page she had closed shone again before her, and said within her heart, 'Charity suffereth long, and *is kind.*' And a voice within—it scarcely seemed her own, and yet it surely was her own, only it was as yet a new voice, and she was not fully accustomed to the tone of it: a voice within replied,—'And I am Charity: it is my name—it is to be my nature; and I must suffer long, and be kind—be kind now to little Alice.'

So, taking the child upon her lap, she sat down in the window-seat, and was thinking what story she should tell her, when the child's arms were thrown more tightly than before around her neck, and she said,—

'Oh, Charity, I *do* love you! You are so good to me. They said just now that Charity was a good name for you, and suited you better than any other; and I think so too, for Miss Mowbray told me to-day at my lesson that charity meant love, and I'm sure I love you, and everybody ought to love you. But *they* don't,' she added, with a deprecating glance across the room to the other window-seat; '*they* don't. I think they hate you; and I know why, too. It's because they're jealous—they're jealous that Mr. Morton likes you so much, and most of all, that you are going to drink tea there to-morrow.'

The words were meant to be a whisper; but Alice Rhodes' whispers were of a nature to reach any ear within any part of the room in which they were uttered; and Alice Rhodes' impetuous volubility was such that it was useless to attempt to check the progress of any communication when once it was fairly started. Charity did, indeed, now lay her hand upon the child's lips, with the words—softly-spoken words—'Hush! hush, Alice! you must not talk like that! you must not repeat anything that is said of me, or of any one.'

But Alice's loud whisper had hushed the occupants of the next window-seat into such intense silence, that every word, both of the child's communication and of Charity's reply, was distinctly heard. Fraulein was speechless with confusion; but it took a good deal to disconcert Ellinor, and she at once replied,—

'Oh, pray don't check her, Miss Helstone; she's perfectly welcome to repeat anything she's heard us say. I'm sure I, for one, haven't said anything I feel at all ashamed of.'

'Then I'm sure, Ellinor,' exclaimed the child, 'you ought to feel ashamed; for you've been saying very wicked things. You said Charity was no better than the little children that sat round the Communion-table, and that it was because Mr. Morton was so fond of the poor foundlings that he had taken such a fancy to her: that's what you said, and you know you did.'

The hot blood rushed to Charity's cheek and brow, and seemed as suddenly to depart from Ellinor's. The latter evidently knew not what to say, and for a moment no one spoke. Then Charity's voice was heard, very trembling with emotion, yet quite distinct, as in tones struggling with tears, nervousness and courage, she turned to little Alice, and said aloud,—

'Never mind, Alice; people may say what they like, and we must not let it make us feel angry. What those young ladies say is quite true: I am not any better off than those little children you see on Sundays. For they have not any father or mother, and no more have I; and they have no home really of their own, and many among them do not even know their name; and all this is just like me. But God, you know, has given them kind friends, and so He has given me dear, good friends, and I must be thankful to Him, and love Him for all that He has given to me. You asked me for a story, little Alice, and I will tell you one which is quite true:—There was a very lovely lady once, who was going on a journey, and she was taken very ill, and died in a house where no one knew who she was or anything about her, and she left one little tiny baby. And there was a good lady in that place, who took the little baby and brought it up as her own, and called it by her own name, and loved it very much, just as if it was her own child. And the little baby grew up to be a big girl, and once she used to be unhappy because she had no dear papa and mamma like most of the children round her; but afterwards God taught her that He was her Father, and that He had arranged and ordered everything just as was best for her; and you know, little Alice, no one who knows that can ever be very unhappy. For to have God for one's father makes one happy, if one has nothing else to do so. And this little girl grew quite happy, and was very thankful, though she had no parents and no home to which she had a right, and nothing that she could call her own, except the gold wedding-ring which was on her poor mother's finger, and which she always wears on hers.'

'Oh, Cherrie!' exclaimed the child, 'you are that little baby! You wear a gold ring upon your finger. I know you are that little baby. And is your aunt the good lady who brought you up?'

'Yes,' said Charity. 'Her name is Mrs. Dorothy Helstone, Alice; but I call her "Aunt Dorothy," because she is just like a dear aunt to me, and takes as much care of me as your aunt does of you. One day, you know, you are to come and see her in her pretty house at Arlington.'

'Oh, I shall love her very much,' said Alice, 'because she has been good to you. And one day, Cherrie—one day, I'm sure you'll find out that you are some grand lady. It's just like the story about the fairy princess in my book, and you know they thought she was some poor man's child, and she turned out to be a great princess. And you're just like her to look at, because you are so beautiful; you've got such lovely hair, and such lovely eyes. M. Perrot said the other day you were not a bit like the other young ladies—yes, he did say so to

Miss Mowbray, after you had gone out of the room; and he said you walked like a queen. And I know you 're much grander than all the rest of us, and I dare say that 's why they 're jealous of you.'

Again Charity's hand was laid upon the impetuous little lips, but this time no interruption arose from the window-seat. Its two astonished occupants had remained as motionless there as though Charity's little, simple story had turned them into stone; and it was only on Miss Mowbray's entering the room, which was a signal for the second bell to be rung, that they seemed to find strength to move and draw near the table.

Charity did so likewise, but her heart was beating so violently that she felt quite sick, and before the tea was over there was a sudden commotion amongst the girls, and to every one's surprise it was discovered that Charity Helstone had fainted. She was taken to her own room and condemned to go to bed, and though she begged to be left alone, it was decided that some one must stay with her, and at her own request that some one was Helen Anstruther. The two girls had liked each other from the first, but since their return a strong friendship had arisen between them. Little Alice Rhodes never kept anything that was on her mind long, without making Helen a sharer in it, and during the half-hour that had passed while Miss Mowbray was herself assisting Charity to bed, and the other girls discussing her sudden illness in the school-room, she had drawn her friend Helen aside, and told her all that had happened before tea, and how certain she was that Fraulein and Ellinor Temple had made Charity ill. So that it was with a heart very full of sympathy that Helen took her seat at Charity's bedside, and asked her how she felt.

'I am not ill,' said Charity, 'and I can't think what made me faint. I was not feeling well when we sat down to tea, my heart was beating so violently; but I did not wish any one to perceive it, so I forced myself to eat.'

'Then,' said Helen, 'I do not wonder you fainted. I'm afraid,' she added, 'that Fraulein had said something to vex you. Do you know, Fraulein is very much on my conscience?'

'Why?' said Charity.

'Because I'm sure Miss Mowbray has no idea what sort of a person she really is, or she would not keep her here, and I think we ought to let her know; I think I ought, being the eldest here. She is very rude to you, though I can't see why she should be.'

'I think,' said Charity, 'it's only because Ellinor Temple does not like me, and she is so intimate with Ellinor.'

'But why should Ellinor dislike you?' said Helen.

'That is my own fault,' said Charity. 'I believe I took a dislike to her when first I came to school, and I showed it. I used to take so little trouble to hide what I felt or thought; I had been spoiled at home, and I have always been so selfish and wilful.

Oh, Helen! how thankful I feel to have gone to Mr. Morton's classes; everything looks so differently now from what it did then. And he is so kind to me!'

'Yes,' said Helen, 'you are favoured, certainly. Ellinor says you are going to drink tea there again to-morrow evening. It is not often that any one is asked to drink tea there; and, Ellinor says, he called himself to ask Miss Mowbray to allow you to come. She was practising in the drawing-room when he came in, and she heard him say so. Do you know I think this helped to make her angry, for we all think so much of Mr. Morton.'

'He is so kind—so very kind!' said Charity. 'I have never seen any one so kind.'

'But he does not generally make much of young people—or of any one, indeed,' replied Helen; 'that is why the girls call him "the Shunammite's Prophet." You must have heard Ellinor Temple give him that name?'

'Yes,' said Charity; 'she did so to-day when we came in from the class: but I could not imagine why.'

'It is very wrong,' said Helen; 'but that is the name he generally goes by amongst the giddy ones here, and I believe it was Ellinor herself who first gave it to him. You know what is said of the Shunammite, that she built a little chamber for Elisha on the wall, and set for him there a bed, and a table, and a stool, and a candlestick, so that when he passed by he might turn in thither. Ellinor says, that if any one wishes to show attention to Mr. Morton, they would have to set about it in the same way, for that he is much too holy a man to be expected to mix with other people; that, she is sure, he only needs the barest necessaries of life; and that it would be much better to keep him in a little chamber on the wall than to have him with the family. I don't think it right of her to turn things into a joke, but I do think Mr. Morton seems somewhere a long way off from us; and it seems strange that you should have been asked there so often, and have grown so intimate with them.'

'Mr. Morton is a long way off from us,' said Charity; 'at least, he is so good that he seems so. And I don't think he makes very much of any one in particular.'

'No,' said Helen; 'I like that in him so very much. Some clergymen seem to be placed on pedestals to be admired and adored, and to be perpetually at the mercy of those amongst their admirers who like to waste his time by pouring all their domestic or personal trials and temptations into his ear. Certainly Mr. Morton is not like that.'

Charity smiled. 'How strange that you should say so to-day!' she said, 'when it was only yesterday that Mrs. Morton was telling me, that though Mr. Morton was so deeply interested in all his young catechumens, he always sought to make them feel that he was not so much a personal friend as a pastoral guide, and would rather check than invite particular confidences.'

'But,' said Helen, 'so much of the difficulty of

life arises from one's own peculiar circumstances or personal feelings, it seems difficult to imagine how one can receive guidance without these being fully understood.'

'Mr. Morton thinks,' said Charity, 'that all general principles bear upon all particular circumstances.'

'Did he say that to you?' said Helen.

'Yes,' replied Charity; 'and I have been thinking very much all these last days how true his words were. For I have never told Mr. Morton anything about my troubles here, or, indeed, spoken to him at all of the things which of late have weighed heaviest upon my mind. I could not do so, if I wished even, for I should be a great deal too shy; and yet if I had told him everything, every little circumstance, all he has said to me could not have been more exactly what I seemed to want. I was thinking so only this evening, Helen, when, as you say, Ellinor did wound me dreadfully; so sharply, that it was all I could do to keep in what I felt. But just before I had come downstairs I had been learning some verses Mr. Morton had marked for me, which, he said, were suitable references to that sentence in the 13th of the First of Corinthians, which he has made me select as my special portion for study these weeks.'

'He often does that,' said Helen: 'he did so with me last year. I went through the Beatitudes. But I suppose he gave you this on account of your name being Charity.'

'Yes,' said Charity; 'and I am sure I am very

grateful to my godmother for giving me such a name, much as I used to dislike it once, if I owe to it all the teaching that Mr. Morton has given to me about it. No, indeed, Helen, I don't think we need tell all our circumstances, or, perhaps, any of them, to our friends in order to receive instruction or teaching.'

'Unless,' said Helen, 'one was in some particular difficulty or temptation, when it would be impossible, perhaps, for any one to give us the best advice unless they knew the details.'

'Oh, of course,' replied Charity; 'that is very different: then one would have to remember a sentence of Miss Edgeworth's, which Aunt Dorothy used often to quote to me, when she said I gave her half-confidences and expected from her whole advice, which she never would give. She said that Miss Edgeworth's words were sound truth,—"Always tell your physician, or your lawyer, or your friend, the whole truth, or he is either a fool or a knave if he prescribes for you or gives you advice." I can see that it must be so in any difficult things, any "case of conscience," as Aunt Dorothy would say; but not in such conversations as Mr. Morton has with us. I think then, to enter on our own circumstances would be a hindrance rather than a help.'

'And so do I,' said Helen; 'at least, I'm sure it would be so to me. My mind would be in such a turmoil of personal feeling, and excitement, and nervousness, that I don't think the teaching poured upon it while it was in that condition would find any resting-place. When the teaching was over, I think the excitement and the instruction would all have passed off together.'

'That's just what I think too, Helen,' replied Charity. 'Whilst Mr. Morton never seems to agitate or excite one, and his words go down deep into the heart, and seem to meet with every hidden circumstance they find there. I believe he tries to set one's heart right; feeling that when the springs of that are in order it will go just as well, and direct us just as surely, at one hour of our lives as at another, by day or night, or in shade or sunshine, as the case may be.'

'Yes,' said Helen; 'get the machinery right, and you may weave all sorts of textures and colours, coarse or fine, bright or dark, with the same facility. Well, I believe that is true, and that a great deal of precious time is lost in picking and unpicking one's circumstances or one's character, because we find that things don't go right, and think the fault must lie in the web and the woof, when all the time the machinery is the thing at fault.'

'The poor, proud, self-willed heart!' said Charity; 'that is just what Mr. Morton says. If I could only remember all he told me to day on that one line,—"Charity suffereth long, and is kind," it seems to me as if I could never feel angry again with any single living creature.'

'Well, Cherrie, you seem to have remembered it to-day,' said Helen.

Charity smiled.

'It was very fresh in my mind then, Helen, and sometimes the passing away of my impressions seems to be in proportion to their strength. What I feel most deeply at the time seems often to pass away most quickly.'

'I suppose that is when one's natural feeling has been a good deal excited,' said Helen. 'But I do think, Cherrie, your forbearance to-night made some impression on Ellinor; as for Fraulein, nothing appears to touch her, but Ellinor really seemed sorry when you fainted, and very anxious for Miss Mowbray to come back and tell us how you were. I was so glad she said I was to come and sit with you, for I used to be so lonely here, but since I have had you I have been so happy.'

'Since Mr. Morton has had me, you ought to say,' replied Charity; 'for I am sure the first half-year I was no comfort to you or any one else.'

'Shall we not say then,' said Helen, tenderly, 'since Jesus has had you?'

'Or,' replied Charity, quickly, 'since I have had Jesus. It seems as if *He* were always offering Himself to every one, and all depended upon whether one would receive Him or not.'

Thus the two friends talked happily together, and when the prayer-bell summoned Helen away from her, Charity could not regret anything that had passed that day. It had all brought forth good—the talk with Mr. Morton, the happy learning of the texts on charity in her own quiet chamber, the scene in the school-room immediately afterwards, which had led to her telling Alice the story concerning herself, and the fainting-fit at tea, which had led to such an unusually long talk with her friend Helen.

CHAPTER XI.

THERE had been some doubt as to whether Charity was to be considered well enough to attend the class at Mr. Morton's house next day, but she begged so earnestly to be allowed to go, and seemed so perfectly to have recovered from her yesterday's attack, that Miss Mowbray gave permission, and with a happy heart she took her place in the cab with Ellinor Temple and another girl, who was also to be confirmed.

The thought had more than once crossed Charity's mind that Ellinor did not seem to take much interest, or receive much benefit from the classes, but she always turned away from it; for who was she, that she should judge another? and besides, could not the same God, who had done so much for her in such a very little time, do just as much for Ellinor in yet less time? But it made her sad to see Ellinor's utter thoughtlessness, and she was always very silent on her way to and from the class, for she could not and would not have joined in remarks on the dresses of the passers-by, or the gay things hanging in the shop-windows.

But to-day she especially wished not to appear unamiable, lest Ellinor should think her mind was dwelling on what had taken place yesterday; and she sought to enter into conversation by asking Ellinor some question on the subject on which Mr. Morton had spoken to them all the previous day, before talking in private to each, as he did daily during this week, the last before the Confirmation. But, unfortunately, Ellinor was not able to supply the information which Charity sought, for the very simple reason that the text which had passed from Charity's memory had never even entered Ellinor's ears; and feeling provoked at this she answered sharply, that 'if Charity wished to note down all that had been said the day before, she would have a good opportunity of cross-questioning Mr. Morton himself on the subject, since she was going to drink tea there again.' Annie Danvers, however, supplied the text, and added her opinion to Ellinor's remark, that 'it must be very nice to go so often to Mr. Morton's. She had spent one evening there after her illness, and it was so pleasant, it reminded her of her own home in Scotland, which she only saw once a-year, and where she was so happy with her own parents and her young brothers. The Mortons seemed such a happy family party.'

Yes, the Mortons were, indeed, a happy family party. Charity thought so that evening, as, after the class, Mr. Morton took her to the drawing-room, where his wife and the young ones were assembled, one and all engaged in some happy occupation. Eleven of them in all there were, yet in that bright, orderly home, each seemed to find his own special place and work; and whilst all were united in a most harmonious whole, each seemed to retain his or her own special individuality in a manner which greatly charmed Charity's mind, for it was new to her. At Arlington Rectory it was very different, and dearly as she loved the Savilles, one and all, from kind Mr. Saville himself down to the last round-faced baby in the cradle, Charity's clear-judging mind could not but perceive that there was a vast difference between the party of eleven in Arlington Rectory and the same party in St. John's Wood, and that the advantage lay with the latter. Not that Mr. Morton could be more holy, more devoted as a clergyman, than her dear, good godfather. Not that Mrs. Morton, sweet and loving as she was, could be more so than soft, tender Mrs. Saville. Charity could quite imagine that in heaven such saints might stand side by side. But they were not in heaven yet, but upon earth; and being so, there was a difference which Charity felt.

The atmosphere of one home might be, and doubtless was, as holy as the other. With the parents faith, love, prayer dwelt, no doubt, as permanently. But at St. John's Wood the spirit of order reigned and discipline was maintained, and when Charity marked the effect of just the influence of this one difference upon the children, she could not but wish that it could be so at Arlington: it would be so good for all the children there, it would have been so good for Edward in particular. Charity wished sometimes that her dear old friends at Arlington could have made acquaintance with her new friends at St. John's Wood, and that Mr. Saville might have learned from Mr. Morton that it was wise and well for fathers, sometimes, to leave the old divines to sleep on the shelves for an hour or two whilst they themselves brought their eyes, and ears, and hearts, into the drawing-room and school-room, and allowed their minds to dwell upon the young ones there; whilst dear, indulgent Mrs. Saville, might have learned from Mrs. Morton, that if mothers win their children's hearts and confidences by tenderness, and gentleness, and patience, and long forbearance, to keep the hearts they win there must be firmness too, and the young will must never learn to feel itself the strongest.

Impulsive, ardent, youthful as she herself was, Mrs. Morton never forgot that she was the mother of that family, and amidst the tones of love, indulgence, sympathy, there always mingled one of consistent firmness, which the children felt, and which had its influence upon them. That home had a peculiar fascination for a mind like Charity's, which had a very strong vein of practical good sense running through the imagination that pervaded it. Her evenings at St. John's Wood were her great delight, and as she watched the system of family training in that large household, the only check to her enjoyment of it arose from the regret that it had not been thus at Arlington; for had it been so, might not Edward Saville have been all that Charles and Harcourt Morton were? Charity's faithful heart clung as fondly as ever to Edward; no other boy would ever be so dear to her. But Charity's judgment was not of that nature which is blinded by feeling, and if she loved Edward she admired the Mortons, and was only too ready to attribute all his faults and all their virtues to the very different training they had received.

To-night, as usual, Charity was introduced into a lovely family scene. The day's work was over, or rather it seemed over to the young folk, for the parents felt that, perhaps, so far as the children were concerned, the most important work was that which was carried on in those evening hours when story-books were allowed to be taken in hand, music was placed upon the piano, games were chosen by the younger ones and all apparent restraint being removed, each was supposed to follow the bent of his own wishes.

The father had come in from the day's work, and brought with him no thoughts of the world without, or the books in his study; the world within his own home was what he was now living in. The mother had finished all her housekeeping cares and parish arrangements long ago; the boys had left their studies for the day; the girls had no more to think about until to-morrow. It was the time for recreation and relaxation, and those who watched, as Charity did, the way in which these recreations and relaxations were provided, would have felt, as she did, that the watchful eye, the matured judgment, and the ready hand of the parents, were just as active here as elsewhere, and that, through God's blessing on these means, bodily, mental, and moral development were making just as rapid progress, and perhaps more rapid progress during these evening hours, than at any other period of the day.

The cheerful drawing-room in St. John's Wood was a pleasant scene to Charity, and as she came into it to-day, and one and all arose to greet her and make her welcome, her smile was very bright. But later in the evening Mrs. Morton remarked that a grave look had taken the place of the smile, and that Charity had laid down her work, and was gazing at the various little groups in the room with large thoughtful eyes, which, when they had that sad expression in them, always reminded Mrs. Morton of another pair of sad eyes, long years ago, in Duke Street.

'You are tired, Charity?' she said.

And at the word Charity started from her reverie, said 'Oh, no, she was only thinking,' and went on with her work.

Mr. Morton was playing chess with Harcourt; but the little incident was not lost upon him; the children used to say nothing ever was lost upon papa; and when they sat down to tea, and Charity was beside him, and all busied in helping themselves and one another, he said quietly,—

'Harcourt is fond of offering you a penny for

your thoughts, Charity, when you are in one of your grave moods. You do not often look quite as grave as you did this evening, when Mrs. Morton roused you by asking if you were tired. Shall I offer you a price for your thoughts, or will you make me a sharer in them without?'

The blood rushed so quickly into Charity's fair face that Mr. Morton regretted having alluded to the subject, and would have turned it off into another channel without waiting for an answer; but Charity replied at once.

'I was thinking,' she said—'perhaps it was very wrong—but I was thinking how delightful it must be for Minnie to have a home and parents, and such dear brothers and sisters. But I know such thoughts are not right.'

'They are very natural,' he said. 'We must not expect that they should not exist.' And he said no more, for Charity's eyes had a brimming softness, which looked as though a word would make them overflow. But later in the evening, when Charity had quite recovered her composure, and was sitting quietly a little apart, resting from a merry game of romps with the youngest of the eleven, whom Minnie had just carried off to bed, he laid his hand upon her head and said gravely, 'Charity envieth not.' It had been their subject at that day's class, and had entered then into Charity's head. And now these three little words seemed to find their way straight down into her heart.

The servant who came to fetch Charity from St.

John's Wood that evening was sent back, and Mr. Morton walked home with her himself. No sooner had she entered the school-room than she saw that something was wrong there. Helen Anstruther was writing a letter at the table, but with a perplexed, distressed look, which said, either that the letter was an unpleasant one to write, or that it was not at that moment the chief subject of her attention. Annie Danvers and another girl were playing draughts very quietly, and looked as though they had just been very suddenly frightened, and had not recovered the shock. Ellinor Temple was the only other girl in the room, and she looked simply in a very bad temper. On Charity's coming in Helen laid down her pen, as though glad to have an excuse for doing so, and began questioning her as to whether she had not had a very pleasant evening; to which Charity replied by giving her an account of the very pleasant evening they had had, and Annie Danvers ceased playing draughts to chime in with enthusiastic remarks of her own, admiration of the Mortons and all connected with them having been her one great enthusiasm ever since a severe illness she had had some months ago, when Mr. Morton's kindness to her, and some pleasant intercourse she had had with the family, had kindled within her a romantic devotion, which was very natural to a simple, affectionate, yet somewhat sentimental nature like hers.

'Don't you remember drinking tea there with me, Ellinor,' she asked, 'and how much we enjoyed ourselves? I was sorry to get quite well and strong again, because one doesn't generally get asked there without some special reason. Miss Mowbray says they have so many people they must ask in their large parish. You know we have never gone there since; and I only went then because I was ill; and you only went, Ellinor, because I was too poorly to go alone. And since then we really haven't heard anything of them, except in church, until the Confirmation classes began; and now, what a fancy they've taken to you, Charity! Why, you've been there ever so many times! Doesn't it make you quite proud?'

Charity laughed. 'They are very kind to me, certainly, though I often wonder why they should be so.'

A most provoking smile curled Ellinor's lip. The look on her face was most expressive. To Charity it just seemed to say, 'Don't you know why? Why, it's just because you're a poor foundling, and the foundlings are known to be Mr. Morton's special delight, his pet *protégés;* and Mrs. Morton's heart goes out to everything that is poor and wretched; and that's the reason, Charity Helstone, why you are such a welcome guest in St. John's Wood,—at least, that's what I think about it, and what I'd say too, only I'm afraid to do so.'

All this that one look of Ellinor Temple's seemed to Charity to imply, and her spirit rose in indignation within her; but remembering words she had heard only that day, that 'Charity thinketh no evil,' she checked the thought as it arose. But it was not only Charity who was struck by the contemptuous curl of Ellinor's upper lip. Helen Anstruther saw it plainly enough, and colouring with that indignation which is to be checked when we ourselves are the subject of it, yet becomes lawful, and even righteous, when it is called forth for another, she said quietly, but very markedly,—

'We all feel how wise Mr. Morton is—we all know how carefully he brings up his children. Minnie has no companions of her own age, all the boys come between her and her little sisters; if he and Mrs. Morton wish her to form a friendship with you, Charity, and that is why they ask you so often to the Rectory, I can't say I, for one, wonder at it.'

Charity blushed, and Ellinor crimsoned, for she was cute enough to know that Helen's speech was not in reality addressed either to Annie or Charity, but simply to herself, in answer to that one scornful smile.

'Really,' she said, 'Miss Helstone is very fortunate to have such admirers within and without. For my part, I should not have thought it was good taste to pay such compliments to people before their face.'

'I never pay compliments,' said Helen, quietly; 'I merely say what I think.'

'Which it is not always usual to do in the presence of people,' replied Ellinor, losing her temper and her judgment together. 'It might have the appearance of flattery, you know, Miss Anstruther; or it might tend to engender vanity, which you, who are so good, ought surely to seek to avoid.'

'Miss Helstone knows I am not given to flattery,' replied Helen, restraining herself by an effort from smiling; 'and as to vanity, she is not likely to be made vain by anything I may say to her, considering what Miss Mowbray has just said of her to us, and which she herself would have heard if she had been here then, and will hear to-morrow. It seems, Charity, you have more marks than any of us in almost every subject this year, and are pretty sure of the prize. But there 's the prayer-bell! Come, we must not wait an instant, for Miss Mowbray has put off prayers already a quarter of an hour, on account of Mr. Morton's message that if you might stay a few minutes longer he would walk home with you himself. You certainly are, as Annie says, a favoured individual.' And Helen's tone was really almost malicious, as, drawing Charity's arm within hers, she hurried her downstairs.

That night, to her surprise, she found that little Alice Rhodes had taken Ellinor Temple's place as her bedroom companion. The child was fast asleep when she reached her room, so there was no opportunity to make inquiries from her as to why this change had been effected. But that it was a very pleasant change for her Charity felt at once. And that there was something connected with it which made it just the reverse to Ellinor she felt also, when that young lady came to the room a few minutes afterwards to fetch something, and retired with such an expression of sullen resentment that Charity did not venture upon a word with her.

Something had happened during her absence, but what she could not imagine. Helen's words returned to her mind, and with satisfaction she reflected that, whatever had gone wrong during her absence, she herself could have had no share in it. On the contrary, Helen's words seemed to imply that something must have happened to raise her in Miss Mowbray's good opinion, since it was but seldom that she expressed such commendation of any one as Helen had repeated to her that evening. And how pleasant a walk home she had had! She did not wonder that the girls were disposed to be a little jealous of the favour shown to her. And with these thoughts came a feeling, much pleasanter to entertain than the humbling shame from which Charity had suffered so much in time past; but, as she at once felt, quite as dangerous, or more so, to her soul's peace and welfare. The same spirit that had borne in upon her heart the words Mr. Morton had said in her ear, 'Charity envieth not,' now gently whispered within the words, 'Vaunteth not itself, is not puffed up, doth not behave itself unseemly.'

And every feeling of triumph or self-exaltation vanished into distance as Charity lay down her head upon her pillow, and fell asleep with humble, happy gratefulness for all that had passed that evening.

CHAPTER XII.

THE next morning, the first news that Charity learned from her little companion was, that there had been some great 'fuss' the evening before. The child did not know what, but it was all about Fraulein; and Helen Anstruther and Ellinor Temple had been concerned in it, for they had been closeted for a long time in the study with Miss Mowbray and Fraulein: but all the result that little Alice knew was, that she had been sent to sleep in Charity's room, while a bed had been prepared for Ellinor in Miss Mowbray's dressing-room. 'And as for Fraulein,' the child added, 'do you know, I think she's going to be sent away, from something I heard Miss Mowbray say: she and Helen had such a long talk last night, and I'm sure they said something about its being much better that she should go away. Perhaps she's going to day, Cherrie! Oh, don't I hope she is!'

This hope of little Alice's was further confirmed when, on coming downstairs, they saw two large boxes standing in the hall, and on entering the school-room found that Fraulein was not there as usual, but that Miss Mowbray was reading in her arm-chair, while the girls looked over their lessons in the half-hour before breakfast. Another circumstance was not lost upon Charity; and that was, that Ellinor Temple's appearance had not been improved by her night's rest in Miss Mowbray's dressing-room. She looked, as one of the girls said afterwards, 'like all the Furies;' and Helen had remarked that, sullen as her face had been before Charity came into the room, it darkened very considerably after that event.

Miss Mowbray's presence, however, maintained the most perfect outward composure, whatever storms might be passing within; and breakfast, prayers, and the reading of the psalms and lessons, passed as quietly—more quietly, indeed, than usual: for, of course, if the mind is occupied with thoughts within which may not find utterance, there will be perfect stillness from its not engaging in anything that is passing without. Before rising from the table, however, Miss Mowbray spoke, addressing herself to Charity,—

'You were not here last night, my dear,' she said, 'or you would have heard then what I now repeat for your sake: that I have finished looking over the marks in the different books, and that you have the advantage over any of the others. Ellinor has almost as many, her music giving her so large a number; otherwise,' she added, turning to Ellinor and speaking very gravely, 'otherwise, as I told you last night, Charity's marks would be much greater than yours, for you are very deficient in some subjects, history and composition especially. But your music marks and . . . ,' she continued, with a little hesitation, 'and your German marks, run up the number of your marks greatly, and bring them very nearly on a par with Charity's, whose number of marks is almost equal in every subject. And this is just what pleases me so much in *your* book, Charity; you have not given your time only to that which pleases you, or for which you have a special taste; but you have worked steadily at everything that has engaged your attention, and that ever since you came to us, though of late with even increased zeal. It is seldom that any mark-book has given me so much pleasure as yours did yesterday. It now remains only to see which writes the best theme, and what marks you have from your French and drawing masters, for me to decide which will receive the prize for general proficiency in all subjects; which, I believe, is the prize which you all most covet, because it is so much the most valuable, though, as you know, it is not a very great favourite of mine.'

'Miss Mowbray always ends up with that remark,' said one of the girls, as Miss Mowbray left the room. 'I believe she isn't a bit grateful to that old uncle of hers, but rather owes him a grudge, for leaving five pounds every year to be given to the girl in her school who should do best in every subject at her Easter examinations. Such a funny old man he was! I remember him so well the first day I came to school; he died six months after, and I was always so glad I'd seen him. He used to dine here every Saturday—a little wrinkled old man, with white hair and large gold spectacles; and he always asked us all round, "Well, and how's the French? and how's the German? and how's the music? and how are you?" and he actually left it in his will that this prize should be given as long as the school lasted. Do you know, I overheard Miss Mowbray say one day to Mr. Morton that it was very kindly meant, and so she must and did feel grateful for the feeling that prompted it; but that if her uncle had understood as much about education as she did, he would have left that legacy out of his will, or have arranged it in some other way.'

'Well, we're glad enough to get the prize, anyhow,' said Annie Danvers; 'at least, those are who do get it: which, of course, I know I never shall, not having Charity's talents, which make her do well in everything she turns her mind to; or any one particular gift, like music, as you have, Ellinor, which runs up your marks in one thing, even though you can't do so very well in others.'

This speech, not being especially agreeable to Ellinor's feelings, so considerably darkened the dark look on the brow, that a good-natured girl present who saw the gathering clouds, and who dreaded a 'school-room storm' above all things, sought to avert it by saying,—

'Music and German, Annie, Miss Mowbray said.

And I'm sure one must be clever to get on in German, for I never can learn it; it's so difficult.'

'Oh, as for German,' said Annie, saucily, 'I don't think much of the German marks, when it's Fraulein that gives them. We know how particular she is in putting them down correctly, and I think Miss Mowbray seems to have found that out at last, for she didn't seem to think very much of these same German marks. And, you see, we've heard nothing of Fraulein this morning. I told you there was a grand fuss last night, and that something would come of it; though Helen wouldn't tell us what Miss Mowbray wanted when she kept her so long in the study. I only hope we may never see Fraulein again, with her deceitful, underhand ways. I'm sure she would be no loss, at least not to most of us.'

'Come, come,' said Helen, 'it's very wrong and very foolish to talk like this, when we're all so busy, too. I'm going to write my theme, and I should advise you, Charity, to get on with yours this morning.'

Yes, Charity had intended doing so; but when she took her desk she felt as if the morning's events had driven all her thoughts away. She wished Miss Mowbray had not told them anything about the marks before the examinations were finished. It made one nervous to feel one had so good a chance. She could not write a word with all this running in her mind; and taking her hat, she went into the garden to breathe the air of the fresh spring morning. It seemed to bring back to her all strength of body and mind, and she was returning to the house, feeling quite light and bright, when, just as she came into the garden-door, the green-baize door leading into the hall was opened, and she saw Fraulein come out of Miss Mowbray's study and go out of the front-door into a cab waiting for her.

It would be a piece of news to communicate to the girls, who, being in the school-room at the back of the house, would know nothing of Fraulein's exit from it. But Charity was not given to news-telling at any time, and this piece of news she felt no inclination whatever to communicate. So she took her place at her desk, and, in a way which surprised even herself, wrote her theme with singular ease, though her mind had been so preoccupied up to the very moment of her commencing it. As Charity laid down her pen and glanced at the pages before her, neatly covered with matter, which she felt was aptly and neatly expressed, she marvelled, and it seemed as if some one must have helped her to write them; for Charity as yet, though she prayed earnestly and in faith, was in that stage of faith when the answer one expects surprises one when it comes. And though she had asked that, if the theme must be written to-day, God would tell her what to say and how to say it, after she had said it she found herself not fully realizing that her ideas and her words had all come in answer to her prayer; and never perceived, perhaps, that the very feelings which made her think she never should be able to write at all, were, in truth, but a preparation for what she should afterwards write so well.

She read her theme over, and felt it was very fairly done. Her own sense told her that Ellinor was not likely to do better. It had occupied nearly all the morning, and she went to her room to get ready for dinner. There lay her little Testament open at the usual page, and as her eye fell upon the words, "Seeketh not her own," Charity prayed that they might find place in her heart also. Mr. Morton had said, that it was the very secret of religion; and was it not the secret of happiness also?

Dinner over, the girls gathered in groups in the school-room, for the morning sunshine had been succeeded by an afternoon of fastly-falling rain, and there could be no walk that day. Charity's face was bright with the brightness from within, and one of the girls remarking how bright it was, said,—'You 're very cheerful to-day, Cherrie; and no wonder, if you know what Alice has just been telling us, that Fraulein has gone away, never to come back any more. You and she were never very good friends, and, really, lately she has seemed to hate you. I should think you were heartily glad to get rid of her; just as glad, Ellinor, as you must be sorry, who were such a great friend of hers. Pray can you enlighten us as to the cause of her sudden disappearance? for our curiosity is greatly excited on the subject.'

Ellinor looked up from the book she was holding in her hand, but not, it was evident, attempting to read. 'I think,' she said—it was the first word she had been heard to say that day, for not even the morning's conversation about the marks had elicited a word from her—'I think you had better ask Miss Helstone that question. It seems to me, Fraulein's enemies have had more to do with her going away than her friends. Some people care little what means they take to get rid of anything that troubles themselves.'

Charity's quick temper prompted an angry refutation of the implied insult, but her eyes had been but lately removed from that little book on the dressing-table. Was it not one of the special characteristics of that charity, whose nature she was so earnestly seeking to possess, that it was not easily provoked? She waited but a minute or two before she answered, but that minute or two were quite enough for the colour in the cheek to have subsided, the heart to have grown calm, and the voice to be under control, as she replied,—'You say I am to be asked, Ellinor, and you look as though I had something to do with Fraulein's going away. If you think so, you are quite mistaken. I know Fraulein did not like me; as Annie said just now, we were never very great friends; and sometimes I used to think her unkind: but I have never made any complaint of her, even to Helen.'

And going to her desk she took out her theme, and began copying it out fair without another word. She was half through her work, when a message reached her that Mrs. Morton wished to speak to her in the drawing-room for one moment.

'She must be quick, please,' the servant said. 'Mrs. Morton was in such a hurry, she had not wished to come in, as she could not stay an instant.'

Quickly running downstairs, Charity left her paper on the desk on the little table in the end-window, her own accustomed place, Ellinor Temple working near it, the other girls around the table. She returned five minutes after to find it gone.

'My paper!' she said; 'where is it?'

Ellinor rose at once and inquired, 'What paper?'

'The paper that I was copying,' said Charity. 'I left it on the table, and it has gone!'

'Oh, Ellinor!' exclaimed Helen, rising from her own desk, and coming forward to the window, 'how could you open that window with a paper on the desk, and the wind blowing like that? Of course it must have been blown into the street. I hope it was not of consequence, Cherrie; for I very much doubt your ever seeing it again. Why, when Ellinor insisted on having the window open for a minute to let in the fresh air, we all remonstrated, saying we should be blown away; and so we very nearly were. Your papers have gone on a journey over the neighbouring chimney-pots, Cherrie. I hope it doesn't matter. What were they?'

'Only my theme,' said Charity, quietly.

'What, not the rough copy and all!' exclaimed Helen.

'Yes,' said Charity. 'I left it altogether on the desk when I ran down in such a hurry to speak to Mrs. Morton. I never dreamt of any one opening the window in such weather as this; especially,' she added, 'when they must have seen there were papers on the desk.' But the words on the page upstairs returning again to her mind she checked herself, and said no more, for she felt that she was growing hot.

'Really,' said Ellinor, pettishly, 'one can't be expected to look all round to see what mischief one may possibly do before one moves to do anything. The room was so hot one could scarcely breathe. I said I was going to open the window, and no one made any remark about Charity's papers.

'Because no one could see from here that Charity had left her papers loose on her desk.'

'And why should I see it either?' said Ellinor.

A voice at the end of the table said something about none being so blind as those who didn't wish to see. And Ellinor crimsoned with anger, and was about to make an indignant retort, when Helen interfered, and insisted upon silence.

'Miss Mowbray has given me the charge of the school-room this afternoon,' she said, 'and I will not hear another word about it. All who have seen what has happened may draw their own conclusions; but I won't have any disputing about it. Charity's papers have been lost, that's certain; and it's equally certain that Miss Mowbray will not allow her to lose anything by it. Either time will be given to write the theme over again, or it will not count at all in making up the prizes. We may feel very sure of that. And now, if you please, we will all go on with our work.'

No more was said, but telegraphic messages passed from one pair of eyes to another. Ellinor saw and understood, and her cheek grew pale with anger. Charity saw, and would have understood also, had not the words on the page upstairs, 'Charity thinketh no evil,' returned to her mind, leading her to resolve that, not even in her heart, would she take up a reproach against her neighbour.

CHAPTER XIII.

THE day of the Confirmation came, and Charity stood in her room ready prepared for church, with the sunshine of spring without and more than the sunshine of spring within. Brightly did the rays of the sun shine upon her brown curls, and make them dance in light from beneath the simple little white cap. Yet more brightly did the rays of the true Light of Life shine into her young heart, and fill it with warmth and gladness. It seemed to Charity the very happiest day she had ever known, and she looked so beaming as she came out of her room to join the other girls in Miss Mowbray's study, that that lady said to herself, she had never really understood all the beauty that lay in Charity's face until then.

She had expected to meet Annie Danvers and Ellinor Temple, but, to her surprise, only Annie was there; and in answer to her questioning look, Miss Mowbray said quietly,—'Ellinor has attended the classes with us, but she will not go with us to the

Confirmation. It is early yet. If you will wait here, I will join you in half-an-hour.'

No sooner had Miss Mowbray left the room than Annie exclaimed,—

'I believe, Cherrie, that Mr. Morton has refused to give Ellinor a ticket: I do, indeed. And I half think Miss Mowbray herself has had something to do with it, for she called on Mr. Morton yesterday. That was where they went in the afternoon, she and little Alice.'

'Yes, I know,' said Charity. 'Alice told me she had had a nice play with the children, whilst Miss Mowbray was having a long talk with Mr. Morton in his study.'

'Well, and I believe the talk was all about Ellinor,' said Annie; 'for after they came home Miss Mowbray sent for her, and kept her ever so long in her room, and when she came out—oh, Cherrie! I wish you could have seen how she looked, and how she behaved all the evening. You don't know, because you didn't come into the school-room much last night; but I'm sure she is not allowed to go with us to-day. What do you think?'

'I think,' said Charity, 'that it's very sad.'

'Well, but,' said Annie, 'I'm sure she doesn't deserve to go. I can't say I'm sorry, for I didn't think she ought to be confirmed; I didn't think she should have been allowed to be, if it had only been on account of her conduct to you. I hope it isn't very wrong, Cherrie, for I should not like to have any wrong feelings, especially to-day; but I could not help feeling glad last night when I thought she would most likely not come with us to-day. Do you think it 's wrong to feel like that?'

'I don't know,' said Cherrie, gravely; 'I don't think it 's wrong to feel glad that Ellinor is not going to be confirmed if she is not in a fit state to be. But I think we ought to feel very sorry for her.'

'I 'm afraid I don't,' said Annie; 'and I should have thought you would be still less likely to do so, because it 's just to you that she has behaved so badly.'

'But I think,' said Cherrie, 'that 's just why I feel more sorry for it. You know, Annie, Ellinor's having taken this dislike to me has made me think a great deal about her, and the feelings I ought to have; and all this time at the classes she has been very much on my mind, because the verses Mr. Morton gave me to study have seemed to fit in so wonderfully with all that was happening around us. Did Mr. Morton give you any particular part of Scripture?'

'Yes,' said Annie; 'he gave me the 103rd Psalm, because I had been so very ill a little while ago; and I have liked learning it very much, and hearing him explain it to me. You know, Cherrie, it 's about God forgiving all our iniquities, and healing all our diseases, and redeeming our life from destruction, so that our youth is renewed like an eagle's. You can't think how much there has been for me to learn in this psalm, nor how much it has made me feel that I really was, as Mr. Morton says, very nearly gone like a flower of the field when the wind passes over it; and that since God in His loving-kindness has redeemed my life, I ought to give it to Him.'

'And I have been studying the 13th chapter of the First Epistle to the Corinthians,' said Charity; 'my own chapter, I call it now, because it's all about charity. And when you were talking of Ellinor, it made me think so much of the verses I was repeating only just before I came downstairs.'

'What were they?' asked Annie.

Charity repeated them,—

'"Rejoiceth not in iniquity, but rejoiceth in the truth; beareth all things, believeth all things, hopeth all things, endureth all things." I'm sure, Annie, if you had heard all that Mr. Morton said about charity not rejoicing in iniquity you wouldn't wonder at my feelings about Ellinor. It seemed to me when he was talking as if he must know all about her; though, of course, I had never said a single word to him on the subject. I am sure, however, he knew exactly what to say to me.'

'But he could not,' said Annie, 'if you hadn't told him.'

'God put it into his heart, I think,' said Charity, gravely. 'You know, Annie, the Bible says that "the preparation of the heart in man, and the answer of the tongue, is from the Lord," and I do think, if we ask God to let our ministers teach us what it is most needful for us to know, we shall find that they *do* teach us those very things.'

'Well,' said Annie, 'and what did he tell you about Ellinor?'

'Nothing about Ellinor, exactly,' replied Charity, smiling; 'but he told me what it was not to rejoice in iniquity, and that where there was true charity in the heart, it would lead one to grieve very much when any one, whoever they might be, fell into sin. Mr. Morton said, that often we felt a sort of natural satisfaction when we heard of some one else having fallen into sin, or saw them do wrong.'

'I believe that's true,' said Annie. 'I think it's because it makes us seem better to ourselves when we see other people act badly, especially if they do something we don't think we should have done.'

'Yes,' said Charity, 'and if it's something that we have done ourselves, then we are glad to find that we are no worse than our neighbours. Mr. Morton said just that, and that this feeling was natural to every heart; but that to indulge it was to do what St. Paul calls "rejoicing in iniquity," and that the charity which came from God inspired a feeling just opposite to this, and that where charity prevailed it must destroy the other feeling, and lead us to grieve over iniquity in others as well as in ourselves, and to rejoice only in the truth.'

'Well, I'm sure I do like the truth,' said Annie; 'and that's why I can't bear to see deceitful people having their own way.'

'Mr. Morton said,' interrupted Charity, 'that the word "truth" in this verse was put in opposition to "iniquity" in the same sentence, and that it meant that we were to rejoice in seeing others do well, never mind who those others were, whether they were our friends or our enemies. There must not be any personal feeling about it. We must so love goodness, all that is right, and noble, and true, and pure, for its own sake, that we must rejoice to see any one do what is right.'

'I think everybody does that,' said Annie. 'Helen said last night we ought to love you because you did right, and were so patient and forgiving.'

'You must not praise me to myself,' said Charity, smiling, 'or you will be doing me harm. You know, Annie, my chapter says "Charity must not be puffed up," so don't make me so.'

'I don't puff you up,' said Annie, 'only I say, and I should think you knew it well enough without my telling you, that you have been very patient with Ellinor, and very forgiving. I thought so when you were repeating those words just now, "Beareth all things:" that's just what you've done, Cherrie. I wouldn't have stood half as much. It makes me angry now to think how she's tried to insult and teaze you.'

'"Beareth all things,"' repeated Charity. 'Mr. Morton showed me that that word "beareth" meant "to cover;" that it was the very same word that was used in the Gospels to signify a roof; and that just as we covered our houses with a roof to keep off the rain and the wind from coming in, so we must cover our hearts with the grace of charity, and not let the drops of unkind feeling, and the breath of unjust suspicion or unchristian resentment, find their way into them: in which case they would be very sure to do much mischief, destroying many holy graces and happy feelings. Those were almost the very words he said, for I wrote them down when I came home; I wanted so much to remember them, because of Ellinor. And do you know, Annie, it was the very day after that my papers were blown away!'

'I never could see the sense of her doing that,' said Annie, 'for she must have known it could not do you the smallest harm; unless she thought that Miss Mowbray would give time for the theme to be written over again, and that you would be too hurried to do it properly these days. What do you think, Cherrie?'

'I don't think at all, Annie—I really don't; I try to keep the covering over my heart just as that dear, kind Mr. Morton, told me to do, so that the thoughts may not find their way through. I say to myself, "Believeth all things, hopeth all things, endureth all things;" and I do believe, that if Mr. Morton is teaching me in my head, God is teaching me in my heart. Mr. Morton said in one of his sermons that it often was so, when God enabled us to receive a truth in our heart, He gave us afterwards the opportunity of carrying out that same truth in our lives, and expected us to do so. I was struck with his saying so, and I thought it must be just like that with all that he was teaching me, and all that was happening at school.'

'Certainly,' said Annie, 'Ellinor has given you opportunity of learning how to endure.'

'Only a little,' said Charity. 'Oh, Annie, when

we think of all that Jesus endured for us, what a very, very little it does seem! How it makes us long to be able to do anything, to show our gratitude to Him! And how good it seems of Him, out of regard for what He knows and sees we are wishing to do, to put it in our power to do something! Nothing we can do can be of any real service to Him, yet He gives us all work to do, because He loves us, and loves the work that we do for Him from love.'

'Yes,' said Annie, 'Mr. Morton told me that, too; and though I am not like you, Cherrie—I haven't half as many thoughts, nor half as strong a will to do what is right, yet I think I do really want to love and serve God, and that He will give me strength to keep the vow we are going to make.'

Thus talked the two young friends whilst waiting in the study, and when they entered the cab which was to convey them to church, any one who had glanced but casually at their faces might have seen in the sober earnestness that rested on them the reflex of what lay beneath. Charity was struck at seeing how small was the number assembled by Mr. Morton within the parish church that day, compared with that which had gathered in his own district church three months before.

But she did not wonder that it should have thus diminished. Mr. Morton's examinations had gone so deep, his public exhortations had been of so serious, his private conversations of so searching a nature, that Charity felt sure she herself would have shrunk from coming, had not Mr. Morton himself urged her doing so, and had not a very unmistakable voice within responded to his wish. Had it been a question of worthiness to approach—had there been any thought of fulfilling, in her own strength, the requirements of God's holy religion—had it been to take upon herself vows of godliness and self-denial, which in herself she must possess the power to perform, Charity would, indeed, not have dared to draw nearer to-day. For the further she went into God's truth the more clearly did she see how all power to understand, to believe, to receive, and to practise, must come alike from Him who sows the seed and brings forth, first the blade, then the corn, then the full corn in the ear. Commencement, continuance, and completion, the whole must be of Him, otherwise it could never be at all. But when Charity felt that it was not a question of all she must be willing to do for Christ, but, on the contrary, a question of all that Christ had been willing to do for her, then was her heart strengthened.

And as Mr. Morton explained to her one by one the various clauses of that most inclusive exhortation, 'Ye that do truly and earnestly repent you of your sins, and are in love and charity with your neighbours, and intend to lead a new life, following the commandments of God, and walking from henceforth in His holy ways;' she felt that she might draw near in faith, to take upon her this holy service, and look forward to the ensuing Sabbath, when she should still further ratify it by approaching the Table of the Lord, to receive His holy sacrament, 'in remembrance that

Christ's blood was shed for her, and to feed on Him in her heart by faith, with thanksgiving.'

The service was over. Charity, in the presence of God and that large congregation, had renewed the solemn promise and vow that had been made in her name at her baptism; she had ratified and confirmed the same in her own person. She had acknowledged herself bound to believe and to do all those things which her godparents had undertaken for her. There was no need for her to feel downcast and disheartened at the prospect of the arduous work before her, for had she not acknowledged that her help was to be in the name of the Lord, who had made heaven and earth? and had she not received the assurance that the Lord, blessed for ever, world without end, would be with her, and with her spirit; and that her prayer should go up unto Him, and be heard by Him, the Almighty and Everliving God, who had vouchsafed to perform the greatest of all His great works upon her, and, giving unto her the forgiveness of sins, regenerate her by water and the Holy Ghost? Would He not continue the work which He himself had begun, and strengthen her with the Holy Ghost the Comforter, daily increasing in her the manifold gifts of grace, and filling her with the spirit of wisdom and understanding, the spirit of counsel and ghostly strength, the spirit of knowledge and true godliness; in short, with the spirit of His holy fear, then and for ever? Defended by the Lord's heavenly grace, would not she continue His for ever, and daily increase in His Holy Spirit more and more until she came to His everlasting kingdom? Charity believed that she would, for God had promised. What He had promised, that she felt He would perform, and she must not suffer her spirit to feel unbelief or fear. It was the Almighty God alone who could make any one either to will or to do those things that are good and acceptable unto His Divine Majesty.

To that great and everliving God had she addressed her humble supplications; unto Him had the fervent intercessions of His saints been also addressed in her favour. The hand of God's servant had rested on her young head, in sign of the Almighty's favour and gracious goodness towards her, while deep within her heart the prayer that God's fatherly hand would be ever over her had found its solemn echo. She knew no father but God. She had been first drawn to come to Him at all in the hope that she might find in Him a father. That hope had been richly realised. And now she had no doubt but that He who had brought her so far would bring her yet further, letting His Holy Spirit be ever with her, and so leading her onwards in the knowledge and obedience of His word, that in the end she should obtain everlasting life through the Lord Jesus Christ. This same Almighty and Everlasting God would indeed vouchsafe to direct, sanctify, and govern both her heart and body in the ways of His laws, and in the works of His commandments; so that, through His most mighty protection, she should be preserved both here and ever, for the sake of Jesus, her Lord and Saviour.

Strengthened by such prayers, fully assured by such promises, Charity rose from her knees, with a heart alike heavy with grateful love and light with eager hope and ardent zeal. As she trod down the aisle, Mr. Morton's eye rested upon her with a look of deeper interest and thankfulness than upon any other of his young charges. The blessing of God Almighty, the Father, the Son, and the Holy Ghost, which had just been pronounced upon those young heads, seemed to have rested in a special measure upon Charity's. It appeared as though she herself was aware of it, and the feeling gave light to her countenance and elasticity to her very step. Never had Charity's bright face looked to Mr. Morton so bright as it did that day, when he stopped to shake hands with her at the church door.

'You go home to-morrow,' he said, 'and we shall not see you this evening, I hear?'

'No,' she replied: 'I do not think I ought to be away the last evening, and I have said goodbye to Mrs. Morton; but only for a very little while.'

On his return home, Mr. Morton entered the drawing-room with a letter in his hand, and said to his wife,—'It is as well, perhaps, that your little friend does not come to you this evening; at all events, you would not have had the satisfaction of telling her that she is not the first of her name in whom you have taken a deep interest. I have heard from Mr. Saville.'

'And what does he say?' asked Mrs. Morton, eagerly.

'Very little, and that little not very satisfactory,' replied her husband. 'At least, it does not in any way clear the mystery connected with these Helstones, who have thus come across our path twice in such a strange way—such a very strange way, that I cannot but believe that He who ordered the first acquaintance ordered also the second, and that there is an intended connexion between the two, which we shall yet see, though we cannot quite do so now.'

'But what does this Arlington clergyman say?' interrupted Mrs. Morton.

'Well, the most important point in his letter,' replied her husband, 'is, that he confirms the information which we had ourselves gathered pretty correctly from Miss Mowbray's hints; and confirms it, too, in a way which leaves no doubt whatever in my mind—not that I had any before, but still it makes the thing plain—that this pretty little Charity is our pretty Mrs. Helstone's only child. As we know, she left this one bitter day in January, sixteen years ago. As we now find, she arrived that same night at a little inn at Arlington, and there gave birth to this poor child. It seems the people of the inn sent for Mrs. Dorothy Helstone, an elderly lady who had lived many years in the village, and who appears to be the good fairy of the place; and this lady then and there adopted the child, which she has ever since brought up as her own.'

'And *her* name is Helstone?' exclaimed Mrs. Morton. 'But there *must* have been some relationship!'

'That is the most extraordinary part of the business,' said Mr. Morton. 'It does not appear that there is any—at least, Mr. Saville tells me that the old lady herself evidently had no idea of there being any; that she had never, in their many conversations about the child, and their many conjectures as to who her parents could be, given him the smallest reason to suppose that she could, by any possibility, be connected with herself.'

'But she *must* be!' said Mrs. Morton, eagerly. 'There is, evidently, some secret with which this good clergyman is not acquainted. We must find out what it is. We shall have to do so, perhaps, from the old lady herself.'

'Perhaps,' said Mr. Morton, 'this will not be so easily managed. Mysteries are not always cleared quite so quickly as people—women especially—would desire that they should be. I do not for a moment doubt that there is some connexion between this child and her so-called aunt. But I do not believe that either of them can have any idea that such is the case. Charity, we know, has not. Nor do I think, after reading this letter, that Mrs. Dorothy can have, either.'

'But if we could tell her all we know,' said Mrs. Morton, 'perhaps she might be very thankful; perhaps it might be the clue to some labyrinth in her own story—the unravelling of some perplexity in her own path.'

'Perhaps,' said Mr. Morton; 'but one cannot act upon a perhaps. And the difficulty is just this, that Mr. Saville tells me this lady's health is in a most precarious condition, and that the medical men say, that everything depends upon nothing being said or done which may occasion the slightest agitation. It seems that she is subject to nervous attacks of a very serious character, which are brought on generally by mental agitation. Also you will see that the old servant, the same "old Betsy" of whom we have heard a good deal from Charity, has been consulted on the propriety or the possibility of her mistress being questioned with regard to the Helstone family, and that all the satisfaction obtained from her was an earnest entreaty that "no one would think of mentioning the name of Helstone to her mistress; unless, indeed, they wished to kill her." Though, as you will see, this old Betsy herself has not any knowledge of any one of that name now living.'

And he handed the letter to his wife.

'What can be done?' she asked.

'Nothing more now, that I can see,' he replied. 'If this mystery is to be cleared, the end of it will come, no doubt, like all other things, in due time. Meanwhile we must wait patiently, and you will see now the propriety of our having said nothing at all on the subject to Charity.'

'I think,' said Mrs. Morton, 'it would have been a comfort to her to feel that we had known and loved her mother, and that she was such a sweet, lovely, loveable creature.'

'But you must remember,' said Mr. Morton, 'that we cannot tell her we knew her mother, without at the same time telling her that we knew her father.

And what could we say of him which it would be pleasing for her to hear? You may be sure that all this has been very wisely ordered. And though I confess that I shall be very glad to know what is the connexion between Charity and her godmother, and very glad on her account to prove that there is a connexion, I have lived to see that God's time being always the best, our wisdom consists in waiting for it.'

Easter was but a very short vacation, yet Charity's yearning love for her godmother prompted her to make a request, which Mrs. Dorothy's yearning love for her godchild caused her very readily to grant. Indeed, she wondered that the idea had not at once suggested itself to her own mind, so fitting did it seem that Charity's first approach to the Table of the Lord should be made in her own dear church, and that she should first taste the privileges of that holy ordinance, kneeling by her godmother's side to receive from the hands of her godfather the tokens of her Saviour's dying love.

Both those dear, honoured godparents, now knew all the story of Charity's young mind. Charity had written it all to Aunt Dorothy, pouring out her very heart in a long, long letter, which told all;—the humiliation she had undergone on receiving Mrs. Dorothy's letter—the passionate struggle that followed in her mind—the wonderful effect of Mr. Morton's sermon—the earnest longing to be a child of the great Father in heaven which those words awakened—the vain attempt to find Him, until Mr. Saville's sermon that last Sunday had opened to her the one new and living Way—the full acceptance her soul had found at the feet of that compassionate Saviour, and all the blessing and teaching which she had since received through the Confirmation classes.

An hour after Mrs. Dorothy had received that letter, she might have been seen still sitting with it in her hands, a look of deep joy upon her aged countenance; such deep joy, that for some time it had seemed unutterable, until at length she might have been heard to say, in a voice tremulous in its earnestness, 'I love the Lord, because He hath heard my voice and my supplication.'

Then, summoning Betsy, she despatched a message for Mr. Saville; and gratefully and joyfully did those two devoted godparents acknowledge together the wonderful goodness of the Lord. Mr. Saville dwelling thankfully on the special mercy the Lord had vouchsafed to himself, in allowing words of his to bring in the first ray of light into the mind that had been awakened to a sense of its darkness by the faithful teaching of her London friend.

That same night was the happy news told to the faithful Betsy by her mistress, and hardly had the tremulous tone of Mrs. Dorothy's voice died away, when Betsy burst forth in broken, tearful ejaculations of wondering thankfulness. 'Well, to be sure!' she cried; 'and the Lord's ways they *are* wonderful, and past finding out. Just to think that this trouble, which I 'd have given all I possess in the world to keep away from Miss Charity—this trouble, which I have worrited and worrited over till I haven't known where I was—just to think that this very trouble should have been the very road which the Lord had Himself marked out to bring the dear lamb into the "Shepherd's blessed fold!" Well, then, ma'am,' continued Betsy, 'I won't be after distrusting the Lord again, if I know it, as long as I 'm in the body. Sure enough He has His reasons for every mortal thing He does; and how could I ever think as He was a-going to let everything go contrary like to Miss Charity without making it up to her! And now, true enough, she 'll have a good friend with her as long as she walks this vale of tears, and won't never feel the lonesomeness of heart I used to feel in the workhouse, before I learnt as there was a God above as had given me all I had.'

And Betsy took her departure to the kitchen, saying to herself several times as she bustled about, putting all away for the night,—'Well, to be sure! 'tis enough to make one drop tears, that 'tis!'

Thus with thankful, happy hearts, did Mrs. Dorothy, Mr. Saville, and Betsy, look forward to soon having their child again with them.

CHAPTER XIV.

CHARITY'S farewell to her London friends was not to be for so short a time as she had imagined; a few days, she expected, would again see her in St. John's Wood: but before that time had passed Mrs. Dorothy, who had accompanied Charity to church on Easter Sunday, and, may be, gone beyond the powers of the failing flesh in the eager, thankful outpourings of the spirit, had been taken so very ill on that very evening, that all thought of Charity's return that week was given up. The illness, it was hoped, would prove but a passing one; but weeks went by before Mrs. Dorothy left her room, and when, at length, they had the joy of seeing her do so, her health, always very shattered, seemed to have given way so much, that it was decided that Charity should not return to school at all. It was her duty to remain with her aunt, and devote herself to her; and it was her happiness also, for, dearly as Charity had loved the old lady in the days of her childhood, she clung to her now with an affection which, while it retained all the warmth and self-forgetfulness of youth, had acquired all the intensity and consciousness of matured years: moreover, all the wonderful union which those feel whose hearts are joined in the best of bonds.

Charity was young to leave school, but her education would not be neglected at Arlington. Miss Danvers had taken her departure, and a very superior governess was engaged for Ellen Saville, in whose instructions Charity was to share. Mrs. Dorothy would give her lessons also from the first masters in the neighbouring town, and Ellen should go with her and share the benefit. She would be a pleasant companion for Charity, and Charity would make better progress than she could do if she were to study alone.

All these arrangements were of Mrs. Dorothy's making, and when she laid her plans before Mr. Saville, for his concurrence and approval, begging that a finishing governess might be engaged for Ellen, and that she might be allowed to defray the additional expense, it was solely for the sake of Charity, their mutual godchild, that the request was made. Nothing was said of the benefit which such an arrangement would secure to Ellen, who was now preparing to complete her own education in order that she might turn her talents to account as a governess—a course rendered necessary by Edward's extravagant follies, which had now been for several years a continual drain on his poor father's purse. The evident benefit to Ellen did not seem to enter

Mrs. Dorothy's mind; or if it did, she did not show that it did. The request was made as a personal favour to herself, for Charity's sake. And no arrangement could have succeeded better.

Six months passed—a year passed—two years, and Charity had grown almost into womanhood, without any one seeming to have any idea that she was anything still but a child: indeed, her aunt often told her that she grew younger in mind as she grew older in years, for as time added inches to her height it seemed also to add brightness to her cheek, light to her eye, and simplicity to her manner. Mrs. Dorothy was as proud of her godchild as the fondest mother could have been of her own and only born. She and Betsy would watch her every movement with delight, and talk of her for hours together; and the two years that passed after Charity's return to Arlington were amongst the very happiest of good Mrs. Dorothy's life—certainly the very happiest that she had known for thirty years. The little home had never been more bright, and though Mrs. Dorothy was now unable to leave it, even to go into the garden, it never seemed dull to her so long as Charity's bright face was coming in and out amongst the birds, and the flowers, and the books.

What happy days those were! Often in later years did Charity look back upon that peaceful time, and own that that spot of life had been very soft and green. The pleasant morning spent in little household cares never seemed wearisome to Charity, because they were for Aunt Dorothy's comfort.

She made the cleverest little housekeeper that ever was seen, for it was Charity's way to throw her whole mind into whatever occupied her for the moment.

That was a part of her character, as Mrs. Dorothy had seen very clearly as soon as her little godchild began to show any character at all. Old Betsy had said truly, that no child in its cradle ever cried as that child did; she had nursed a many in her day, in and out of the workhouse, but she had never had her cap torn off her head, or her collars crumpled into pieces about her neck, in the vigorous way in which little Miss Charity would set about it when once she was in a passion. When she was in a rage, it was a thorough rage; when she laughed, which she did sometimes for no reason at all but because she was so happy, she could not help it; her peals of clear, ringing laughter were so merry, that others could not keep from laughing, too, for very sympathy. When she found a book that interested her, the little figure would be bent well-nigh double over it, and the large eyes riveted upon its pages, while she was utterly and entirely unconscious of everything that was passing round her. Either she would not do a thing at all, or she would do it with all her might.

That had always been her way, and it was so now. She did not seem to be conscious of it; there was no effort in it. Charity was one of those who did nothing with an effort, but everything with a will; as if the self she ruled came gladly to the work, and had no need to be driven up with the whip and spur.

And Betsy was not far wrong when she described her young mistress's housekeeping to her friend the miller, and told him that, if he could only see it, he 'd say with her that it was the prettiest thing in the world.

'There 's never a cloud on her pretty face,' she said to him one day, as Charity left the kitchen, after ordering a sack of flour, with as much grace and courtesy as though the miller had been a nobleman, and his white cap the order of the Garter; 'there 's never a cloud on her pretty face. As you see her now, so you see her always; morning, noon, and night, she 's always the same—a bit of sunshine wherever she goes. If I 'd nought else to do in life but watch her and her pretty ways, I wouldn't find it dull. And that 's about all my poor mistress has left on earth to do, and I believe she 's satisfied, and don't want for anything beyond Miss Charity. She says to me sometimes, "Miss Charity 's a very good housekeeper, Betsy?" "Yes, ma'am," I 'll say, "it seems to me she 's good at anything she puts her dear little mind and her pretty little hand to do." "That 's just it, Betsy," she 'll say in answer. And then she 'll go on to tell me how she is as clever at books, and all them sciences people are so much given to in these days, as she is in everything else. My mistress says, it 's just as easy for Miss Charity to put down the ideas that are in her clever little head upon paper, as it is for her to set down the housekeeping accounts in the books, and that she does one as well as the other. The masters over at Burleigh say it's just a pleasure to teach her; and the governess up at the Rectory, who, they say, is the cleverest lady that ever was educated, you should hear what she has to say about our young lady. And then, Mr. Brown, as you said just now, she 's so pretty-spoken: no airs or graces; no thinking of herself, one may say, at all. That's what I love most in her. God bless her! she 'll come down here in the morning in her plain cotton frock, and she 'll give all her orders in as pretty a way as can be, just as though it would be very polite in me if I 'd be pleased to do them all. And yet she isn't careless about how things are done—not she! there's no fussing about one, and looking *at* one, till one does not know whether one's on one's head or one's feet, as I 've seen with many mistresses, especially with them as are young and inexperienced. She just gives her orders all so prettily and clearly, and trusts to their being done; but, somehow, she must give another look round afterwards, for she finds out quick enough when a thing is forgotten: but then there 's no fuss or scolding, only, "Betsy, I think you 've forgotten this or the other." And that not only because I 'm an old thing, who brought her up, and she has got a kindly feeling for me; she 's just the same with the girl Phœbe Dawson, who comes in of a morning to help. Why, she 's the same with the very birds and the other creatures: she 'll go to them after she 's done all she 's got to do in the kitchen, and I hear her talking to them as though they had the sense to understand: which, for all we know, they may have. Then she 'll just settle her flowers, and arrange my mistress's arm-chair and footstool, and she 's upstairs helping her aunt to dress and getting her into the parlour. There isn't a morning that I don't stop my work to listen to her singing the Morning Hymn to Mrs. Dorothy, and then I hear her sweet voice reading the psalms and lessons, regular every day, one after another. And so she 'll go on the whole day, as happy as a lark. And looks like a queen when she puts off her morning frock and comes down in her black silk to give me her directions about her aunt before she goes up to the Rectory, or over to Burleigh, to some of her fine lessons. It 's my opinion she has a grander look about her than any one of my lord duke's daughters we had in church last Sunday. I sat and made my remarks on them, and compared them with our young lady, and that was the conclusion I came to; the same I reached years ago: but there's many years they haven't been down here, and they 'd grown beyond recollection.

'Just so, Mrs. Betsy,' at length interrupted the miller, 'and I was going to say a word on this very subject; only, when once you begin about Miss Charity, there 's no stopping you, as you say yourself. Not that I can ever hear too much of her, for the matter of that, for she 's been a prime favourite of mine ever since she was as high as your table there; and all you say is only just the fulfilling of what I told you many times in years gone by—that the metal was good, and you 'd find it would prove so. And so it has. Well, she would have her head once upon a time, and she had it: and now it 's been as I said, she's got the same spirit in her yet: but it's taught and trained, and she's a thorough-bred—that's just the truth. And you mark my words, and see if, come what will, the spirit that she's got in her don't keep her up and make her run till she drops; which is, you know, Mrs. Betsy, the nature of them creatures as are thorough-bred. But what I was going to say, only I was waiting for room to put it in, is, that the eldest son of my lord duke, as you call him, is coming down himself to put the place to rights; and they say —I had it from some of his own people—that the family's going to live here mostly in the winter times, because the second son is lately married, and his father has made over the other place to him: which, I believe, the young ladies don't like at all, because it's much gayer than this. But this place is much the best property, and it's all going to be put in order for the eldest son, who is to be here next week. And a fine gentleman he is, and grandly thought of in parliament, where he does all he can for the poor. If all one hears is true, it will be a lucky day for Arlington when he comes down to see about the property.'

'And is he married, too?' asked Betsy.

'No; nor yet going to be,' replied the miller: 'so you see, Mrs. Betsy, it's a fine chance for your young lady. You say she ought to be a queen; but since she can't quite be that, I suppose you'd be satisfied in seeing her my Lady Huntley—eh?' And the miller laughed, a laugh with something in its tone of which Betsy did not quite approve.

'I don't see what there is to laugh at, Mr. Brown,' she said: 'it 's my belief our young lady 's good enough for any lord in Christendom, even though he should be the prime minister, and sit at the queen's right hand. That 's just my opinion.'

'No doubt it is, Mrs. Betsy,' replied the good-natured miller; 'and it 's mine too. I had no intention of hinting otherwise. I agree with you that Miss Charity 's more than good enough to be my Lady Huntley; and why shouldn't she be so, too, one day? "Many a true word said in jest," you know.'

And the miller ended his long parley with his friend Betsy, or, rather, her long parley with him, by wishing her a good afternoon and riding homewards. Betsy watched him and his pony wending their way up the hill. She raised her eyes a little higher, to where the turrets of Huntley tower soared upwards to the sky, seeming to raise themselves above the little village in protection of the place and people. She looked around on the woods, which extended far and wide on either side—all the Huntley property, one of the richest and largest in all the country.

'"Many a true word said in jest,"' she said to herself; 'well, that 's true. I wonder what made the miller say that, now? They do say that "coming events cast their shadows before them:" that 's another proverb; and I suppose there must be truth in all such sayings, or they wouldn't come to be sayings. My poor old first mistress of all used to say, that she felt a kind of horror come over her the first day that ever *he* showed his dark face inside the Briersley parlour; that was like a thick, cold cloud, that wrapped itself round her, and made her shiver to the very core, and the feeling never left her. Well, it does make me feel queer like to hear of a young lord up at Huntley Tower, who must see my pretty lady every Sunday of his life in church, and meet her often enough besides, for the place isn't so big but what the few people that live in it must come across one another pretty often. Well, I don't think he'll see my young mistress once without wanting to see her a second time. And they say he's so handsome, and so clever, and so good, and likes to speak up for the poor, who lie so near Miss Charity's heart. Well, as I tell my mistress, "It's time she should be leaving off her lessons, Mrs. Dorothy." She says, "Keep her a child as long as you can, and that while she is willing to go on with her education she would not for worlds be the one to break it off." I wonder if she remembers that she was a married woman herself at that same age? May be she does, poor dear! and that's the reason she likes to keep the lesson-books in Miss Charity's hands as long as she can, and see if getting her learning into her heart may keep it from turning to other thoughts which mayn't prove quite so profitable.'

But, at this moment, Betsy's imaginations and anticipations were interrupted by the entrance of the subject of them, those same lesson-books in her hand and a bright colour on her cheek. She had just come from the Rectory, and as she stood there in her black silk dress, with the neat white collar and cuffs, her plain jacket setting forth to advantage the graceful line of her slight figure, and her bright brown hair falling still in the clustering curls of childhood from under her black hat and feather, old Betsy's lively imagination represented her standing just as she now stood, only with Lord Huntley at her side; and the picture was pleasant to her mind. She felt that he or any one else might so stand, and be satisfied.

'Well, Miss Charity,' she said, 'and so you've come from the Rectory! It seems to me it was most time you'd finished your lessons, my dear.'

'Oh, not yet, Betsy,' said Charity. 'I'm in no hurry to be made a woman of, I can assure you.'

'Well, but, my dear, one can't be a child always.'

'No,' said Charity, 'unfortunately; therefore the next best thing is to be a child as long as one can.'

'Somehow, Miss Charity, I think you'll always be a child in some things; you'll always be light-hearted, I do believe.'

'I'm feeling very light-hearted to-day, Betsy, at all events; for I've just heard a very good piece of news, and one that I know will please Aunt Dorothy as much as it seems to please Mr. Saville.'

'And what may that be, Miss Charity?' said Betsy, feeling that the miller had been beforehand with Charity, but not wishing to mar her pleasure in communicating a piece of good news by saying so.

'Why, Betsy, all the Huntley Tower property is going to be restored, and the family are coming to live here again! It's quite true, for Lord Huntley has written himself to Mr. Saville and told him all about it, and Mr. Saville says it will be just the making of the place. The Castle is going to be all repaired, and the gardens laid out freshly, and the plantation put to rights. And the cottages on the estate are to be all put in order; and Mr. Saville says there will be work for all the people round about, to say nothing of the advantage it will be to have a resident landlord, and such a landlord as he says Lord Huntley will be. For he 's such a good man — very clever, and as good as he is clever. I must go and tell Aunt Dorothy, for she 'll brighten up at such news. It seems as if it was to be a blessing to everybody.'

And Charity passed on to the sitting-room, leaving Betsy to add with renewed vigour a few more stones to the castle she was building. The only further remark she made to Charity was to say, as she was leaving the hall,—

'Miss Charity, my dear, I really think you ought to be leaving off them long curls, and doing your hair some other way.'

'Well, I really think I might do that, Betsy,' said Charity, laughing; 'for even Mr. Saville makes fun of my long hair. But whatever made you think of that just now?'

Betsy could have told her, but did not.

CHAPTER XV.

THE summer passed and the winter came, and six months later, though it scarcely seemed six weeks, so quickly had that time flown amidst the many changes that had marked it, the ground lay covered with snow, and the ice in Arlington Pond was thicker than it had been seen for years.

The time had flown quickly, because every one had been so much occupied; but it seemed long to look back upon, for so much had been done. The winter was more severe than could be remembered 'within the memory of the oldest inhabitant,' and yet 'the oldest inhabitant' could not remember a time when winter's trials had been so little felt. The wind howled piteously around the walls of the cottages, but did not pierce through; for Lord Huntley had seen that every cottage in the village was weather-tight. The hail and rain beat unmercifully upon the roofs, but not a drop found entrance in the little rooms beneath; for Lord

Huntley had seen that not a slate or a thatch wanted repair. Old men and women cowered over the grate, but they did not murmur as they did so; for Lord Huntley had furnished the coals, and they were plentiful and burned brightly. Little children wound their way to school with blue cheeks and red little noses, but yet feeling warm and merry within; for Lord Huntley had provided the linsey cloak and woollen jacket which each boy or girl rejoiced in. Working men came in from the day's labour with appetites sharpened by the intense cold, but ready to do credit to the hot soup which Lord Huntley had placed it in the power of every industrious wife to provide for them.

The landlord's heart and purse had come to the help of the good Rector's head and experience; and the Arlington poor were spending the pleasantest winter they had known for many a long year, in spite of the very remarkable cold that prevailed everywhere.

Even in old Betsy's warm kitchen it was cold to-day, and though she had made up the parlour fire only half-an-hour before, she thought it must need replenishing; and accordingly, coal-scuttle in hand, paid it and her mistress a visit of inspection. The old lady was sitting in her arm-chair, watching the bright coals, and, for all we know, building as pleasant castles among them as Betsy had ever built up in the air amongst the turrets of Huntley Tower; for she started when her old servant opened the door, and seemed as though suddenly roused from a reverie.

Not an unpleasant one, however, as Betsy satisfied herself by one quick glance at her mistress's well-known countenance. The brow, wrinkled by age, was not, however, now drawn together over the eyes. There was no nervous twitching of the mouth. The hands were not pressing one another in a sort of nervous sympathy in the lap, but lay quietly resting, with the knitting-needles still within the fingers.

'Why, Betsy, there was no need of coals,' she said; 'you've only just made up the fire.'

'Yes, ma'am, that's true,' said Betsy; 'but it's terribly cold, and I thought Miss Charity would need to find a good blaze when she came back from her frolic.'

Betsy had not quite courage to confess that another motive, besides replenishing the fire, had brought her to the parlour at that moment—even the hope that her mistress might say something to her on the subject of the visitor whom she had just shown out of the front door. But since Mrs. Dorothy did not begin the subject, as Betsy had hoped she would, Betsy would do so herself.

'My Lord Huntley will have been sorry not to find my young lady at home, ma'am,' she said, as she swept up the hearth very carefully, and not with too much speed.

'Lord Huntley did not come to see Miss Charity, Betsy,' said Mrs. Dorothy.

'But he inquired, ma'am, if she were within,' responded Betsy. And seeing that the old lady's countenance did not wear the expression which always told her, without any need of words, that it was well not to pursue a matter further, the old servant took courage to say,—'My lord asked for you, ma'am, and said it would be a favour if you could give him only a few minutes' conversation on business; and then, ma'am, he inquired whether Miss Charity, or "Miss Helstone," as he calls her always, though no one else seems able to find the way to do so —whether Miss Helstone were at home also. And I did think, ma'am, he seemed somewhat disappointed when I said "No, she was not; nor wouldn't be all the afternoon." His countenance seemed to fall like, as though he'd have been better pleased to hear that he was going to have a sight of her pretty face when he got inside the parlour.'

Mrs. Dorothy smiled. 'Very likely indeed, Betsy,' she said. 'There are not many young men in the world, I suppose, who wouldn't rather see a pretty young lady like Miss Charity than a poor old woman like me.'

'Lor, ma'am, that's not what I meant at all!' exclaimed Betsy. 'That's not my Lord Huntley, ma'am! For the matter of that, I know he isn't a bit like other young men. It's my belief, now, he'd a great deal rather be sitting here with you, ma'am, than with half the young ladies you could give him. He's that sort of gentleman, that somehow he seems to walk along the road wrapped up in his great thoughts and plans; and I believe all the ladies in England might just walk past him without his so much as knowing they were there. But when it comes to be a matter as to whether Miss Charity is there or not . . . well, ma'am, I believe he *do* know, and he *do* care. I 've thought so many times before, but the look on his face to-day made me just set down the matter for sure in my mind. He 'd got his business, no doubt, ma'am—he 's full of business, and all of a sort worth attending to, which is more than can be said of the business of most young gentlemen of his age: but he 'd room for other thoughts besides in his mind this day. There was a bit of pleasure at the back of the business, and I was sorry enough to be the means of driving it away by telling him my young lady was not at home.'

'Lord Huntley and Miss Charity have many interests in common,' said Mrs. Dorothy, the discouraging tone now just tinging her voice: 'they are both engaged heart and soul in their work amongst the poor, and there is no stronger bond of union than that of doing good together.'

Betsy put the finishing stroke to her hearth by sweeping up the two or three tiny coals that had fallen whilst she had been speaking, and disappeared. But when she got back into the kitchen, she relieved her mind by saying the rest of what remained upon it to herself. 'No doubt, that 's just the truth. They 've got a good many interests in common now, and it 's my belief they 'll soon have a good many more. I don't know what my mistress means by saying "There 's no stronger bond of union than that of doing good together." It's a strong-enough bond, no doubt: my Lord Huntley and Miss Charity seem to find it so, anyhow. But I should have said, there were one or two ways of making the bond stronger still, if I'd been asked. Not that I know much about such things myself—thank the Lord and my ugly face, as I've said many times. But my mistress, she ought to know something about it—to her cost, poor thing! And my Lord Huntley, my name's not Betsy if *he* thinks there couldn't be a stronger bond of union between him and our pretty lady than that of visiting the poor and doing good amongst them. It's my belief he wouldn't be against a visit to the parish church together, to see what Mr. Saville might be able to do in the way of strengthening the bond. I wonder, now, whether my mistress told him where my young lady was? Anyhow, I'm glad I had the sense to do so. And it won't be my fault if he goes back to Huntley Tower to-day without having had the wish gratified, which I could see plain enough was lying at the back of that look of his. Unless I'm very much mistaken, it won't have been for nothing that I told him my young lady had gone down to skate on the Huntley Pond with the young ladies and gentlemen from the Rectory.'

Betsy was not mistaken. To the Huntley Pond Lord Huntley took his way at once. And there, amidst the groups which were gathered either on the banks of the pond or on the ice itself, he was not too absorbed in his 'great thoughts and plans,' as Betsy termed them, quickly to discover which was the particular group he sought, and which the particular figure in that group which at once became to him all the group together.

Having found what he wanted, he seemed, however, contented to approach no nearer to it; on the contrary, as soon as he had drawn near enough to the pond clearly to discern 'the young ladies and gentlemen from the Rectory,' and in the midst of them the tall slight figure of 'my young lady' herself, he withdrew to a greater distance, and walked up and down a particular piece of ground there, apparently so buried in meditation that more than one passer-by, who took off his hat or made her bow to him, as the case might be, arrived at a conclusion which might have been expressed in old Betsy's very words,—'Lord Huntley was too much absorbed in his own thoughts to take notice of what was passing around him; the fairest face in the United Kingdom might have passed him, and he would not have seen that it was fair—he was wrapped up in his own thoughts.'

Not so completely wrapped up, however, but that a sharp and sudden cry from the ice reached his ears almost before any others. Not so completely wrapped up, but that he saw at half a glance, indeed without any glance at all, towards the spot where one group was skating, in gay rivalry each of the other's skill, which was the figure that had disappeared from it. Not so completely wrapped up but that, although he was further from the scene of the accident than any other spectator of it, he was the first to reach the spot, and that with such marvellous speed that, before the brave young boys had had time to take the plunge, which any one of them would have risked, Lord Huntley had freed himself from his heavy cloak and under-coat, and had plunged beneath the cold dark water. Nothing was to be seen, at least nothing to the outward eye; but Lord Huntley saw — saw with a vividness which made every nerve in his body quiver with the most intense actual pain, a slight form shivering in a death-agony; two fragile arms, beating the pitiless waters in a fierce struggle for victory and life; features, every line of which he knew by heart, convulsed with terror;—all this Lord Huntley saw, or seemed to see: those who marked the look upon his face, and never afterwards forgot it, could scarcely believe that he did not really see it. The cry she gave could not, they said, have reached his ears at the distance where he stood. They told him afterwards it must have been the united cry of all who saw the accident that startled him from his meditative walk, and brought him in an instant to the spot.

It might have been so; he did not contradict them: but to him it always seemed as if the piteous cry for help which Charity had uttered when she sank had reached his very soul. For that loud cry of many eager, terror-stricken voices, if heard, was forgotten as soon as heard. But that one pitiful cry in that dear, well-known voice, 'Oh, help me! help me!' it sounded in his heart, and kept repeating itself there as he too struggled beneath the water.

While above, the ice was being broken up on all sides, and anxious faces were bending forwards with ever-increasing paleness, as more than one came forward to help with their best efforts.

At length, the first and strongest effort was crowned with that success for which hearts had prayed that, until that morning, had never framed a prayer. Charity Helstone's pale, dripping form, was borne to the shore in Lord Huntley's arms. He would resign her to no one. A strength not his own—a strength that seemed beyond all that was possible to nature, was in him. He ordered one of the young Savilles, almost imperatively, to fetch the carriage from Huntley Tower, and see that a bed was laid in it. He desired another to get his horse at once from Mrs. Bryce's little inn—a favourite horse he was known never to allow any one to mount but himself—and ride off instantly for the doctor.

All these orders he gave without consulting even Mr. Saville, who, however, himself set off to Ivy Cottage, to break the tidings of the accident as gently as possible to Mrs. Dorothy, and prepare her for the sight of Charity's turgid countenance and lifeless form. He felt thankful that Ivy Cottage was as near as any other house, and that, therefore, Charity might as well be carried there as elsewhere, for he knew what agony of mind it would have been to Mrs. Dorothy to have had her darling, for all she knew, dying in some cottage, and she herself unable to go to her. Indeed, he doubted whether anything could have kept the old lady from her niece under such circumstances, or which would have been likely to injure her most—the effort of leaving the home which she had not quitted for months, or the intense agony of remaining in it with every thought and imagination actively interested elsewhere.

But Ivy Cottage was one of the nearest houses to Huntley Pond. Therefore to Ivy Cottage she was carried, and the strong arms that bore her, inspired with far more than their usual strength by the anxious hearts that beat within their owners' breasts, had well-nigh reached their destination before the Huntley Tower carriage met them, just in time to bear the precious burden up the steep hill that led to Mrs. Dorothy's residence.

Mr. Saville and old Betsy were waiting at the door—Betsy as calm and self-possessed as those who knew her best would have expected her to be. Just within the hall stood Mrs. Dorothy, and even in that moment of intense excitement it struck more than one of those present how much paler a pale face could become under agitation. It might have been said of Mrs. Dorothy that she was at all times 'as pale as pale could be,' yet now the hue of her aged cheeks had whitened by many degrees; yet she had lost none of her usual composure, and it was she who gave all the orders, and herself followed to the bedroom—Charity's own room—where every preparation had, in that short time, been made by those few hands.

But all efforts for long seemed in vain. Charity lay still as death, and after every attempt at restoration had been made which either Mrs. Dorothy's or Mr. Saville's skill could suggest, there was no sign of returning animation.

It was at this moment that Edward Saville, with a hardiness and strength of will which Lord Huntley admired and envied, left the group of anxious watchers and waiters in the parlour, and found his way into the room where Charity lay. In an instant he had stretched forward, and was breathing, with all the force of his strong, healthy lungs, into the pale, parted mouth. Again and again was the warm respiration, into which his very soul seemed poured, forced into the lungs, which to all appearance had ceased their action for ever, until at length there was a sigh—faint, indeed, but still a sigh; at sound of which new strength seemed to enter Edward's soul, and again he poured forth the warm living breath which was to bring back life more precious, better worth preserving, than his own.

And then, for the first time, Betsy spoke. 'See!' she cried; 'see! she moves her finger!' It was true. There was a nervous twitching of the little finger—then of the hand—of both hands. The sighs were louder, and soon became gasps—eager, panting gasps for the dear breath of life. Mr. Saville laid his hand again upon the heart, and instead of the despairing look with which till now he had done so, pronounced that he could feel it beating. Every effort was redoubled, till at length the faint returning spark of life had been nourished into a steady, though somewhat feeble flame.

Before the doctor arrived the power of swallowing had returned, and all he did was to order hot wine and water, to desire that the patient should be kept very warm and very quiet, and to pronounce that all danger was over and that life was safe.

'And almost a miracle, too,' he added, on returning to the parlour, 'if, as you say, the young lady had been nearly a quarter of an hour in the water. We owe it to you, young man,' he said, turning to Edward; 'you have saved her life.'

'No,' he said, 'it was Lord Huntley who did that. Would that I had been on the spot when she fell in! Then none could have taken the plunge before me.'

And, saying that he would soon return to see how Charity was, he was the first to leave the house.

CHAPTER XVI.

CHARITY'S recovery was very rapid. She had, as the doctor said, everything in her favour—youth, health, strength, a cheerful buoyancy of constitution, and all the care that the most devoted attention could secure to her. A fortnight after the accident and she lay on the sofa in the pretty parlour, a little pale and somewhat weak, but otherwise well. The room looked very bright and gay; on each table stood lovely bouquets: it would have surprised any one to see such a wealth of rare exotics in that humble little parlour, had they not known that every day Lord Huntley himself brought the loveliest choice his hot-houses could supply.

Old Betsy's face had grown quite radiant since the accident, and it was with a most triumphant look that she would usher my lord into the parlour when he called, or, if she had orders to deny him, bring in herself the messages, and the lovely baskets of fruit and flowers he had left for Charity. This triumphant look on Betsy's face was not lost on Mrs. Dorothy, if it was on Charity. But it did not seem to find any response there, and this Betsy was quick enough to remark. Lord Huntley's daily visits—Lord Huntley's marked attention, so different from anything which the most extreme politeness or the deepest interest could have excited, did not seem to afford Mrs. Dorothy by any means the same delight that it afforded old Betsy. On the contrary, there was a troubled look on Mrs. Dorothy's countenance which Betsy could not understand.

'It was no wonder her lady should dread the very sound of marriage,' she would say to herself; 'but she could not, in the very nature of things, suppose she was going to keep that sweet flower of hers to herself all her life, without any one's wanting to lay their finger on it. Her mistress might have the sense to know, that it had only to show its pretty head for a many to be wanting to gather it, and therefore she would have thought, that when a young man such as my Lord Huntley showed such evident signs of wanting to transplant it to his home, she might have made him more welcome than she did, instead of, on the contrary, seeming rather disconcerted like at the sight of him.' Only the day before yesterday, when she told her mistress that he was riding up the street, she had said, quite put out like,—'Lord Huntley again! why, he comes every day!' And when Betsy had replied, which for the life of her she could not help doing, Miss Charity not being there, 'Why, yes, ma'am, it seems to me that's what he means to do;' she was sure she had heard her mistress say to herself as she left the room to open the door to him,

'I 'm afraid so.' What there was to be afraid of Betsy could not quite make out. It might have helped her to a conclusion could she have overheard the conversation that took place that evening in the little parlour between Mrs. Dorothy and her adopted child.

It was evening, and there would be no more visitors that day. There had been enough, and too many, for both Charity's returning and Mrs. Dorothy's failing strength, and both one and the other looked somewhat exhausted as Betsy cleared away the tea-things, made up the fire, and left them to what they called their 'best hour,' the quiet time before evening prayers, when Mrs. Dorothy always rested for an hour in her large arm-chair, with her feet on her footstool. Before the accident this stool was always Charity's seat, but now she lay on the couch on the opposite side of the fire: a book was in her hand, from which she had been reading aloud to the old lady; but the 'best hour' almost always ended by the book being laid aside, whilst they talked pleasantly together.

To-night, however, though the reading had ceased almost as soon as it had begun, for Charity's voice was weak, conversation did not at once begin. Mrs. Dorothy lay back in her arm-chair, and looked, Charity thought, very worn. She had no doubt seen too many visitors that afternoon, and she had been growing weak of late. Charity did not like to think that there had been a change in Aunt Dorothy since her accident, and yet she could not shut her eyes to the fact that her aunt's voice was many degrees weaker, her cheeks many degrees more shrunk and pale, and her step many degrees more feeble, than they had been only one fortnight before. She was greatly changed since that day when Charity left her knitting in her parlour, and went off gaily to enjoy an afternoon's skating on the Huntley Pond; and this thought made Charity resolve to take as much care of her as possible, and keep her from over-fatigue. She must not see so many visitors another day. There had been too many this afternoon. Mr. and Mrs. Saville had called; Edward had come, as he generally did, in the twilight, and remained until Betsy had brought in the tea. Lord Huntley had been there for so long in the afternoon, and Mrs. Dorothy had talked a great deal too much to him about the poor people. It must not happen again.

Charity had just arrived at this conclusion when, as though some similar thoughts were passing in her aunt's mind, the old lady said abruptly,—

'Lord Huntley has been here every day this week, my dear.'

'Yes,' said Charity: 'I was just thinking about it.'

'Were you, my dear?' said Aunt Dorothy, in a tone which showed the interest inspired in her mind by this very simple piece of information; 'were you, my dear? and what were you thinking?'

'That his visits fatigued you, dear aunt; that we must not allow him to come so often. You can't tell him, perhaps, but I can give him a hint that you are not strong, and not equal to seeing many visitors.'

Mrs. Dorothy's countenance lost the look it had acquired,—'I was not thinking of myself,' she said. 'Lord Huntley's visits are not to me, Charity.'

'To you and to me, too, I suppose, Aunt Dorothy,' said Charity.

'He does not give me his lovely flowers, Charity,' continued Mrs. Dorothy; 'and though I am growing old and feeble, it is not concern for my health that brings him here: his anxiety is all for you.'

'He has been so anxious that I should recover from my accident,' said Charity. 'He is so very, very kind!'

'You do not think he will come as often when you are well, Charity?' asked Mrs. Dorothy. There was something peculiar in the old lady's manner which Charity felt, but did not understand.

'Aunt Dorothy!' she said, fixing her large, childlike, blue eyes on her aunt, with the same wondering look in them which Mrs. Dorothy had always been so fond of, 'Aunt Dorothy, what do you mean?'

'I only wanted to know, Charity, whether you thought Lord Huntley would come to see us as often when you get well as he does now?'

'I should think not, Aunt Dorothy: he comes to see how I am getting on.'

'And it is anxiety about your health brings him here—nothing else?'

'And I suppose because he likes to come, Aunt Dorothy,' said Charity, the blue eyes never changing in their wide-open look of simplicity. 'I think Lord

Huntley likes you and me very much Aunt Dorothy: don't you?'

If Charity had been on her footstool at Aunt Dorothy's feet, the withered hands would have been laid very caressingly on the child's head. As she was not, it was only by the tone of her voice, the loving, tender, almost pitying tone, that one could have seen how the child's simplicity touched the old lady, how it went to her very heart to be obliged to say one word which might open Charity's eyes to the reality of the life before her. It seemed such a pity to let in any of this world's light upon a mind which was so happy in its utter simplicity. For Charity's sake she was most unwilling to do so, but for Lord Huntley's sake it must be done. Mrs. Dorothy had seen plainly enough that day, that if she did not open Charity's eyes to the truth he soon would. She hesitated a minute or two, and then she said,—

'I think, Charity, Lord Huntley is very fond of you; I think it will depend on you whether he continues these visits or not. You are nearly well now; he will soon have no reason for coming daily to see you.'

'Then, Aunt Dorothy, you may be sure he will not come so often,' said Charity.

'No, Charity, I am not at all sure of that. Lord Huntley likes coming here. No doubt he will continue his visits, if he thinks they are pleasant to you also.'

'They are very pleasant, Aunt Dorothy,' she said. 'I like Lord Huntley very much indeed. No one can help liking him—he is so good; so very, very good; and so kind: he is kind to every one, but so very kind to me.'

'That you would be glad to see him every day of your life?' said Mrs. Dorothy, quietly.

'Oh, I don't know about that,' replied Charity, quickly. 'I like to see him very much, especially now, when I cannot get out; and he brings me just the news I am longing to hear, about my poor people. But if I were well—no; then I don't think I should care about seeing him so often. It would be an interruption, Aunt Dorothy—wouldn't it? I don't think that one would care about daily visits from any one when one was quite well and strong, and able to go about; unless,' she added, 'it were from some one that one knew very, very well, and loved very much, like Mr. and Mrs. Saville, or Edward. They don't seem like visitors.'

'Why not?' asked Mrs. Dorothy.

'Oh, because one is so intimate with them; they seem like a part of one's own self, and one goes on just as one would if they were not there. But if Lord Huntley were to come here every day of the year to see me, I should never feel like that with him.'

'Why not?' again asked Mrs. Dorothy.

'Because he is a stranger to me, Aunt Dorothy.'

'Not quite a stranger, Charity,' said Mrs. Dorothy; 'you have known him for many months now, and you must remember he saved your life——'

'It was Edward saved my life,' interrupted Charity. 'I always like to think so.'

'My child,' said Mrs. Dorothy; and but for the darkness Charity might have perceived the shadow that crossed the old lady's face: 'my child, Edward brought back the sinking powers of the life which, through God's mercy, Lord Huntley had saved. But you owe your life to Lord Huntley: we must never forget that.'

'I never wish to do so, Aunt Dorothy; I would be grateful to him all my life.'

'Only,' said Mrs. Dorothy, 'you would not wish to show your gratitude by allowing him to spend every afternoon with you.'

She spoke lightly, but the words had a heavy sound behind.

'No,' said Charity, laughing now quite gaily, 'that I should not like.'

'Then I think, my dear, we must, as you say, give him a little hint about not coming quite so often now that you are getting better. I will do it to-morrow; he said he was coming again then.'

'Oh, Aunt Dorothy, let me do it. It will come best from me.'

'No,' said Aunt Dorothy, 'I think not, Charity. Old women must have their way. And now, my child, I shall ring for Betsy; it is time for both of us to go to bed.'

The next day it so happened—or was it so arranged?—that Mrs. Saville's usual daily visit to Charity was paid before that young lady had left her bedroom to come into the parlour, and that Mrs. Saville and Charity were still talking there when

Lord Huntley was ushered into the sitting-room, where Mrs. Dorothy sat alone. That she was not there also did not seem to afford any disappointment whatever to Charity; though, after Betsy had come into her room and announced the fact of Lord Huntley's arrival in the parlour, she turned from other subjects to tell Mrs. Saville that 'Aunt Dorothy meant to give him a hint not to come quite so often;' adding, 'I wanted to do it myself, and I thought I could have managed it quite easily, for dear Aunt Dorothy has been so weak and poorly lately, I really think it does her harm to see people, strangers especially; and somehow, I always fancy she is nervous, and not quite at her ease with Lord Huntley. I would rather have spoken to him myself, because I should be so very sorry for him to be the least bit vexed. He has been so very, very kind to me, and I like him so very much. It almost seems wrong of me, though, not to like him even more than I do, when he risked his life to save mine. Do you know, Mrs. Saville, I've been calling myself bad names this morning for even allowing myself to feel that it will be a little bit of a relief to me when he does not come every afternoon.' And Charity's blue eyes looked straight into Mrs. Saville's, who returned the look with a loving, motherly kiss.

Meanwhile, Mrs. Dorothy in the parlour was making but poor work of it with Lord Huntley. For Lord Huntley, though he was some ten years older than Charity, and had received, as Betsy boasted, 'the finest education money could give,' and had had all the experience of life that would be gained by public schools, having a private tutor, going to the University, travelling on the Continent, and being a member of Parliament, proved in this little matter as simple as Charity herself, and was so dull at comprehending any of Mrs. Dorothy's hints, that at length she had to tell him plainly how grateful she was for all that he had done for her niece, who was, indeed, to her as her own child, her very darling child; she owed that precious life to him, and never could she feel grateful enough to him for that great benefit and all his subsequent kindness; but——

But here Lord Huntley interrupted her. He was a man of few words; Mrs. Dorothy had heard people say that they did not believe it was in Lord Huntley's nature to express himself strongly on any subject. But Mrs. Dorothy could never have said so after listening to the fervent manner in which, in few, but powerful words, he poured forth the feelings of his heart on the subject of Charity, adding that he had but been waiting till Charity should have recovered from her illness to say all to her which he now said to Mrs. Dorothy. It was in vain that Mrs. Dorothy sought to check him; Lord Huntley would have his say.

'You will not speak to her, my lord?' said Mrs. Dorothy, gravely; 'you would find her quite unprepared. God knows,' she added, fervently, 'God knows, Lord Huntley, how gladly I would give my child, my darling, my only one, into your keeping.

I am very old, and very weak. My days, I feel, are numbered. Could I see my Charity safe in the care of such a man as you are, I should go down to my grave in peace. I should feel as if the life you had saved once, were perhaps rescued from worse destruction than even those cold waters would have brought to her. But I would not have you speak to her as you have spoken to me, for I do not think the child's mind is prepared for it. Later, perhaps; but not now. You will not speak to her yet?'

But Lord Huntley would not promise. His mind was made up; and if Lord Huntley had a fault, it was, perhaps, obstinacy, a too inflexible will where once he had arranged his plans, and thought he saw his way clearly. May it not be so with all such characters? Every disposition, it has been well said, has the 'faults of its good qualities;' and are not the high-minded and conscientious, the brave in action and unshrinking in right-doing, also at times the unbending and unchangeable, sometimes to their own cost as well as to that of those around them? Be that as it may, it proved so with Lord Huntley. Mrs. Dorothy had advised, but he would not listen.

Before many days had passed he had spoken to Charity, and received her answer. She had gone for her first walk, and had met Lord Huntley. How many a walk he had taken up and down that street in expectation of this event it does not behove us to inquire. Mrs. Saville was with Charity; but Lord Huntley had made a third in the walk, and he had offered to see Charity home from the Rectory, and Mrs. Saville had left them to return together. When Charity came in, even old Betsy saw that there was something more the matter with her than the fatigue of the walk, and ere Charity had been many minutes in the parlour, all that had happened in that last quarter of an hour had been sobbed into her godmother's lap; sobbed forth as freely and as fully as ever had been the story of her early grievances, of her misdemeanours, or her repentance.

The old lady soothed and petted her; she rang the bell, and made the wondering, troubled Betsy, take her young lady's walking-things off, and lay her on the sofa, and bring her some tea. But no rest could Charity get that evening. She would not stay upon the sofa; she was happy nowhere but at her aunt's feet; and there, at length, she sat quietly, whilst Mrs. Dorothy talked to her of all the happiness that might be hers if she could learn to love such a man as Lord Huntley. At the words 'learn to love' Charity started up, the old fire of childhood in her eyes.

'It is just that, Aunt Dorothy,' she said; 'I should have to learn to love him. and that is a lesson I can never learn. Oh, Aunt Dorothy! that was just what made me say I could not marry him. I know he is a good man, and would make me a good husband, and I know he would be kind to you, and that it would be delightful for you to have a lovely home for you to live in, and to be able to do just as much for my poor people as ever I should like. I felt all that while he was talking. But, oh, Aunt Dorothy, it would be dreadful to be married and not to like to be always with one's husband—to feel that there was some one else one would rather be with than be with him.'

'And you think you should feel that with Lord Huntley, Charity?'

'Yes, Aunt Dorothy, I know I should; for, even now, I like so much better to be with Edward.'

'Edward is like a brother to you, Charity,' said Mrs. Dorothy, with an inward prayer that he might never be like anything else.

'Yes, Aunt Dorothy, just like a dear brother. But he is not my brother; and if I were married I don't suppose Lord Huntley would think he were: nor, indeed, should I wish him to be.'

'No, my child; no, of course not,' said Aunt Dorothy, sadly.

And no more was said that night. Betsy came to insist upon her mistress going to bed. Mrs. Dorothy insisted upon Charity's going too. And each, to please the other, went; though, as neither of them closed their eyes, it might have been better if each had followed their own inclinations and remained where they were: for then, at all events, some of those weary hours would have been relieved by converse and by sympathy.

CHAPTER XVII.

A GREAT change had that visit of Lord Huntley's, and his subsequent conversation with Charity, made at Ivy Cottage, and amongst its inhabitants. A gloom seemed to have fallen upon every one. Old Betsy had had her own misgivings as soon as she perceived that Lord Huntley's daily visits ceased, and she gave herself and her mistress no rest until, by persevering, yet respectful importunity—for it was remarkable to see how, in the dignity of Mrs. Dorothy's character, and the right-mindedness which marked Betsy's, familiarity never even approached contempt—she had obtained the information she desired, or rather, we should say, dreaded, and discovered that Lord Huntley and Miss Charity were never likely to be what it was her dearest wish on earth to see them.

It was not to be expected that Betsy should receive this news without some signs of the real sorrow she felt.

The only castle in the air she had ever been known

to build had come down with a crash, and Betsy's face bore marks of the trouble of mind its ruins occasioned her.

Charity's bright face, too, had grown very thoughtful; the large blue eyes were clear and truthful as ever, but there was a deeper look in them than Mrs. Dorothy had ever remarked before that melancholy evening when she and her godchild had talked so long together. Some of the happy, thoughtless mirth of Charity's childhood, had certainly been washed away with the tears that she had shed that night over Lord Huntley's disappointment. It was so painful to grieve others—so much worse than being grieved one's self. Charity's troubles at school had never caused her half so much sorrow, had never made her heart ache half so truly, as did the remembrance of that short walk with Lord Huntley that cold afternoon, and the recollection of the words that he had said to her, and the words that she had said to him, and the miserable parting they had had together. It was not alone weakness from her recent illness that made Charity's step heavier upon the stair as she came up, and Charity's face many shades less bright when she came in, and Charity's voice less merry when she spoke.

Aunt Dorothy knew and felt this, and her own face and voice assumed a graver look and tone, and she leant more heavily upon her gold-headed stick, and her weakness became more evident every day. Whilst day by day another fear pressed more and more painfully on Aunt Dorothy's heart, as day by day she marked other signs—signs which she knew too well, and from the very first indication of which she shrank and quivered as though a finger had been laid upon some old wound within, which made it open and bleed afresh.

Nor were these signs lost on Betsy; she marked them too, and recognised them well, though nearly half a century had passed since last she had noted them. It was not without drawing her own conclusions that Betsy noted, that whilst the lovely hothouse flowers Lord Huntley had brought day by day had been left for her to tend so long as they lived, and when they withered for her to throw away, the one winter-rose that Edward Saville brought was kept in Charity's own little room whilst it lived, and Betsy never saw it afterwards, till one day she found Charity reading her Bible, and saw amongst the leaves a dried flower, which she felt rather than knew was the same. Betsy longed to take it out and put it in the kitchen fire. It would have given her the truest pleasure to watch it crackling and consuming there.

But she said nothing to Mrs. Dorothy, for she was not sure as yet whether her mistress perceived anything amiss, and she was ill enough already,—what was the use of troubling her too soon? Besides, what could be done? 'If Miss Charity had been silly enough to refuse such a man as my Lord Huntley . . . well, there was no doubt she'd be silly enough to accept such a man as Mr. Edward Saville. When young folks were bent on self-destruction, it was pretty much the same with them as with the moths—they'd never let be till they 'd burnt themselves up alive: she 'd seen that once before, and now, no doubt, she must make up her mind to see it again. And what if it did break her heart outright, and her mistress's, too? Well, they were soon going to where the broken hearts would be healed. It was a selfish sort of comfort to take, perhaps, but still it was a comfort to feel that she wouldn't, most likely, live herself, and certainly her poor mistress wouldn't live to see Miss Charity's dear heart broken, as it certainly would be broken, and no manner of doubt about it, if she let Mr. Edward once get it into his hands. She 'd do her best to keep off that trouble; she 'd pray as hard as ever mortal prayed: but, somehow, she hadn't much hope of her prayers being heard, for, really, it almost seemed as if what the poor people said was true, and there was a fate over some things. It always made Mrs. Dorothy mightily angry when any one said so, but, for her part, she couldn't shut her eyes to the fact that some particular kinds of misfortune did seem like to run in families. There was her own family, in which for three generations not one son had died in his bed, but must needs be killed by some accident. Hadn't her grandfather been crushed by a tree he was helping to cut down for the Squire in the Briersley Park? was not her father killed by a fall from the house he was helping to build? was not her only brother crushed by a load of gravel rolling down the bank above him and smothering him alive at his work, with the pick-axe in his hand?* If she had

* A fact.

ever married—which, thank God, she'd never been tempted to do—and had had a son of her own, she'd have expected to see him brought home killed from his work every day of her life; because, somehow, it appeared to be the fate of the family. There seemed as if in some families there was a sort of evil genius, which kept its place amongst them from generation to generation, and was not to be driven out anyhow. And that was why she could not keep herself from despairing about what the end of it would be when she saw Mr. Edward coming and going, and Miss Charity looking for him and after him, with the very inside of her dear heart in her blue eyes—just, for the life of her, as Miss Dora had done in days gone by. Oh dear! oh dear! it was a weary world, to be sure, and the sooner folks were rid of it the better for them.'

It was thus that Betsy communed to herself in the kitchen, while in the bedroom above, where Mrs. Dorothy had remained all day—for it had been a bad day with her, and she had not left her room—the old lady lay back on her pillows, whilst Charity told her all—every word—that Edward Saville had said to her that day, and all—every word—that she had said to him in return.

There was a pause, broken only by some sobs, which found their way from poor little Charity's over-laden heart, and then the old lady said,—

'One hour, Charity, my child! my dear, dear child! leave me for one hour and then come to me again, and you shall hear a tale from my lips.'

'A tale, Aunt Dorothy!' exclaimed Charity; 'a story! Of what?'

'Of my life, Charity. Come to me in an hour, and you shall hear all that your godmother *can* say on this subject.'

One hour later, when the last rays of daylight were dying out one by one, and leaving the quiet bedroom in a strange dimness, Charity took her seat by the old lady's bedside, and listened to the words that came from the pale lips—came soft and low, for there was but little strength left in Mrs. Dorothy's voice; yet quite composedly and collectedly, for when once a heart that has suffered deeply resolves to tell the story of its suffering, the effort by which it does so is not perceived by others. The reluctance has been struggled with and overcome out of sight, and beforehand.

Charity was evidently agitated, her little hands shook, and the roses that to Betsy's and every one else's delight returning health had begun to paint anew in delicate colours upon her soft cheeks, had vanished for the day. But Mrs. Dorothy was no paler than usual, and her voice scarcely could be said to have an additional tremor in it, as she said quietly, taking within her own the trembling little hand that Charity laid upon the coverlid:—

'You must not expect me to tell you the story of my poor life in many words, Charity, my child; for, indeed, I have little power to do so: nor can I see much of it myself, standing as I now do at this distance from it, save the chief events or periods that stand out from all the rest in strong relief.

'My childhood I remember well—indeed that is the time which, as a whole, I remember best; and it was the happiest childhood that ever mortal was blessed with. I cannot remember even one passing shadow ever crossing the clear sky of that bright period, nor do I believe there was one. My father and mother were very wealthy, and I was their only child. They were devoted one to the other, and both to me, and though I had no companions of my own age I never had a wish for any, or had a lonely moment. My mother—you know her picture well, Charity, and it is the image of her—was a grave, earnest-minded woman, with far-reaching thoughts, and she was my instructress, and made learning such a pleasant thing to me that I never knew what it was to mourn over a lesson. On the contrary, I always looked forward to the hour when I should carry my books to the pretty dressing-room which adjoined my mother's bedroom, for I knew it would be a time of delightful interest to me; and often, when the lessons were over, I would beg to remain longer, whilst my mother told me some interesting story connected with the many objects of interest in that room; for it was filled with curiosities and relics from other countries, all sent or brought home to her by my father. He was a naval officer, as you know, Charity, and they had been engaged seven years, nearly all of which time he had been on active service, and my mother waiting and watching anxiously at home; so that it is not surprising that they should have loved and valued each other as dearly as they did, or clung thus fondly to me, their only child. My mother would tell me long stories of those years of separation, and I loved to listen to her, and loved her dearly, tenderly.

'And yet I think I loved my father yet more—my noble, brave, lovely, tender-hearted father! Never did I hear one harsh word from his lips. No one who knew him had ever seen a frown on his brow, or heard him raise his voice, which was so peculiar in its deep, manly, earnest tones. And yet it seemed only necessary that he should speak to be instantly obeyed. It was so in our large household, and on the estate. He saw to everything himself, and I used to ride with him on my pony, and glory, child as I was, in the love and respect which I saw he everywhere excited. And our faithful old man-servant, who had accompanied him through all his services, would tell me that it had been just the same thing on board ship. He never raised his voice, but his word was law; he had no need to punish, yet there was no one who kept those under him in better discipline.

'But I will not talk of him now, Charity, though I could talk for hours of all he was in himself, and of all he was to me. My mother had an anxious, thoughtful mind. My father was all practical life and sunshine; and I remember well how, when I was still a child, I used to think it the prettiest thing in the world to see him forcing my mother into cheerfulness. Every anxious thought of hers, that showed itself like a small cloud in the domestic sky, the sunshine of his character seemed to meet and disperse. So that all was bright, all joyful. Life was one long holiday. My mother was my teacher, my counsellor; my father was my companion and play-fellow. I carried all my joys to him; I forced him to share in all my occupations, and he seemed to enjoy them to the full as much as I did. His great idea was love: no one was ever to be unkind, no one was ever to speak harshly of a fellow-creature, no one was ever to bear malice.

'Our old servant, Allen, used to tell a story of him which was characteristic. There had been some great quarrel between two officers in the station where they were, and my father happened to pass one of these officers one day, as he was standing in a group of friends, detailing the injuries he had received, and inveighing against his enemy. Just as my father and Allen passed, the officer exclaimed, in a tone of revenge, 'I will never forgive him!—no, never!' He was almost a stranger to my father, who had only just joined the station, but words like these seemed to enter his heart, and going up to the officer he laid his hand upon his arm, implored him not to allow such a fearful resolve to remain registered above; nor would he leave him until he had persuaded him to retract it.

'I used to think we never could have lived without my father—certainly that my mother could not, for his bright, buoyant character, seemed the cork jacket which surrounded her more desponding nature, and kept it always up. And yet I have sometimes thought, that had some kind of sorrow come—had he seen me in trouble or disgrace—that my father could have borne it perhaps even less bravely than my mother did. It was the every-day cares of life that had no power to annoy him. Had a great grief come, I can believe that it might have washed away the elasticity of his character, and that he would have been crushed altogether. And I am thankful that he did not live to see the clouds gather over his darling's life.

'I told you that we were rich, Charity; but on my father's death the greater part of his fortune was to go to his nephew, who was in the army, and was abroad with his regiment. I had never seen this only cousin; and I well remember the day when my father received a letter from him, saying that he had sold out of the army, and would be on his homeward way before this news reached us. He would come, he said, to us at once; for he had no other friends left, and he looked upon Briersley as his home. I remember my mother looked more grave than I had ever seen her before, and that as she put forth one objection after another to my cousin's coming to us, I was surprised to see that my father did not, as was his usual habit, combat her objections with his ready hospitality: but, instead of reflecting the sunshine of his feelings upon her, appeared to catch the gloom of hers. I had been feeling delighted at the idea of having a guest at Briersley, especially one bearing our own name, and I asked my mother why she did not seem to wish that my cousin should come. She would have hesitated about answering, but my father, who never kept anything from me that it was in his power to communicate, and who used often to say that "the less mystery, the better policy," replied to my question at once, saying that this cousin of mine, Roland Helstone, had been but a wild young fellow in his youth; that he had been left an orphan when quite a child, and brought up by his mother's relations, who had indulged him in every whim, until he had grown to be insufferably conceited, over-bearing, and extravagant; and that finally he had insisted on going into the army, and had exchanged into a regiment in America that he might have a share in the fighting that was going on there. I recollect saying that I supposed then he was brave, if he had no other good quality, and that my mother replied, "she did not call it bravery, for she believed his desire of fighting arose not from any wish to serve his king or country, and leave a glorious name behind him, but merely from an innate brute force of character, which made resistance a pleasure to him; for, though he had plenty of courage, she had never known him kind to anything or anybody, even to one of the animals on the place, and that a really brave man was always tender." And I recollect that my father reproved her in his gentle way, and said, "It was not right to think worse of the young fellow than perhaps he deserved, and certainly his name had been honourably mentioned in the account of almost every engagement that had taken place, though private news might not have been so satisfactory."

'After that time there were frequent conversations about my cousin Roland, and whether or not it would be advisable to receive him at Briersley; my mother being always very decided in her opinions and expressions that he ought not to be allowed to come to us, and my father never seeming to get beyond the conclusion that, "after all, he was the son of his dead brother; and though the young man had, no doubt, been very wild, and extravagant, and somewhat wanting in respect and submission, his campaign might have done great things for him, and *à tout pécheur miséricorde.*" This saying being one of my father's favourites, he used often to quote it; adding, that it was the best thing he knew connected with France or the French. Thus matters went on, and the question of my cousin's coming to us or not was still much on all our minds, and as undecided as ever, when he settled it himself by appearing one day in our quiet breakfast-parlour, just as we had finished breakfast, and were preparing to read the morning psalms, according to our usual custom.'

Mrs. Dorothy paused; and Charity, interested as she had now become, entreated her to tell her no more. But Mrs. Dorothy assured her that she only ceased speaking because her voice was weary, not from any inability to speak of what was to follow; and refused Charity's next request also, which was that she should say no more then, but tell her the rest another day.

'No, Charity, no,' she said; 'you shall hear all. I will tell you all, and all at a time. It does not hurt me to do so, and my child need not distress herself. As I speak of things now to you this evening, it does not seem to me as though I spoke of myself, but of some one else whose story it was my duty to tell to you to-night, since it may be the means of keeping you back from the same precipice. You shall hear all, Charity—at least, all that it is necessary to tell.

'Roland Helstone, as I say, appeared that morning quite unexpectedly in our pleasant breakfast-parlour, and that day is vivid in my memory still. I fancy I see us all now, just as we were then: my mother sitting at the top of the table with the breakfast things before her, and her Prayer-book in her hand; my father at her right hand, adjusting his spectacles, whilst I was leaning over him to find his place—the seventeenth morning of the month—the 17th of June. And a lovely June morning it was, too, with the window open, the birds singing gaily in the trees without, though the logs of wood were crackling brightly also in the grate within. There was no sound of wheels or bell to announce, as usual, the approach of a visitor long before the arrival, and give us time to prepare for the reception. There was just the sound of a hurried, heavy step, outside, which I had scarcely time to think could not be Allen's, when the door opened quickly, and a young man came in;

tall, very, very handsome—oh, how handsome he looked then!—and with a military air of command about him such as I never saw before, or since.

'My mother did not know him in the least, and looked bewildered, and half frightened. But my father had no sooner seen him than he rose hastily from his seat, whilst the spectacles he had just put on fell upon the ground, as he held out his hand, exclaiming, "Roland Helstone! my brother's son, and the very image of his dead father! It is well you wrote, my boy; for had you come upon me in this way without my knowing you were in England, I should have thought . . . yes, I 'm not superstitious, but I believe I should have thought it was a vision of your father, as he was thirty years ago this very month, when he and I parted on St. Katharine's Dock. I stood on board my ship and watched him standing on the quay to see the last of me; and he looked—yes, in every limb and feature he looked just as you look now. It was my last sight of him on earth—at least, I thought so till now; but I see him again now. By Heaven, I do!" It was but seldom my father used even such expressions as these; he had been accustomed to them on board ship, but he had learnt to think them wrong, and would always check himself, and Allen too, in the use of them. But now he repeated the words, "By Heaven, it *is* Roland!" And as he shook my cousin's hand and held it between both his own, I saw my father moved in a way I had never seen before. The tears forced their way into his eyes and coursed each other swiftly down his sun-burnt cheeks. My cousin laughed gaily. "Of course it is Roland," he said; "and much obliged I am to you, uncle, for your hearty welcome. I hope," he added, turning to my mother, "I hope my good aunt is equally glad to see me?"

'His turning to my mother made me do so also, and oh, I shall never, no, never forget the look on her face that day. She was as pale as death, lips and all; and I, who had never seen my mother overcome before, saw that she trembled from head to foot. She was ever the most courteous of English gentlewomen; my father used, laughingly, to tell her sometimes that her extreme politeness bordered on formality: but that day all power of even feigning a welcome seemed taken from her. She took my cousin's extended hand, but I am sure that her own must have been as cold and as like death as the hue upon her cheek; and I do not think she *could* have returned the shake, had she striven to do so. "Yes," she said, apparently quite involuntarily, "yes, it *is* Roland again." I can remember now the sound of those words. Looking back upon them, I have often felt as if my mother, when she uttered them, must have felt upon her the shadow of what was to come. I stood a quiet spectator of the strange and sudden scene. But I guessed then what I afterwards learned was the truth. No one had ever told me anything about my uncle Roland; I had scarcely ever heard more of him than his name: but I felt that day that there must have been two sides to the picture which the remembrance of my uncle presented to the mind—an earlier one, probably, of youth, and beauty, and innocence, and perhaps a later one of sin and misery; and that, whilst my father's eyes were riveted upon the former, the latter stood as vividly before my mother's. And as with the father, so with the son. The image before my father was one of beauty and vigour. His eyes rested upon it with a feeling of satisfaction. My mother, on the contrary, looked not at what she saw, but she felt instinctively that there was a reverse to that picture, and she trembled.

'Charity, I cannot tell you much of the months that followed. Indeed, I scarcely remember much that happened during that summer: I only know that it was, or rather seemed to be, the happiest of any I had ever known; it was unlike any that had gone before, and oh, most unlike any that have come after. The only drawback to the delight of those days was the dark cloud that rested on my mother's brow, the desponding tone that had stolen into her voice, and which not even my father's brightness—for he was bright—could dispel. Charming as my father always was in my eyes, I had never seen him in as bright a light as I saw him that summer. Roland's knowledge of the world, his acquaintance with countries in which he had himself spent many years, his military experience, the engagements he had seen, all these things were a delight to my father, and cheerful as our home had always been, it had never been as cheerful as it was that summer.

'As I say, Charity, the depressed state of my dear

mother's spirits was the only passing shadow across that sunny path. Once I spoke to my father on the subject, but he only said, "Dorothy, my darling, there are few women like your mother; indeed, I have never seen such a woman, and I doubt if there is another such to be found anywhere: but so long as there's a bit of mortality about flesh and blood, I suppose it must stop short of perfection, and I believe just the one thing that keeps your mother back from being fairly perfect is, that where she takes a prejudice she can't get over it. It's always been the way with her, God bless her! And perhaps I ought to be glad of it; for I suppose, if it weren't for this one small portion of human infirmity, she would be altogether unfit for this lower world. It's the only fault I've ever seen in your mother, Dorothy; so let us be thankful for anything that helps to keep her amongst us. She has taken a prejudice against your cousin Roland. It will be difficult to overcome it; for where your mother feels, she feels very strongly. But we must do our best to convince her that she is mistaken."

'This was an easy command for me to follow, but all my powers of persuasion seemed to fail, and my mother's gravity remained unmoved by all our mirth and merry-making. At length, just as the bright tints of summer were changing into autumn's hues, my mother fell ill of a fever, and a great change came over us all. It was not, the doctor said, a dangerous illness—he never thought it very serious; but it was a long, wearying illness, week after week passing whilst we watched the different crises of the malady. For a long time she was quite deaf, and light troubled her greatly. The room was kept darkened, and my father and I took the nursing by turns; Roland being the companion and the comfort of the one whose turn it was to seek relaxation and refreshment without, while the other watched within. We used to ride out on alternate days, my dear father and I, for neither of us would have consented to leave the house unless the other had remained in it.

'Roland rode with my father one day, and, of course, the next he rode with me, it being my father's turn to stay at home. And thus I learned to depend on him more and more. He told me stories such as I had never heard or read before, for my life had been given more to out-door amusements than to much acquaintance with books, and I had read few, if any, more exciting than the volumes of history, travel, or science, which were to be found on my dear good mother's carefully-arranged bookshelves. Of novels or romances I knew nothing, and almost as little of poetry. But Roland's stories were all romance and poetry to me. I listened to them by the hour. They fired my imagination, warmed my blood, excited every pulse of thought or feeling. My father would often come out to meet me as we returned from our ride, and as he helped me to alight he would tap me on the cheek and say,—" No need to fear lest the long nursing should hurt me while I could boast such a bloom as that, and that he thought the rides with

Roland did me more good than those with him: we young folks could gallop faster, and he was growing an old man." Ah! that dear father did not guess how much more the heightened colour in my cheek told of mental than of physical excitement.

'At length the time came when I lived for Roland, thought of him, dreamed of him; when even my dear father, my early, kind, loving companion, and my mother, my good, devoted mother on her sick-bed, were figures in the background—quite in the background, and at that time but dim and indistinct. Whilst the one figure of Roland Helstone occupied all the foreground—all, all!'

Mrs. Dorothy paused, and Charity, who had been listening—listening so intently that she did not lose a single word—burst into tears.

'Oh, Aunt Dorothy,' she said, 'you loved him! you loved him as I love Edward!'

'Yes, Charity,' said Aunt Dorothy, emphatically; 'I loved Roland as you love Edward. People call it love; I called it so myself.'

'It is love!' said Charity. And as Mrs. Dorothy made no reply, she turned the affirmation into an interrogative form,—'Oh, Aunt Dorothy, is it not love?'

'I should not call it so now, Charity, for love is of God. And the love which God gives, inspires, allows, brings no sin—no misery. But it was a strong, devoted, powerful, passionate, idolatrous attachment.'

'And it ended?' exclaimed Charity.

An evident tremor passed through Mrs. Dorothy's frame, but she had begun to answer Charity's eager, almost imperative question. 'It ended, Charity, as such attachments do often, do generally end—as it is in their nature that they should end.'

But at that moment there was a knock at the door, and before time had been given for it to be answered, the door was opened, and Betsy appeared.

'Mrs. Dorothy, ma'am—Miss Charity, my dear, this really must not be! My mistress will kill herself if she talks any more. You've been in here more than an hour, my dear—more than an hour by the clock in the kitchen, which I've been watching till my eyes ache, and my heart too, knowing how my mistress will be to-morrow if she exerts herself like this to-day. I've been up to the door a dozen times at least, and would have come in long ago, only my mistress said she was not to be disturbed on any account. But there! I could not for the life of me have kept away any longer. Miss Charity, my dear, you'll say good-night, and come away with me now, there's a dear young lady. And I'll get my mistress comfortable for the night, though I don't believe she'll sleep one blessed wink after exciting herself to talk like this. Just look at the bright spot in her cheek! That comes from weakness, and my mistress is fairly done up. Now go, my dear; say good-night, and go.'

Neither Mrs. Dorothy nor Charity offered any resistance to Betsy's authority. Mrs. Dorothy, indeed, was fairly exhausted, though she would probably have wound herself up to the effort, and concluded the story she desired to tell, had it not been thus interrupted. And Charity, though deeply, intensely interested, felt it a relief to have a conversation concluded which she saw was straining every nerve her godmother possessed. She leant over the bed to kiss the old lady, lovingly, tenderly; and as she did so Mrs. Dorothy whispered,—'You shall hear the rest to-morrow. Meanwhile, you will not see Edward?'

'Aunt Dorothy!' exclaimed Charity, 'have I not promised?'

CHAPTER XVIII.

'IT kills you to talk as you did last night,' said Charity, as Mrs. Dorothy called her to her bedside, and bade her resume the seat where she had spent such an interesting hour on the previous evening. 'I am sure it kills you, Aunt Dorothy; you look so pale and ill to-day.'

'And I am ill, Charity; but I have more to say: and I must speak, and you must listen. If your life is to be blighted, if your happiness in this world is to be shattered beyond all power of recovery, and your very soul's salvation perilled, at least it shall not be for want of warning from one who knows—yes, Charity, who knows all that is involved in a fall from that precipice on the very brink of which you are now treading—yes, treading with your eyes fixed on the flowers beneath your feet, whilst you cannot or will not raise them to look at the danger, the misery, that lies but one step in front of you. Charity, you said truly yesterday, that as you now love Edward Saville so I once loved Roland Helstone,

—obstinately, blindly, passionately, with a devotion that sprang from youthful ardour, from excited feeling, from the admiration kindled within me by the charms of his personal attractions, and the powerful fascination of his mind, manner, and talents, but wanting—utterly wanting in that reverent respect and that well-founded faith and trust which, unless a woman feels, and knows she can feel for a man, she is worse than mad to marry him. But, as you say, I loved Roland as you love Edward; and as you would marry Edward, so I would, and did, marry Roland.'

'And your parents, Aunt Dorothy?' said Charity; 'your mother,—what did she say?'

'Ah, Charity! had my mother been amongst us then, I believe things might have been checked before they had reached a point which placed them beyond the power of check from any human hand. But my mother lay many weeks in her sick-room, and when she recovered, when she was well enough to listen to news, the first thing we had to tell her was that I was the promised wife of Roland Helstone; that my father had given his consent—a willing one, even, for my cousin had wound himself around my trusting father's warm, loving, unsuspicious heart. We were engaged, my mother was told, and only waiting her perfect recovery to be married. To this hour, Charity, I remember my mother's face, and the expression of hopeless misery that fell upon it. But she attempted no remonstrance—not a word. It would have been useless to have made any, and my mother, seeing this, was not one to waste her words or efforts.

'The first time she entered the church, from which she had been absent for several months, was to be present at my marriage. She was so pale, so motionless, so intensely grave, that I remember the resolution with which I forced myself, as it were, to believe that her looks arose from her illness, not from anxiety on my account. And I felt glad that the people around should think so also. The simple villagers who crowded to the church to see the Squire's young lady married, knew how near death the Squire's wife had been; and I was glad to think they did, for otherwise what conclusion would they have drawn from that pale face, trembling step, and smileless countenance? It was a lovely day, late in autumn, when the retreating summer, which had for some weeks been out of sight, seemed to turn back to give us one of those last looks before disappearing, which come so pleasantly upon us just because we know they are the last. The birds sang gaily in welcome of such a day, the flowers shone brightly, and the clearness of the blue sky added to the gay tone of our pretty village bells as they rang forth their merry peals. To all these pleasant sounds I gave diligent heed, Charity, with that singular power which we possess over our own hearts, when our will is resolutely bent in one direction, whilst I just as firmly turned away from the word of warning which even then was whispering within, would I but have bent my ear to listen.'

'But, Aunt Dorothy,' interrupted Charity, 'I do not see that you were so wrong. Your father had given his consent. He liked your cousin and your marriage, and there was no real ground for your mother's prejudices.'

'Charity,' replied Mrs. Dorothy, 'it was not my father's consent that ought to have satisfied me, neither was it my mother's prejudices that should have withheld me. Within my own heart there was a knowledge, a knowledge which God Himself had given me, and from which I could not turn without turning also from Him who gave it, and that knowledge should have kept me back from ever thinking of Roland Helstone as my husband.'

'But, dear Aunt Dorothy,' again urged Charity, 'I thought you told me that you were not religious when you were young. I thought you said once that it was trouble and sorrow that brought you to God.'

'And I said truly, Charity, my child,' replied Mrs. Dorothy. 'I never sought the bread and water of life until I had tasted to the full of the wormwood and the gall. No, Charity, there was no real religion within me at that time. But there was a knowledge of right and wrong; there was a light shining, though it was in a dark place, and scarcely sufficed to show me men even as trees walking. Still, the light was there. I can scarcely imagine any child brought up by my dear, thoughtful, earnest-minded mother, having grown to womanhood without it.'

'Then your mother was pious, Aunt Dorothy?'

'Truly so, Charity, according to the light she then possessed. For we had no Mr. Saville in our village, Charity; perhaps there were not then twenty villages in England that had. The clergy in our day and in our neighbourhood thought it no harm to follow the hounds, to sit late over their wine, to join in all the somewhat coarse merriment of their neighbours. My mother had very few religious advantages, Charity; but had she possessed them, hers was a heart richly to have benefited by them. The pure explanations of Gospel truth, which are so abundant now, that, alas! the very richness of the provision tempts our hard hearts to value it the less, would have been eagerly, gratefully enjoyed by her, had such a blessing been placed within her reach. But she had all she really needed in the Bible she loved so well, and she had faithfully instructed me in that holy word. She had taught me, Charity, that life should be a preparation for death; that our existence in this world must come to an end; that our souls would live for ever in eternity; and that, whether they lived in happiness or misery must depend upon the state in which they were found at death.

'All this I knew and believed. And I knew too that Roland, if he knew it, did not believe it. I remember feeling shocked, on the first Sunday that he spent with us, by his reading the newspaper in the afternoon when my mother and father were taking their after-dinner nap, and we were left alone; and every Sunday he did the same. Before my mother he never did so, for he looked upon her, with reason, as a very devout woman, and he respected her feelings. But he never seemed to consider that I cared at all for religion. What reason, indeed, had he for supposing so? He never put on the semblance of anything like regard for religion when we were alone; and though these ways distressed me at first, I never told him so, and at length I grew accustomed to them. Before our marriage he always accompanied me to church.'

'And afterwards, Aunt Dorothy?' asked Charity; and her voice had a tone of anxious interest, which told of something even stronger within than sympathy in the sad story of her aunt's suffering life.

'Afterwards, Charity? Ah! it is just of that "afterwards" that even now I can scarcely speak. And yet it is just of that "afterwards" that I *must* speak, if I would warn you, my child. For as surely as it came to me, so will it come to you. Charity, you think now, that if you marry Edward Saville he will be a different man when he is your husband from what he is now. You say to yourself that he is wild, thoughtless, irreligious now—careless of his interests for this world even, and utterly indifferent to anything and everything that may, and you know does, lie beyond this passing life. But you think that he loves you; that his affection for you, and yours for him, will work wonders; that his parents' prayers and my prayers—perhaps even your prayers, Charity—will all be heard; and that, when once Edward Saville is your husband, he will be an altered character—a changed man, and you will be happy. He tells you so, your own heart tells you so—that poor, little, wilful, ignorant, blinded heart, which is so ready to work its own ruin; and you, Charity, you believe that it will be so?'

Charity's head was laid upon the old lady's pillow, and the sobs were coming fast from her agitated heart; but amidst them all she found breath to answer,—

'Yes, I do believe it; I do think it will be so.'

'Then, Charity,' replied Mrs. Dorothy, and her words were so unlike in their whole tone and tenor to the usual calm diffidence with which she was wont to speak, that they entered deeply into the inmost recesses of her godchild's soul, and fell there like a prophetic warning from another world, 'then, Charity, it will not—no, it will not be so: do not hope it, or expect it, for it will not be.'

'Aunt Dorothy!' exclaimed Charity, starting up, with more of the pride and fire of her childhood in her eyes and voice than Mrs. Dorothy had seen since her return from school, 'how can you say so? *You* do not know! Have you not taught me yourself that God can do anything?'

The excitement of Charity's manner inspired the old lady with perfect composure, though five minutes before she had been on the point of pausing in her story, from want of physical power to proceed with it. She held out her hands for the hand which Charity, in her agitation, had withdrawn from them, and taking it gently again, she stroked it caressingly, and said,—'Listen to me, my child; listen as you may perhaps wish to have done when I am, as very soon I must surely be, lying by your poor mother's side in the churchyard, and there is no longer power to warn or to hearken. Charity, you say truly, God is a sovereign. He is a great and an Almighty King. He does according to His will in the army of heaven, and among the inhabitants of the earth. None can control Him. None can counsel Him. None can stay His hand, or say unto Him, "What doest Thou?" All this I have learned, Charity; and learned not only in the teaching of His word, but in the far deeper teaching of His dealings. But, Charity, I have learned too, that just because God is a sovereign, and a great sovereign, therefore must He maintain the greatness of His own character and His own laws; and if those laws of His—those warnings and those threatenings, are slighted and broken, is it not the very sovereignty of God to which you, in your ignorance, would look for mercy, which is engaged in your punishment? Charity, my child, it is so, and I have found it so.'

Charity was silent, and Mrs. Dorothy continued. 'I remember, Charity, a remark Mr. Saville made to me only a few days since, which has fastened itself on my mind, no doubt because as it entered it found an anchor there in the deep experience of my own life. "Moses," he said, "could not pray himself into the land of Canaan, after once his own conduct had caused God to declare that he should not enter it. And why could he not? *Because God's governmental holiness had to be maintained.*" My child, it is worse than folly, it is sin, to run into danger and temptation with the delusive hope that God's sovereignty will be engaged in rescuing us. It may be shown so. There are no limits to control God's grace. But, so far as we can judge of His words and works, His sovereignty is engaged on the other side. I speak as, perhaps, only those can speak who have *felt* it so.'

'You were miserable, Aunt Dorothy!' exclaimed Charity. Then hastily checking herself, she added, —'Forgive me, dear Aunt Dorothy! I did not mean to ask you. I do not want you to tell me anything that it must make you wretched to talk about. But I am so unhappy myself, I scarcely knew what I was asking.'

'But I mean to tell you, Charity,' said Mrs. Dorothy. 'It was just that I might tell you of this "afterwards" that followed me, and which, I believe, will just as surely follow you, that I called you here to-night. I cannot tell you in detail, my child; that, indeed, would kill me, as you say. Indeed, through God's mercy, the details are all buried with the "dead past," and were I to attempt to dig them up they would but distress you, and could do no good. Once they used to trouble me in thoughts and dreams; but not now—not for a long time. God Himself has buried them deep down in answer to my earnest prayer, and of late years He has granted richly my request that I might forget all which it was good not to remember, and remember all which it was good not to forget. Thus, scenes—such sad scenes of sharpest suffering and sorrow as I would fain spare you from, have long passed from sight. But this, Charity, remains; that such a sinful marriage as mine was brings misery: not, indeed, always such misery as it brought to me, but misery.'

Again Charity's face was raised, and Mrs. Dorothy remarked its expression, and knew the thought that prompted it.

'Not always, Charity,' she repeated, 'such misery as it brought to me; for different characters need different chastisement, and the wise Parent above never errs in laying upon each the exact amount which each requires—always, we know, the very least which will suffice to effect the desired end, for He doth not afflict willingly. But mine was a nature that required severe reproof, for it would have passed by slighter. And, Charity, so is yours. The thought of all my lengthened suffering makes me shudder, as I think that just such a life as I led for years might be in store for you, even though the one last crushing blow should be spared. And even though the blow that laid me low would never fall on you, doubtless there are many others quite as crushing in their effects. Listen, Charity, and I will tell you what has never yet passed my lips, and which, once told to you this night, will never again be heard by mortal ear.

'After my marriage we went to America. It was a very unexpected trial to me and to my parents, for though my cousin had often spoken to us of some little property he possessed in that country, he had never said a word about the necessity of his returning to see after it, and we could not understand why such a necessity should exist after we were married: for my father was wealthy, and was willing to give us any money needful to settle whatever difficulties the possession of this property or the parting with it might involve. But my cousin was firm in declaring that he must go himself, and that it was my duty to go with him; and between my love for him and my unwillingness to part with him, and my desire to travel and see for myself some of the sights which he had so often described to me, he had no difficulty in bringing my inclinations to agree with his wishes. My father's opposition, though very strong at first, was soon overcome. He had been such a traveller himself, that he thought less of distance or of danger than most people did in those days. At first he could not bear the idea of parting with me; but when once the matter was decided, his buoyant, cheerful mind, led him to make the best of it, and he was constantly assuring my mother that after all, since I would no longer be with them, they would scarcely feel the separation more if the winter were passed in America, than they would have done had we yielded to his wish and spent it in Ireland, looking after some property there which belonged to my father, but which, like Briersley, would hereafter be my cousin's. Moreover, he told my mother it would be an advantage to me to travel, and would supply a deficiency which there had doubtless been in my education, from their never having been able to part with me.

'But nothing my father could say had any power to remove my mother's feeling on the subject. She opposed our going to the very last. My father accompanied us to London, and saw us embark; but my mother could not be persuaded to do so, and when I gave her my last kiss, her parting "God bless you, Dora, my only one! God protect you!" was uttered in such a voice that I have often felt since as if the sorrow that came after might have been a severe shock, but could have been no surprise; for from the first she seemed to have been prepared for it. My father saw us on board ship, and we left him waving his handkerchief to us from the shore. That was my last sight of him, and, thank God, no shadow fell across his path deeper than the disappointment which I know my prolonged absence must cause him. For we had gone to America with the intention of remaining the winter, and two years passed, and we were still there; my parents continually writing to persuade us to come back, my cousin as constantly making arrangements which postponed our doing so.'

'And you were happy then, Aunt Dorothy?' asked Charity.

Mrs. Dorothy answered very calmly,—'Happiness, Charity, even earthly happiness, remained at Briersley—at least, it did not come with me to America. It hovered about me during the first weeks of my marriage—never, indeed, assuming a very solid or satisfying shape, but flitting over me in the form of excitement, and pleasure, and amusement; but long before the first three months of married life were over every dream of delight had disappeared. The reality stood before me, a reality of misery, mortification, and remorse. I accepted my fate, and resolved, having as I then realised no other resource, to make the best of it.'

'And your parents, Aunt Dorothy?'

'They never knew what I was suffering. The thought of what that trial would be, especially to my mother, made me careful in concealing everything which would give them uneasiness. It was of my mother I thought most, yet I almost think she would have borne up under the grief better than my father. He had such a singularly loving, susceptible heart; once wounded in its most sensitive part, I do not think he would ever have rallied. Thank God he never knew. Two years after I had left home the tidings reached me of his death. It was almost, I believe, a source of relief to me to know that his sudden illness was caused by a shock received in a fall from his horse, for had it been otherwise I might have tormented myself with thinking that he had pined for me, his former companion and delight, and had fretted at my long absence, for which he had been so wholly unprepared; and I might have reproached myself for not having yielded to his often proffered entreaties, and returned alone to visit Briersley, if my cousin could not be prevailed upon to return with me.'

'And would your husband have allowed you to do so?' asked Charity.

'My cousin,' replied Mrs. Dorothy, who, as

Charity could not help remarking, never once used the word 'husband'—'my cousin often wished me to return for a time, at all events: but I never could be persuaded to leave him. He often left me for weeks together, sometimes even for months, and often I had scarcely money enough to live upon. I, too, who had never till then known what it was to have one wish ungratified!'

'But your parents, Aunt Dorothy,' said Charity, 'they would have supplied you with any amount of money?'

'Yes, Charity, had I chosen to own to them that I was in need of it. But I was too unwilling to cause them pain; too much attached still to my cousin—too proud, perhaps—to confess, even to them, my wretchedness and humiliation. My father made me a very handsome allowance. It was paid quarterly, to my cousin, and when the money was due it generally found him at home; or rather, I should say, with me. For, Charity, our house was not his home. Aunt Dorothy will bring her child to this last point in her sad life, and then, Charity, my child, you must seek your room, and, I hope, your God, and leave me to the quiet of my own room and the support of my God; for when once this point is reached I shall have no strength for more, and must be left alone. For my home, Charity, was not Roland's. I had often wondered where he could go when he left me; where those weeks and months were passed, and how he could spend so much money. But I had never suspected the dreadful truth—who could have suspected it?—until it burst upon me one awful day. I had been alone for many weeks—alone in my dreary lodging; and I had received no news of Roland, save one letter which he had written soon after he first left me, saying that he was going far up the country and would be absent on business some time. My health was very delicate just then, and I felt more depressed by his continued absence than I had ever been before. At length my money was all gone, and in my difficulty I tried to earn some, and painted flowers, which I endeavoured to sell to the stationers' shops in the town. Weak and ill as I then was, I would walk five miles to the town, and go from shop to shop seeking to dispose of my paintings; but I never thought once of writing home to my parents, or of leaving America and finding my way somehow to Briersley.

'At last the day, the fatal day came. I had determined on selling some of my things to procure money, and with this object in view I was turning over a closet in my room, when I came upon a cash-box which had once belonged to my father, but which my cousin had so much admired at Briersley that my father had given it to him. It was of Japan workmanship, and had a secret lock with a very curious key, such as no workman in England could ever have either constructed or picked. My father had brought it home in some of his voyages, and used to keep his money in it, and he had given it one day to Roland; but, somehow, I never remembered having seen it from that day to this, and its very existence had passed from my mind until I suddenly came upon it in this closet. It was a very massive box with heavy gold clasps, and a great deal of very curious carving about it, and the thought struck me at once that I could probably obtain a very good sum for it, if I carried it to the town. It was locked, and my husband, of course, had the key; but I had a duplicate key of my own somewhere in my little dressing-case. I had never thought of this key since my marriage, and my husband did not know that I possessed it, for I had never had occasion to think of the cash-box since my father had given it to him. But when it was my father's he kept one key and I the other, and many and many a time had he sent me to that box to fetch money or papers for him.

'Scarcely thinking what I was doing, I ran upstairs and fetched my key, and opened the box which I had never set my eyes upon since last I had seen it in the little breakfast-parlour at Briersley. It was full of letters—all, as I saw, directed to my cousin —all in the same hand—a lady's hand, which I had never seen before. I never stopped to reflect for an instant; but I opened one after the other, and read —yes, read and understood, though my head was swimming, and my hands and arms shook so violently that I could scarcely hold the paper. But I read and understood, and at once realised my position. I knew now where Roland was, where the money went. The letters were from a lady signing herself "Catherine Helstone," and writing to her husband, and of her children—his children. Yes. And she was his wife, and they were his children. These letters told me that, plainly enough. When Roland Helstone came to Briersley three years before, he left a wife and family in the woods of America, in wretched circumstances.'

'But, Aunt Dorothy, you were married to him?' interrupted Charity.

'I had thought so, Charity. Before God, I was his wife; but he had never been my husband, and now, even in my own sight, I was no longer his wife. That was the first idea I fully comprehended. And at once my course was taken. That very day I left the lodging. There was one person in the neighbouring town on whom I felt I could rely. He was the clergyman of one of the churches there, and though I had never spoken to him I had often, in days past, attended his church, and I knew he was a good man, with a holy heart of love. I went to him that night, Charity; strength, not my own, was given me to go to him, and to tell him enough of my story to elicit all his sympathy and aid. I did not tell him my name, and he did not ask it. He never seemed to doubt my word in anything. It was his own proposal that he should lend me money to return to England at once, and he insisted upon my doing so as a first-class passenger, and also that I should remain at his house for the two days that must pass before the next ship sailed. The long walk into the town, added to the shock of the morning, had made me very ill, and I dreaded lest I should be prevented going on board. But the kind care of that good man and his wife seemed to put new strength into me; and when the morning for the ship's sailing arrived, I had in a measure recovered my strength. He saw me into my berth himself, and, as I learned afterwards, secured for me the captain's attention and respect; and it was with extreme difficulty—it was only, indeed, on my insisting upon it as a personal favour to myself, and a comfort to my poor agitated mind—that I could prevail upon him to let me leave with him a valuable ring, which had been given to me by my dear father on the day of my engagement. His wife made me promise that I would let them know of my arrival in my own home, should it please God to bring me safely there; adding, in her true woman's consideration for my feelings, that there would be no need to sign any name—initials would be enough: those which were on the ring I had left with her husband, and which had the letters "D. H." set in brilliants.

'When she left me her tears flowed freely. I wished mine could have done the same, but every drop that it would have relieved me to shed seemed frozen somewhere in my brain, and pressing upon it. I could not thank them as I longed to do; but I remember that I strove to return his warm grasp with my cold hands, and that the tears which her parting kiss left upon my rigid cheek seemed to refresh it, like drops of God's rain upon parched and withered ground. I only found out how much she had felt and thought for me after she had left when, on opening a box which she and the good clergyman had prepared for me as a provision for the voyage, I found, amidst many other things, an assortment of little baby-clothes, and a gentle loving note from the giver, saying that, though I had not told her so, she could not help fearing that I might need these things before I reached my own dear home, and reminding me in a few earnest words of the great Father above, whose love was extended to all the works of His creation; but whose heart went forth in special favour and protection towards those who, but for Him, would be fatherless. Her words were very precious, and, Charity, her gift remained carefully treasured by me for many, many years, until I had need to use it for one of whom we are not speaking now.'

'You mean for me, Aunt Dorothy!' exclaimed Charity.

'Yes, Charity; you were the first to wear those little garments which love, Christian love and pity, had so carefully prepared, and gratitude had so carefully treasured. For myself I had no need of them, or, at least, but one amongst all those little articles had I any need to use. My kind friend's fears were not realised. The winds were favourable, for He who holdeth them in His hand continued His loving-kindness towards me, and we had a short and prosperous voyage. One night I remained in London, for I would not risk the shock my sudden arrival at Briersley would have been to my mother, then a widow of three months' sorrowing. I told her very little; only enough to prepare her for seeing me. It was sufficient for her to know that I was returning in sorrow—that I had left Roland for ever. The truth would be better told when I was with her; and her grief and horror would be tempered by the sight of me, and by the knowledge that, at least, I was safe and with her.

The next day I returned to Briersley, and that evening, Charity, a little baby was born; but through God's mercy, as I have never ceased to remember, not born to live and die, but to die and live again in a world where none are fatherless—none suffer shame or sorrow. The child—my child, was dying when it was born; they placed it in my arms; for a few short seconds its little cheek rested on my breast, and then it grew very cold, and they insisted on taking it away. My mother herself had dressed it in one of the little white robes that I had brought with me, and I did not fail to write word that in that little dress its body was laid to rest, whilst the happy, ransomed soul, winged its way to heaven, scarcely touching this sad earth as it passed by. The clergyman had been sent for, and a name was given—the name of "Henry," so loved and honoured by me because it had been my father's. It was my mother's doing, but had I been able to be consulted it would have been my own wish also. It was just another proof to me of the tender, watchful care of the good God, who had never ceased to protect me and provide for me from the moment that I had left my lodging, and who had many times in judgment manifestly and graciously remembered mercy. No other name was added. To me my baby was Henry—only Henry. He had no other name, save the "new name" which none knew but Him who called him to receive it, and enjoy the glory and the rest of heaven without enduring the conflict and the tribulation of earth. That name alone stands on the grave in the village church of Briersley, just below my father's. The dear name of "Henry Helstone" had scarcely dried upon the stone where it had been so newly engraved, when the words, "And to the memory of his grandson Henry," were added, with the date of his birth, and the text, "Taken away from the evil to come."'

'Oh, Aunt Dorothy!' exclaimed Charity, 'how marvellous it seems that you should ever have recovered!'

'Nature is very strong, Charity, when God does not withdraw His upholding hand; and I had now everything to help me, youth, and health, and the tenderest care and nursing, and, best of all, an object still left to me in life. For my dear mother, who, Allen told me, had been pining away ever since my father's death, seemed to take new life and strength on my return. Her one desire was to cheer me; to forget her own trials, in order that she might soothe and comfort me. Mine was to do the same for her sake. Thus we lived for one another, until, unconsciously, time came to aid with its unfailing help, and the griefs which we had so resolutely been keeping out of one another's sight gradually passed in a measure from our own. We left Briersley at once, and lived for many years in London, near my mother's relations, and after her death I came here.'

'And Briersley?' asked Charity, 'and . . . and . . .'

'And Roland,' replied Mrs. Dorothy, calmly. 'Briersley was let at first, Charity, and it passed from our sight, my mother at once resigning the life-interest she had in it. Since then it has been sold, and has changed its name. It was not long in Roland's possession; indeed, it was not for very long that anything belonged to him. Not many years passed before we heard of his death from that same clergyman, who, though he never seemed to do so, must have known more about him and me than I supposed. And, Charity, God's mercies are very great; he died humble and repentant. It had been my never-ceasing prayer, and it was granted. And now, Charity, go, my child, go; the story of Aunt Dorothy's life has never been told till now. But it has been told to you this evening, Charity. If, after hearing it, you can make shipwreck of your life's happiness by joining your destiny with one whom you may indeed love, but whom you have no reason either to revere or to trust, then my effort has been in vain, and God has not seen fit to answer my prayer.'

CHAPTER XIX.

CHARITY did go to her room, and locking herself into it she sat down on the floor, her usual habit when greatly touched or excited, and leaning her aching head against the little iron bedstead in which she had slept from a child, and, consequently, in which she persisted in sleeping still, the troubled thoughts passed quickly through her bewildered brain, not one amongst them remaining long enough in it to form either a purpose or an action.

Half an hour had passed thus when there was a knock at the door, and in answer to her hastily-given assurance that no one could come in, Betsy's voice informed her that 'Mr. Edward Saville was in the parlour, and particularly wished to see her.' Charity started to her feet and unlocked the door. Betsy remarked the agitated face and the tear-stained eyes instantly, although not seeming even to look at her young lady, and said, quietly,—

'I'd better tell Mr. Edward you can't see him,

Miss Charity; you 've got a headache, I know. I 'll just tell him so, and send him away.'

'No, Betsy, no! I will go down: I want to speak to him. Are the candles lighted in the parlour?'

'No, Miss; the fire was burning bright enough; for I didn't think you 'd be spending all the evening up in my mistress's room, talking; which, it strikes me, is about as bad for you as it is for her; and I kept up the fire, but I waited to light the candles till you should come down. I 'll go and light them now, Miss Charity, and tell Mr. Edward you 're coming.'

'No, Betsy,' said Charity, quickly; 'don't light them, and don't disturb me. I want to speak quietly to Mr. Edward. I 'm going down now.'

'But you 'll just smooth your hair, my dear,' said Betsy, somewhat imploringly; 'and if I were you, Miss Charity, I 'd wash my face a bit. You don't look like yourself to-night, my dear; you see, you 've been too long upstairs, and when one gets talking like that, one forgets sometimes that one isn't very smart.'

And Betsy set down the candle she held in her hand on the looking-glass. Charity cast a glance at her pale face and dishevelled curls, and in obedience to Betsy's request passed the brush over her hair in a listless way, and bathed her burning eyes in fresh water; then, without another word, ran downstairs to the parlour. Edward stood by the fire, and she went straight up to him, and holding out her hand, said,—

'Good-bye, Edward: you 're going away next week; but as far as I am concerned, let it be good-bye now. I 'd rather say it this evening and have it over, than go on seeing you every day and have to say it at last.'

'But why say it at all, Cherrie?' he exclaimed. 'Part we must for a time, I know; for I must not dream of marriage, or, rather, I must dream of it; it will be, for some time, my one thought by day and dream by night: but I must be content to wait to carry the delicious dream into reality till I can afford to keep a wife, as such a wife as you, Cherrie, ought to be kept. But why ever say good-bye to me, since you can keep me just as closely in your heart when I am away as when I am near; and more closely, too, Cherrie? You and I must never say good-bye to each other: why should we?'

'Because we must, Edward,' she said, calmly, her face growing more and more pale. 'Edward, I cannot—dare not marry you.'

'And why not?' he asked, impetuously, almost angrily. 'Did you not own to me only yesterday that you loved me with something different from a sister's love? When I told you of all that Huntley had told me, and how he had said that he believed one reason why he could not win your heart was because it already belonged to another, and that other was myself; when I urged you to tell me if his supposition was true, you would not own that it was so: but you would not deny it, and your silence led me to suppose that Huntley was right, that my dearest wishes were likely to be realised, and that our early, happy affection, had ripened in your heart as well as in mine into something even stronger than its childhood's force, though I am sure that was pretty strong. Only yesterday, Cherrie, we were sitting happily in this room together, and you seemed as unwilling that I should leave as I was to go, and now you talk of saying good-bye to me for ever! But I know what it is: our old godmother has been talking to you. This is her doing; she hates me, I believe, and would gladly make you hate me too; and she has been putting some of her sanctimonious ideas into your pretty head, which is half too full of them already.'

'Oh, Edward!' exclaimed Charity, 'pray don't talk like that! Aunt Dorothy is good—oh, so good! and kind, too! We have both of us great reason to love her, and be grateful to her.'

'Great reason, indeed!' interrupted Edward. 'I have, especially, when she sets you against me, and blights every hope of happiness I have. I thought she would do it if she could; she told me as much on Sunday.'

'Oh, Edward!' was again all that Charity could answer.

'Yes, she did!' he replied, speaking in the loud, eager tone, which always frightened Charity, and, somehow, made Edward seem less dear to her than he usually was. 'Yes, Cherrie, she did; not in so many words certainly, but that was the pith of what she said. She sugared it over with fine speeches, and good advice, and a lot of loving expressions towards my father and mother and myself: but take away the coating she covered it with, and the inside came just to this—that I was a wild young fellow, without any fixed character or principles, and that the less you had to say to me the better. Now, Heaven knows, I don't want to pretend to be any better than I am; that's not my way, and never shall be. I know I don't care much for religion—perhaps they gave me too much of it when I was young; I had a surfeit of good things then, I believe, and may be that's one reason why such things seem stale to me, and I can't pretend to have the relish for them that some folks have. Anyhow, I know I haven't been able to take the delight in church-going and psalm-singing that the rest of my family seem to do. But I love to go to church with you, Cherrie; the pleasure of having you at my side will be quite enough to make me willing to go there every Sunday, and twice a Sunday, too, if you like; to say nothing of how gladly I shall do anything that pleases you. And as for the psalm-singing they're so much addicted to at home . . . well, I own I used to find it dull work with only Miss Danvers and Ellen's voices to listen to; but since you've come home, Cherrie, there's no one listens more attentively to the Sunday singing, or enjoys it more than I do; and oh, Cherrie, if I had you for my wife to sing to me on Sunday evenings, don't you suppose I should find more happiness by your side listening to you than in gossiping the time away with some other young fellows as careless as myself? No fear of my not keeping the Sabbath, as Aunt Dorothy calls it, properly, if you were keeping it with me. And as for extravagance—for Aunt Dorothy told me that, with my extravagant habits, it was madness to think of marriage—I suppose I can change my habits when I've a motive strong enough to make me do so.'

The thought flashed across Charity's mind at this moment of all Edward knew of the poverty in his own home, and as he spoke of no motive strong enough to lead him to a little economy and self-denial, she remembered, if he did not, the thin worn face of his mother, toiling incessantly from morning to night to assist in the care and teaching of the little ones at home. But she said nothing; indeed she never could find much to say when Edward talked; and he continued,—

'Only give me a motive for economy, and I shall be as saving as Mrs. Dorothy herself. Don't you think it will be pure enjoyment to save money instead of spending it, when I know that the money I save is all to be spent one day on your sweet face, instead of on my good-for-nothing self? I don't want to be a hypocrite, or make out that I've been steadier in past days than I have been. I know I have given my father trouble, and spent more money than I ought to have done. I know I haven't always had the best of characters, or kept the best of company. But let bye-gones be bye-gones. As you would say, Cherrie, who are so fond of quoting poetry, "Let the dead past bury its dead." If I'd loved you,

Cherrie, seven years ago as I love you now, my life would have been a very different one. I did love you always, ever since I can remember how happily we used to play together; and you never worried me as Ellen did, but were always my favourite and friend. But I was a boy, then—a child. It was very different. Ah, Cherrie! if I had known then how I should feel now, I should have led a different life. But I was young, and I got into bad company; and then I had not courage to tell my father, and things went wrong; and I know there's a great deal to regret. But now, Cherrie, now that my one thought is of you—my one desire to please you—to work for you—to be worthy of you—do you not see for yourself—Cherrie, you must see, that I shall be an altered man—an altered man, I say!'

The words fell heavily on Cherrie's heart. She seemed to have heard them before. Something within bore witness to their fallacy, and she answered,—'It needs a stronger motive than any earthly love to make such a change. Aunt Dorothy says so, and I believe her.'

The mention of his godmother's name was unfortunate. Edward stamped his foot impatiently upon the floor,—'Aunt Dorothy again!' he said. 'Have you no will, no feelings, no words of your own? Cherrie, you loved me yesterday—you were ready almost to give me your promise yesterday; would that I had remained a little longer with you and obtained it, instead of leaving you to the canting influence of your old-maid godmother! Cherrie, you know you loved me yesterday, and I know it too: do you not love me now?'

And Edward laid his hand upon her arm, and fixed his eyes on hers.

Charity burst into tears. 'I loved you yesterday, Edward,' she said, 'just as I love you to-day—just as I always have loved you, and always shall. But you say truly; yesterday, had you stayed a little longer, my promise might have been given. Yesterday I would have promised to be your wife, and to-day I cannot.'

'And if yesterday, why not to-day?' he asked.

His look, which had such power over her, was turned away from her now, and fixed moodily upon the floor; there was a coldness in his tone which cut Charity to the heart, but if it chilled it strengthened also.

'Because,' she said, 'yesterday I thought of what you wished, Edward, and—and of what I should wish, of enjoyment and happiness in this life; and now I am thinking of what is right—of what will bring happiness in another life.'

'In short,' Edward interrupted, 'Aunt Dorothy's last sermon is fresh in your mind. Perhaps, Cherrie, if I go away now and come again to-morrow, the impression may have passed away, and you may be a little more like your dear old self. Come, Cherrie,' he added, recovering his temper and resuming his own warm, winning manner, 'come, Cherrie, don't let us make shipwreck of both our happiness in this world, for the sake of the strait-laced scruples of a saintly old godmother, who, having one of her own feet in the grave, looks upon things in general in what you may call a somewhat one-sided view, and cannot be supposed either to understand or sympathise with young people like ourselves. As I say, don't let us make shipwreck of our best hopes, and sacrifice our best feelings and interests, to a passing impression, however powerful it may seem.'

Again the words fell familiarly on Charity's ear. Edward's own voice seemed again repeating Aunt Dorothy's warnings. The very weapon he sought to use turned, by a power stronger than his own, against himself. 'Not make shipwreck of her best hopes!' 'not sacrifice her best feelings and interests to a passing impression, however powerful it might seem!' Just what Aunt Dorothy had so earnestly begged her to remember, whilst she strengthened her entreaty with the experience of her own life. Oh! how little Edward had known of his godmother when he said she could 'neither understand nor sympathise.'

'Cherrie,' continued Edward, 'you see the truth of all I say: you do not really wish to follow our godmother's advice, and cast me off for the sake of her, or your silly scruples. Only think that, when once you have spoken the word, it will be too late to retract. My ship sails next week. It is to be a new life for me. I shall sail in a new vessel, with a new captain, to a new world; and if you will only throw off the influence of others, and be your own dear self, and act for yourself, as I know, as I can see you wish to act,—then, Cherrie, I shall sail too with new hopes, new principles, a new object,—in short, as I said before, a new man.'

He paused for an instant, but Charity did not answer, and he continued,—

'But the word that you speak to-day, it will be too late to retract to-morrow, Cherrie. Think—reflect.'

The sobs choked Charity's voice, but it was firm enough for Edward to understand as she answered,—'I have thought, I have reflected, Edward. I love you very much. What Lord Huntley said is quite true. I never thought of being married to you or to any one else till he spoke to me that day. For one grows up almost without knowing how old one is, and I had always thought of myself as a child, and never dreamt of having any other home but dear Aunt Dorothy's, after I had seen how wrong it was to think of leaving her to be a governess. But when Lord Huntley talked to me that day, oh, Edward! then I did feel that he wasn't like you, that I could never like to be with him half as much as I like to be with you, or tell out my heart to him as I can to you. I know he is very good, and noble, and I like and respect him very much. But I felt that day that he never could be such a dear companion to me as you are; that I should always like you best, and love best to be with you, and so I could not marry him.'

'Just so, Cherrie!' Edward interrupted. 'Huntley said so to me, and I felt that he was not mistaken. You are a right-minded, noble-hearted girl, Cherrie, and so you would not marry where you did not love. Almost any other girl but you would have been tempted by the offer of such a man as Huntley, and such a position as he would have been able to give you. But rank, talent, wealth, what are these things compared with affection? You refused Huntley because you had a heart, Cherrie; and knowing the value of that heart, you would not sacrifice it to any earthly ambition or prospects whatever—you would not crucify your better nature to your lower one, and cease to be a woman, a true, pure-minded, loving woman, with her heart beating freely within her, that you might become a lady with a coronet pressing upon her head. Cherrie, I honour and respect you, and love you ten thousand times better, if possible, than I did before, for the motive that led you to refuse Lord Huntley. Shall not the same motive now lead you to accept me? ought it not to do so? or are you to sacrifice now that very heart, the value of which you seem to know so much better than most women do, and, as it were, commit a moral suicide, by destroying those very feelings and affections which are, and which you feel are, a woman's life, the source of all her energy and strength? Cherrie, you must be blind if you do not see, that just the very reason which led you to refuse Huntley should—ought—must lead you to accept me. You let your heart, your true, loving, woman's heart, speak to you then. Vanity, ambition, all the lower passions of the mind, must have spoken also, and many a woman would have listened to them, and been led by them to sacrifice herself. But in you, Cherrie, the heart, the true, warm heart, spoke out louder still, and you listened, and were saved. Let that same heart speak now, and I know, I feel, that I shall be satisfied with its answer.'

It almost seemed that, as Edward spoke so eagerly, vehemently, passionately, Charity's own heart made an attempt to second and strengthen his words, for she pressed her hand upon it as though she would control its powerful workings by a physical effort, whilst she answered,—

'No, Edward, I dare not—I *will not* let my heart speak now. You are right. It did speak then, and, thank God, I listened to it; for I felt that its teaching then was true and pure. But now, Edward, I hear a truer, purer voice than that of my own heart. It is the voice of my soul. If Aunt Dorothy has had anything to do in this, it has only been because God has allowed her, in His mercy has made her to be so. For all she may have said to me, my own soul had told me before. I am very weak, Edward, only a very weak beginner in the right path, and I dare not hinder my progress by joining my steps with one who is not even attempting to walk in the same direction. I should not lead you right, but you would lead me wrong. I know it would be so—I feel it would. God gave me strength to turn a deaf ear to every lower thought some time ago, and listen to the voice of my own heart. He will do so now, and will strengthen me. He *is* strengthening me to turn a deaf ear to my own voice that I may hear His. I could not sacrifice the feelings of my heart. I could not crucify my own will and wish for any earthly gain or prospect. But for heavenly hopes—for my soul's good—I believe, I am sure, God will give me strength. Oh, Edward! do not tempt me, for I am very weak.'

And at that moment the door opened, and Mr. Saville came in. For an instant he stood in the doorway, apparently hesitating whether to enter or retire. Then he came forward into the room, without, however, appearing to notice Charity. In an instant she had disappeared, and a moment after was locked into her bedroom, in the very position in which she had been when summoned by Betsy an hour before to her interview with Edward Saville—on the floor by the side of her little bed, her burning head leaning against the cold iron, and her hands pressed tightly together. But then there had been no settled thought, and no definite purpose within her perplexed and troubled brain; now, though her head ached violently, though she felt sick, dizzy, bewildered, and very, very unhappy, one thought within assumed a defined shape, and her mind rested upon it, or rather returned perpetually to it from its various tossings to and fro. There was a promise to God's children in His word that no temptation should happen to them greater than they were able to bear; or that, with the temptation, He would make a way of escape. God was faithful, and He had fulfilled His word. If the spirit was willing, the flesh was weak; and Charity's was fast failing when Mr. Saville had so unexpectedly opened the door in search of Edward. It was no chance act, though it was to recall him to the Rectory that he might see a friend who had, 'by chance,' arrived that evening. Charity had begged Edward not to tempt her. He certainly would not have hearkened. But God did, and Mr. Saville's entrance was the way of escape.

Meanwhile Edward, on being thus interrupted, looked as he felt, thoroughly annoyed and irritated; and on hearing why his father had thus suddenly come to fetch him, refused to return to his home, and declared he had no wish to see that friend or any other—he had lost the only friend in the world he cared to possess. He accompanied his father to the Rectory, however, and after spending a very miserable evening there, announced his intention of returning to London with his friend the next morning, and remaining there until the ship should sail in the course of the following week. His mother remonstrated, and Ellen implored, and the younger ones entreated; but his father said nothing. Afterwards, when he and his wife were left alone, he said quietly to her,—'Edward has proposed to Charity, my love, and she has refused him;' and he told her of the conversation he had been the means of interrupting.

'Oh, Edward, and I thought she seemed so devoted to him!' was the reply of the tender mother; 'and with her affection to steady him, he might have been a different character.'

Mr. Saville smiled, a very grave smile. '*Might* have been!' he said. 'Ah, how many a fair young bark has gone down into hopeless misery, and been lost for ever, by striking upon the rock of what *might* be!'

'But surely,' urged the wife, 'affection is very powerful—such strong affection as Edward seems to have for Charity? You do not suppose that he has no heart, Edward? You surely think that he loves her?'

'You will think me very harsh,' replied Mr. Saville, 'if I say that he loves her as much as a man can love, who loves himself better than any other object in the world. He admires her very much, certainly—no man but must do so, for one rarely sees beauty such as hers, and he has set his heart on making her his wife; and where Edward's will is once fairly involved, it would be very difficult to decide between strength of resolution and strength of affection.'

'But,' said Mrs. Saville, 'you think she loves him?'

'Yes, I do,' replied her husband; 'and I am inclined to believe, too, in the report that has gone about in the neighbourhood, that she has refused Lord Huntley for his sake. Few people seem to credit it; perhaps it is scarcely to be expected that they should, since I do not suppose there are ten young women in the county who would not sacrifice anything and everything they possess to make such a marriage. But I have thought a good deal about it, and I have come to the conclusion that Huntley must have proposed for our penniless, nameless little godchild, otherwise I cannot account for his conduct towards her. Lord Huntley is not the man to pay any girl such attentions as he paid to Charity, and then suddenly draw off and cease them altogether. He is the most honourable, high-principled, and, I really believe, Christian young man, I have ever met with; and I feel sure he would not behave so to any girl, least of all to one in Charity's position.'

'It seems strange that she should have refused him,' said Mrs. Saville, 'for he is, as you say, so superior to other young men; his energy and devotion in doing good to the poor are as great as his talents: and, moreover, he is so handsome. It seems curious to think of such a man not being able to win the heart of a child like Charity.'

'Unless the heart were not hers to give,' said Mr. Saville; 'which is another reason for my believing that she does love our poor boy, and, therefore, could not listen to Huntley. But for this, I believe that a heart like Charity's, so warm and true, and so thoroughly simple and unsophisticated, would have been very speedily and very strongly attached to a man like Huntley, who has in himself *every* thing to secure love and trust.'

'And what a position it would have been for her, poor child!' said Mrs. Saville. 'Such a husband—such a fortune—such means of doing good! Certainly things do sometimes seem to go very contrary to what one would imagine best.'

'*Seem* to go contrary,' said her husband, gravely; 'but, thank God, never do so. The straightest-seeming things are often those which, in the end, prove to have been the most perverse. The crookedest turnings are often found all to lead to the right end; our smoothest walking, at the last, often proves to be over the stones which were roughest to our feet at one time, when, so to speak, they each stood up under them, sharp and separate, while at God's command we stepped from one to another. But let those same stones be fitted one into another by God's hand, and polished into shape and smoothness by our submission, and I think we shall find them a very solid and a very safe, even a very easy, support for our feet.'

'We must hope so,' said Mrs. Saville; 'but some of these stones pierce one pretty sharply now. Edward is a perpetual thorn in my side, and I had thought this desired marriage of his would have been the means of removing it.'

'Say, rather,' replied her husband, 'that it would have been the means of planting it in Charity's side also. I cannot myself see that any other result would have been produced, and, therefore, I cannot but feel thankful that Charity should have refused him, as I feel sure she has done.'

Thus did Mr. and Mrs. Saville talk together that evening, while Edward flung his things into his portmanteau in preparation for the morning's journey to London, and Charity sat still on the floor, with her head leaning on the iron bedstead.

CHAPTER XX.

THE little remaining daylight had long given place to the dark clouds of night, when Charity was roused from her position by some one knocking at the door, and opening it before she had time either to grant or refuse admittance. Of course it was Betsy, who, setting down the candle out of sight of Charity, who, she saw, could not stand the light so suddenly introduced into that dark chamber, began such a series of remonstrances as might have been expected from her, and carried them on the more violently because she thought that Charity would not wish her to know either of the two facts of which she felt, in reality, quite as certain as though she had been present at both the conversations, of which she had not heard one single word.

Betsy knew perfectly that Mrs. Dorothy had been giving her godchild the story of her life; or, at all events, the sketch of some scenes in it. Otherwise, she would never have been in the state in which she had found her on going to her room a short time after Charity had left it. And Betsy felt equally certain that Charity had that evening parted from Edward Saville with different words, and in a manner which differed greatly from that in which they had parted on any other evening. Otherwise, he would not have slammed the parlour door after him in that fashion, utterly regardless of the old lady in her sick-room just above; nor would he have spoken to his father in the passage in the impatient tone which had fallen upon Betsy's ear, as she sat at her solitary supper in the quiet kitchen.

'Well, these are pretty doings to be sure!' was Betsy's conclusion. 'My mistress trying to hasten the few days she 's got to spend on earth by talking away the little breath she has left, in direct disobedience to the doctor's orders that she should keep perfectly quiet; and Miss Charity crying the pretty blue out of her dear eyes, and the bright colour out of her sweet cheeks, for the sake, as I do believe, of that good-for-nothing young scamp Mr. Edward, that I haven't got the smallest patience with—no, nor never had! Hasn't he spent money that might have saved his poor mother's hair from turning grey before its time, and kept the flesh on her poor bones? All the village says he 's near broke her heart by the wild sort of life he 's been leading since he 's been away; and now, I do believe, he 's had the impudence to come and ask our pretty dear to give him leave to break hers also!

'The coolness of men is wonderful, to be sure!

and makes me thankful that I never had anything to do with them. "It's an ill wind that blows nobody good," they say, and that's one good my ugly face has done me; it's kept the men at their distance. There! I do wish I might never see another of them —at least, not until he'd learnt sense, and manners, and the right way of behaving, like our good parson, or the miller, and such-like, whose brains seem to have come with their grey hairs. For as for the young ones, they seem made to bring trouble and sorrow. There was that handsome young fellow that must needs come across the Atlantic, years ago, to fetch our dear little lady's heart and break it! Well, he's dead and gone, and many 's the time I've prayed I might have the good God's grace to think upon his memory without cursing it, especially as they say he died repenting of his sins. I thought I'd come to think of him in a right sort of way at length; but this last month the old feelings seem all to rise up again at the sight of Mr. Edward's face, and the sound of his voice, coming troubling round here after our pretty flower —for all the world just as Mr. Roland used to do at Briersley! I've thought many times that it was a good thing for him, and for me too, that he had leave to come and go without asking me to let him in and out. It's my opinion, if I'd the opening of our front door to him, he'd have seen pretty sharp that, so far as I was concerned, he was no welcome visitor here; and I'd have shut it after him pretty much as he did himself this evening: unless, indeed,

I hadn't done it out of respect for my poor lady's nerves, which he never seems to think of—not he! though he did have that long talk with her last Sunday, and must have seen that she had scarcely any strength left in her body. But I dare say he didn't see it; the like of him don't seem to see anything but just what concerns themselves. There, I 've no patience with them! I wish there 'd never come another near us, unless indeed it were such as my Lord Huntley: but there isn't many such, and now he never comes near the place. Folks seem to have found out that he came after Miss Charity, and that she must have given him a hint not to come any more, or he 'd never have dropped off so sudden: but the miller, he says that 's a piece of folly he 'd find it hard to believe of our young lady, and I don't wonder he says so. With such a set of men as there are in this world, to go and send away about the only man of her own age I ever saw worth anything—a nobleman, too—and such a noble man, with a noble heart inside as well—and so good to the poor people Miss Charity 's so fond of; it does seem, to be sure, as though she must be clean mad to refuse him. The miller was saying last night as how he had a grand house in London, and a large estate in Derbyshire bigger than this one, and more money than he knew what to do with; and that, for his part, he wasn't going to believe that our young lady, who had such a good set of brains of her own, and had received the best of schooling besides, would ever be so foolish as to say "No" to an offer like that. "He only wished

Lord Huntley would come and ask her," he said, "for it would do his heart good to see such a sweet lady mistress of Huntley Tower! There! I couldn't, for the life of me, let him guess the truth: I'd have been ashamed to do it.

'But, so far as this young Mr. Saville is concerned, she shall not throw herself away upon him if old Betsy can help it; for another thing the miller told me was, that he had shown what sort he was like in the village already, though he hadn't been here but three months, and it was a thousand pities such a pretty young lady as ours should be left to walk about so much alone as she is now. And there, again! it's pretty much the old story over again. But anyhow I believe Master Edward's gone off to-night with something he doesn't like, and it won't be my fault if ever he gets anything in this house he does like.

'My lady's ill, and, God knows, I don't want to trouble her; but I'll give her a hint how the ground lies some day, though it's my belief she's got one already, and that it's just this that has set her on talking to Miss Charity about herself: for she *had* been talking of herself I know, or she'd never have brought on one of her attacks. I must go and see after them both, and it's a mercy they've got some sensible person to do so; which, perhaps, they never might have had if I'd had a pretty face like theirs to help to turn my hair grey, and fill my face with wrinkles. Why, it's only to look at my mistress and at me, to see how little good often comes of having a pretty face! Hasn't it just been through her great beauty that my lady got into all her troubles? while here am I, who never had an offer in my life to trouble my head or heart, as strong and active as many a woman of forty! The miller says I don't look a day older than his eldest daughter; but I never heed his foolish talk, though, for the matter of that, I think she does look pretty near as old, having had, no doubt, her share of trouble and worry, through marrying early and having a large family.'

And Betsy ended her long soliloquy by taking a bedroom-candlestick and setting forth to see after her mistresses, old and young. Her first visit was to Charity, for she had administered a soothing draught to Mrs. Dorothy an hour before, and knew that she would find her pretty much as she had left her then. But Charity's appearance altogether took her by surprise. She had been prepared for a pale face, and eyes more deeply stained with tears even than they had been in the earlier part of the evening. But a change for which she was altogether unprepared seemed to have passed over her young mistress, who, so far as Betsy could judge in the uncertain light, looked ten years older.

'Miss Charity,' she said, 'I've come to help you to go to bed, my dear: you don't know, perhaps, that it has struck ten.'

Charity did not know, and, now that Betsy had told her, did not seem to care. So Betsy tried another tack, which proved more successful.

'Your aunt has been very ill, Miss Charity,' she said.

At once Charity was all attention, and eager to go to her.

'No, my dear,' said Betsy; 'she 's best left quiet. She 's taken one of the soothing draughts, and you know it isn't good to disturb her while it 's taking its quieting effect on the nerves. I 'll be going in by-and-bye to see after her and light the lamp, and I 'll bring you word how she is. Meantime, my dear, do you get to bed. It will vex your aunt to hear that you are still up, and she 'll be worrying about it, thinking that you 'll be hurting yourself. And indeed, Miss Charity, we ought to keep everything from my mistress that can possibly distress her. It 's my belief that she 's been talking to-night of things which she had better have left alone—if she had consulted her own health, that is to say. You must not mind my talking so free, my dear; you know I love my dear lady, and was her faithful servant long before you were thought of, and I know every turn in her countenance, and every tone of her voice, as, I suppose, none can know but those who have had but one object in life to think about, and have thought of that one object for years and years with all their heart and all their understanding. My lady was but fifteen, Miss Charity, when I went to live with her first; as I 've told you, I dare say, many times.'

Yes: Charity had heard this one fact from Betsy's lips many times before, but hitherto it had never afforded her much interest. Until now, all she had known of Mrs. Dorothy's history was that she had been rich—that her parents had been rich, but that the money had been lost to them in some way, and only a sufficient portion of it left to enable Mrs. Dorothy to live as quietly and economically as she was now doing, and had done ever since Charity had known her. She had no relations that she knew of in the world, and having, as Charity had always supposed, never married, she had formed no near connexions, and seemed to have no closer or more devoted friend than Betsy the faithful maid, whom, as Betsy herself had often told her, Mrs. Dorothy had persuaded her father to take out of the workhouse and into her service. This much concerning her aunt's life Charity knew, and it had seemed to her very ordinary and somewhat uninteresting. But now a new light had shone on everything connected with Mrs. Dorothy, and in reply to Betsy's allusions to the past she said, quickly,—

'Oh, Betsy, you knew dear Aunt Dorothy when she was only fifteen, and you have known her ever since you lived with her at Briersley?'

'Yes, Miss; and I've lived with her ever since: we've spent our two lives together—all except the earliest steps in it, and just one gap afterwards, when, for a time, I was not with her. God knows, I wish I had been!"

'You mean, when she was in America?' said Charity.

'I thought so!' replied Betsy. 'My lady has been telling you somewhat of her own story, and it's been too much for both of you. I knew how it was when she rang her bell, and I found her with her teeth chattering so that you could hear them almost before you opened the door, and her poor, thin frame, shaking and shivering for all the world as though she had an ague-fit. I knew well enough it was no ague-fit, but only just that she 'd been touching that one particular nerve which she, nor any one else, can't even now set their finger on without putting the whole body wrong. I knew she 'd been talking to you, my dear; and though I 'm grieved to think she 's done herself harm, no doubt, and done away with any good the doctors may have wrought for her, yet it's a relief to me that you should know the truth about my dear lady: it will be like another bond between us, Miss Charity, and she 'll seem all the dearer to you now you know how much she has suffered."

'She *has* suffered!' said Charity; the thought crossing her mind how light was even the pain she was herself then enduring compared with Aunt Dorothy's heavy, heavy sorrow. 'Oh, Betsy, how she has suffered! I don't wonder you love her as you do. I wonder you didn't go with her to America; and what a comfort you would have been to her!'

'I wished enough to go, Miss; and my young lady she wished it, too. But *he* prevented it. He was clever enough to manage that, and anything else he 'd fixed his bad mind upon. He had my old master's ear, and he made him believe that it was no use at all to take a young girl like me out to that country: he said I should be sure to marry as soon as I set foot there, and that would be a very bad thing for me. He was only going, as he assured my master in his hypocritical way, for the winter; and since our young lady could not take her lady's maid with her, who had been in earlier years her nurse, because it was impossible that she should leave Mrs. Helstone who had been so ill, it would be best for him, he said, to engage an experienced servant in London to attend on my young mistress during the voyage. But he knew what he was about—trust him for that! He wrote my mistress word that they had found just the person they wanted, and she might feel quite easy. Just the person *he* wanted, he ought to have said. We found out afterwards, that he had engaged the services of a young woman who was going out in the same ship to some situation in America, and who was to wait on Miss Dora on the voyage and leave her when the ship arrived in port. It was just like him! part and parcel of the cool, calculating way in which he carried out all his plans.'

'But,' said Charity, 'did not Aunt Dorothy beg that you might go with her? She is so fond of you, Betsy.'

'Yes, Miss, now, after thirty years of living together; but the love was all on one side then, Miss. Miss Dora was fond of me, and good to me, as she was to everything; but it was just the love that came from pity. She used to visit the workhouse with her dear mamma every week, for my old mistress had trained her from her earliest years in her own ways of piety and charity. They came regularly every week to the house, and whilst Mrs. Helstone she was reading to the poor creatures in the sick-wards, Miss Dora she would have a class of children in the workroom. Ah, Miss Charity! I think I see her now, and never—no, never could my words tell you what she was like in those days. She just seemed like an angel of loveliness coming into our poor place from another world. But if I were to begin to talk of that time I could talk for hours, and you must be going to bed, my dear.'

'But I like to hear you talk, Betsy; I do indeed, for my mind is full of Aunt Dorothy, And it's troubled, too, about other things. Stop here a little and tell me about Aunt Dorothy: my head aches, and it does me good.'

'Well then, my dear,' said Betsy, 'you get ready for bed, and I'll stop a bit. There's your dressing-gown—now get your hair down, and let me brush it for you. My fingers ought to be accustomed to them long curls, for I've had enough to do with them in other days; though it's a good bit now since I've felt how smooth and thick they were.'

And assisting Charity to change the merino dress for the white dressing-gown, Betsy tenderly loosened the velvet band that fastened the long brown curls, and began to brush them as gently as she used to do in bygone days. 'My lady had just such curls when she was young,' she said, 'only they were many shades fairer; not brown like these, my dear—which are just the colour of the nuts we used to gather—but with a golden hue upon them, Miss Charity, for all the world like the colour of your bright birds' feathers. I never saw hair of that colour anywhere else than on her pretty head, and I think it helped to give her that angel look she had—that, and the large blue eyes and delicate skin, and the faint colour in her cheeks, which was never more than pink when she was with us at Briersley, and every shade of which had gone when she returned from America. As I say, I was a workhouse child, and a very miserable one; for my heart was as heavy within me as a stone, and the only happiness I ever knew was when it was Miss Dora's day for visiting us. Sometimes she rode over with her papa, for he was one of the visiting magistrates, and then she would come in with all her bright hair falling from under her black hat and red feather over her blue-cloth riding-habit, which set off so well her light, little figure; and sometimes she drove over with her mamma, and then she was lovely, too, in her soft muslin dresses in the summer, and in her furs in the winter: for I don't suppose the Princess Charlotte herself was more grandly dressed than she was. The girls, and the matrons too, would rave about her from week's end to week's end, but I—I believe I loved her better by far than any amongst them. But, somehow, I never could talk about her; I just kept her in my heart and pondered over her, as the Bible says, till one day she had me alone in the little linen closet, and coaxed me to tell her all my heart, and then she got her mamma to take me out and let me live at Briersley with them. And there I lived for three happy years, till he came and took our joy and light away; and never did I cease to fret for her till she came back, broken-hearted and broken-spirited.'

'And you have always lived with her ever since, Betsy?' said Charity. 'Tell me, was it a long, long time before she recovered her spirits? Do you think she ever forgot him? I wonder whether she ever heard anything about his other wife and the children? I think she must have thought a great deal about them.'

'She did a deal more than think of them, my dear, as I know; better, perhaps, than she thinks I do. You see, Miss, trouble like ours draws the hearts of a household together, when those that rule and those that serve feel the blow alike. And after the shadow fell on my young lady . . . well, it seemed as though my old mistress and I entered the cloud together; and she would often talk to me of her—master, too, being dead, and she having no one to speak to but me. It was Mrs. Helstone that told me that he was dead; they had had a letter from a clergyman in America to say so. Miss Dora, she never named him to me in all her life, and I believe she never did even to her dear mamma, without there was real necessity to do so. But after that news came I observed, that when I carried the letters to the post there was often one in Miss Dora's writing to some "Reverend" in America; and, thought I to myself, "that's the clergyman that wrote about his death, and Miss Dora she's going now to find out about the wife and children." And very soon I knew how right I had guessed, for the letters to the clergyman stopped, and instead of them there were constant letters to a Mrs. Helstone, and often these would be registered letters, and I knew there was money inside, and knew too why my sweet lady dressed so plain, and where the money went. Those letters went on for years, Miss Charity; but they've stopped now, and very glad I am of it. I think the mother must have died, Miss, for the letters to her ceased all at once, and there were others to some of the family for some time afterwards. But not for a very long time now. It's years since I've seen anything of the sort. It's no curiosity that has made me take notice of all this. It's just because my mistress is the one interest of my life, and all that touches her touches me pretty near as close. I used to remark, too, Miss Charity, how often she would have one of her attacks after one of those letters had gone out or come in . . . But now, my dear, you're pretty near ready for bed. I'll see after my lady and then come back to take away your light.'

Betsy's report of her mistress was, that she felt sure she would have a good night; Betsy had herself done her best to secure this being the case, by just saying, as she raked out the fire and lighted the lamp,—'I think, ma'am, there's been some difference of opinion between our young lady and Mr. Edward this evening. He went away very disappointed like; and from a few words he said to his papa in the passage—loud enough, ma'am, for me to hear him in the kitchen—it's my belief he'll come here no more.

Miss Charity 's been having quite a long talk with me, ma'am, while I 've brushed her hair; for, you see, I thought it would not do to have her vexing her dear heart over any words she might have had with Mr. Edward. She wanted to come into your room to-night, ma'am, but I told her you had been poorly, and it would be best to leave you quiet, and she has gone to bed. I 'm going now to fetch her candle.'

'That is right, Betsy,' said Mrs. Dorothy, gently; 'it was best to leave me quiet. But take her my dear love, Betsy, and my blessing.'

Betsy carried the message very faithfully; and when she tucked her former charge and present darling into her little bed she could not help adding, 'And with your aunt's blessing, Miss Charity, which is worth a great deal, take mine, too; which is not worth much, I know, save that it comes from a loving heart; and love, they say, makes all things of value.'

And when Charity fell asleep that night, which after a time she did, if her dreams were somewhat troubled and bewildered, their very diversity took away from their painfulness. For self and Edward were not the only figures that returned in night visions to her imagination. She dreamed also of Aunt Dorothy as a golden-haired, light-hearted girl, and again as a grave, earnest woman, with bowed figure, pale face, and white hairs—of Roland Helstone—of the widow and the children—and of dear, faithful Betsy.

CHAPTER XXI.

TWO years passed away, and Mrs. Dorothy Helstone, who had seemed so near death at one time, appeared to have had granted to her, like Hezekiah of old, a fresh lease of life. Whether anxiety of mind had been the chief cause of her sudden failure of strength two winters before, and that, on the anxiety being removed, her health of itself began to recover, or what the cause of the sudden change was, they did not quite know. But certain it was, that after Edward Saville had taken his departure, not to return for several years—after Charity's cheeks had begun to recover their former healthy hue, and her step to grow light, and her voice mirthful again—after Lord Huntley had left the temporary charge of his newly-arranged estates in the hands of a steward almost as wise and good as himself, and gone abroad for a year—certain it was that, after all these changes had been effected, Mrs. Dorothy was daily observed, as Betsy said, to be 'picking up her strength again;' and two such happy years were spent at Ivy Cottage as do not, we believe, often fall to the lot of our fellow-creatures in this life, where such times of resting are, we know, intended but to be green pastures in the desert—still waters, where pilgrims who have buffeted in rough waves before, and will soon, perhaps, have to meet yet more stormy billows, are allowed to stay for a while, to sing praises for past deliverance—songs of joy which they could not have sung whilst earnest, struggling supplication, engaged all their force and faith, and to prepare for fresh conflict further on, when the Lord may have yet higher work in store for His refreshed and strengthened servants.

Betsy never remembered a happier time than those two years which she and Mrs. Dorothy and Miss Charity spent together, when, as she said, 'without were no fightings, and within were no fears.' The miller was still her chief friend and confidant, for Betsy, like most of us, was given to strange contradictions and inconsistencies, both of character and conduct; and whilst for ever inveighing against 'the men,' and pronouncing them to be, as a race, the embodiment of all that was selfish, and heartless, and tyrannical, she had never been known to admit a female friend either into her kitchen or her confidence, whilst the miller was a welcome visitor any day, and almost every day. To him Betsy would repeat, on an average about four nights a-week, the story of all the trouble of mind she had gone through that winter.

'Never did she go through such a time before,' she would say. 'Other times, one trouble would come, and when that was gone, another; but that winter everything seemed to come together: there were verses in the Bible which she had never understood before, that had had a light upon them in her mind ever since,—such as when David talked of all the waves and billows going over him at once, and one deep calling unto another. It had seemed just like that, and her mind had been like Noah's poor dove, that could not find any rest for the sole of its foot anywhere. There was Mrs. Dorothy like to die; and Miss Charity all but carried off, first by drowning and then by Mr. Edward—which, for her part, she should have thought the worse fate of the two; and poor Lord Huntley, that was as good as gold, and made of sterling stuff, head and heart, right through to the very core of him, gone off from the very place where it seemed as though the Lord had sent him to be a blessing to all who came across him. Well, one comfort was he was back again now, and Miss Charity and he very good friends, and there was no saying what mightn't come of it yet. Her mistress had told her, many times since then, that no good ever came of building castles in the air; and certainly she'd begun to think so too, when the only one she ever built came tumbling down about her ears: but she wasn't so sure but what the scattered stones were coming together again now. Well, she'd just leave them alone, and not seek to put her hand on them again. She'd heard say the Lord wasn't fond of having His people meddling in the affairs of His providence, and that oftentimes, even when He meant to give them a good thing, and may be had got it a-preparing for them, if He saw them putting their foolish fingers to the work and making themselves too busy about it, He would just throw the whole thing down, even though He should mean all the while to build it up again when they'd learnt the lesson of leaving the Lord to do His own work in His own way, and keeping themselves quiet, meanwhile, at the bit of business fixed for them. Joseph was to sit on a throne, and wear a royal robe and a gold chain, but he had to go through the pit and the prison. Moses was to lead the people and be their ruler, but he must keep Jethro's sheep till the right time came. David began his life at court by playing the harp before King Saul, and very nearly got killed by a spear cast from the very throne on which it was promised he should sit one day. The Lord had His own ways of bringing about things, and there was no more use in trying to hasten them than there would be in seeking to prevent them. For her part, Betsy had come to think it was not a bit wiser for us to be meddling with the ways of the Lord, than it would be for a little baby to be put to manage the United Kingdom. She had come now to stand out of the way and watch the Lord's works, and see what particular little bit of the work was given her to do day by day and hour by hour, and she'd grown this way to be as contented as the day was long; indeed, there wasn't a cross anywhere now, except that the girl Phœbe never would be what she ought, and that Miss Charity was a deal too indulgent to her.'

Thus would Betsy talk by the hour in the kitchen, whilst Mrs. Dorothy and Charity held just as pleasant communion in the parlour. The cottage was not quite such as it used to be, for a few additions had been made. Now that they were no longer new, Charity had grown to look upon them as improvements, but at first it had gone to her heart to see a stone of the old place touched; and she would have had yet greater difficulty in reconciling herself to the change, had it not been made for an object which lay very near Charity's heart—in order that there might be room in the cottage to receive her friend Minnie Morton. Charity had never been able to summon courage to leave her godmother, even for a day, to visit her friends in London; so that Mrs. Dorothy had planned that Minnie should come and spend the summer with them, and a very pleasant summer it had been. Mr. Morton had brought her to Arlington himself, and had come down to fetch her; and Mrs. Dorothy had soon formed a warm friendship with one whom she already knew so well through Charity, and to whom Charity owed so much.

When Mr. Morton returned to London, it was to tell his wife that her long-cherished wish was gratified, for the good clergyman had, with the peculiar skill and tact which belonged to his character, soon found an opportunity of telling Mrs. Dorothy all that he knew of the name of Helstone. And it was a relief to him to have done so, for he felt with his wife that the information, such as it was, might, perhaps, prove of use to Charity in future days, though he had not wished to force the communication upon her godmother against Mr. Saville's and Betsy's wishes, having learnt, a good way back in his own experience, the lesson which Betsy had reached at length, that 'to everything there is a season, and a time to every purpose.' Ah! what a difference in the life of each one of us might there not be, if only the purpose and the season fitted one into the other, instead of, as is so frequently the case, being independent of each other, and at variance! Like other things which God hath joined together, these cannot be put asunder.

Mrs. Morton was eager to know all that her husband had to tell, and disappointed to find how little that all was. He had prepared Mrs. Dorothy's mind very gently, he said, for hearing that he had met with Helstones before he knew either Charity or herself; since it was evident, from what he learnt from Mr. Saville, that that name had power to arouse within her the strongest and most painful emotions. She had begged to be told all that he himself knew, and he had told her all; how that, when first he entered upon his ministerial work as a curate in a crowded part of London, he found two young persons of the name of Helstone living in a wretched lodging, in a small street in the district committed to his charge, a young man of about two or three and twenty, who might or might not have been a gentleman—he had always himself believed that by birth he was such, but that want of education, and still more, want of principle, had lowered him from the position which otherwise he might have occupied—and a young woman, his wife, who was most evidently and undoubtedly a lady—a lady by birth, by appearance, by mind: 'such a lady,' Mr. Morton said, emphatically, 'as your sweet Charity—the same, indeed, in feature, in mind, in voice, and manner, only that she was far younger—younger even than Charity was on the day I first saw her in the vestry of my church. Mrs. Helstone was a mere child, as ignorant as a baby of the world and its wicked ways, and living only from hour to hour at the will of her husband.'

'I told her,' continued Mr. Morton, 'as little as I could of him, since there was no good to tell; but she seemed to seize at once the idea of the wretched sort of gambling, wild, reckless life he led, and fully to understand how the misery of her existence in one year did the work of ten in the young wife's looks and health. And then I told her how suddenly our acquaintance with them had come to an end, and how one day, when you had gone to see the poor young wife, with your heart, as usual, full of loving sympathy, since there were circumstances in that poor creature's condition which aided in attracting you most powerfully to her at that time, you had found her gone—fled—none knew where, on a cold, biting day in January, with the snow upon the ground, and a piercing east wind finding its way into one's very bones.'

'And what did she say?' asked Mrs. Morton.

'Nothing, just at first,' replied her husband, 'poor old lady! She covered her face with her hands, and the first words I heard her say were to herself rather than to me; something about it's seeming as though there were truth in Betsy's words, and that the same misfortune reproduced itself from one generation to another. But after a little while she recovered her composure completely—you have never seen anything more dignified than that old lady's perfect self-possession—and then she told me there had once been a family of that name, cousins of hers, in America, in whom she had been deeply interested, and that so long as the mother lived she had kept up her connexion with them; but that, on her death, the family had become dispersed, and, one by one, had ceased correspondence with her. One son, the eldest, had run away from home when quite a youth, and had never been heard of since. This evidently was the man whom we had known in London—Roland Helstone; and Charity was no doubt his child. And having said this, she begged me to call her maid, and leave her; which I did, almost regretting that I had ever spoken a word to her on the subject; feeling as if, perhaps, Mr. Saville had been wiser than myself, and it would have been better never to have mentioned it to her. For, though she never lost her self-command throughout the interview, when she begged me to leave her I could see there were stormy feelings at work underneath that calm exterior; and the next day she could not leave her room, and I heard that she had been very ill in the night. She sent for me to wish her goodbye, and I think she must have gathered something of what I was feeling from my face, for she said, "There is nothing to regret. You would not have been suffered to tell what you did if it had not been much, much for the best that you should do so:" the very thought with which I had been comforting myself before. And then she added,—"If my maid has told you that I have been ill, you must not let that trouble you. I often have these attacks—it matters very little whether I have one more or less; besides, I am very old, and very near the grave. And it has done me more good than harm to have talked with you yesterday. Charity was dear to me before. I had thought, as dear as she could be, but she is yet dearer now."'

'And she told you nothing of her own connexion with these Helstones?' asked Mrs. Morton.

'Nothing.'

'And did she mean to tell Charity all that you told her?'

'She did not say so,' replied her husband. 'You know now all that passed between us.'

Mrs. Morton could have wished that it had been more satisfactory. And it was a great satisfaction to her mind when, some time afterwards, she learnt that Mrs. Dorothy had told Charity, and had told her at once. That same evening, when Charity came to read the Bible as usual, before parting for the night, and after reading put her arms round her aunt's neck, and kissed her long and lovingly, she felt Mrs. Dorothy's arms close round her with a strength which almost startled her, while a voice, which at first the frightened girl feared must be that of fever, said, 'Charity, my child! my own precious child! you are no nameless orphan—you are as much a Helstone as I am myself. None can ever say my darling is nameless, and has no claim but that of charity on all that will so soon be hers. It is all yours, my child; not from love alone, but in law—by very right—house and property, all that I have, are yours!'

At first Charity could only think that weakness had produced delirium; but scarcely had she raised herself from her aunt's arms, and gazed upon the calm features, the quiet, steady eye, than she felt there was no fever there. 'Aunt Dorothy! dear Aunt Dorothy!' she cried, 'what do you mean?'

And in the same room, and at the same hour, with the shades of evening gathering fast around them, Aunt Dorothy told her another story; not so long as that which she had related two years before, but, to Charity, quite as intensely interesting—or, perhaps, more so. 'And thus you see, my child, you are Charity Helstone. Who shall say that God did not lead your dear young mother here—that He did not summon me from my bed that night to receive her last sigh, and hear her last words—that

He did not, as my eyes fell upon the "C. H." marked upon her soft, white linen, at once suggest the right name to adopt—the right course to pursue? Who shall say that God did not Himself order everything that happened then, and before, and since?'

'He did, Aunt Dorothy! He did!' cried Charity, in much agitation.

'Of course He did!' replied Mrs. Dorothy. 'We talk of God's works being wonderful. They are, indeed! But now we see but a part; in heaven we shall see the whole. Then, Charity, will be the time for full understanding, and for full admiration. Charity, *your* prayer is heard. You have both name and home. My name and home are just as much yours as mine.'

'But oh, Aunt Dorothy! my poor young mother! And my poor, poor, father! Oh, what a world of strange trouble it is!' And Charity laid her head on the bed and sobbed aloud.

'Your dear mother is in heaven, Charity,' said Mrs. Dorothy. 'None who saw her die could ever doubt that. I have always felt that months of sorrow and discipline had doubtless prepared the way for the reception of that "pardon" and that "peace," which evidently came to her so fully in her last moments, and brought such a bright glory over her dying features. Your mother, Charity, is among the redeemed in heaven. There is a text upon her grave which says, "His compassions fail not." Let us cling to that thought when we remember your father. I feel I have a chain of mercy in my hands,

—a chain of rich, providential goodness, wrought by God Himself. There are some links missing still. We shall have them yet; if not now, in heaven.'

'Oh, Aunt Dorothy,' exclaimed Charity, 'I will pray—pray—pray!'

'Yes, my child. I have been doing that a long, long time; and, one by one, the prayers are all coming back in blessings. Now kiss me again, and go away to bed. But before you send Betsy to me, tell her what I have told you. It is due to her that she should know first, what others must know soon, that you are my own. But tell her not to speak to me to-night; for I am weary, and must rest.'

Betsy's excitement knew no bounds. In her first joy of hearing that Charity was no nameless orphan—that, if not 'a fairy princess in disguise,' as little Alice Rhodes, now a girl of sixteen, and a frequent visitor at Ivy Cottage, still persisted in calling her, she was what Betsy considered still better—a real, true-born Helstone. In her joy at hearing this, Betsy for the time forgot that she had *his* blood in her veins, that she was *his* grandchild. She did not realise this fact, happily, until some time afterwards, when Charity had gone away to bed; and then she comforted herself with the reflection that there was not a grain of him, or the like of him, in her—not a look, or a tone, or a turn: which was true.

Who that fair young mother could have been Betsy longed to know. Very lovely she was, as she remembered; and Miss Charity was, no doubt, the image of her in her loveliest days. Ah! it was the way of such as he to choose the fairest flower! She had seen that twice already—one had got the flower, and one hadn't, thank God! And this was the same old story coming up for the third time. Well, she would like to know who the mother was. If Miss Alice were here, she'd say at once that *she* had been the 'fairy princess,' and prove her point that way. As for the father, Betsy's one great desire was that she might never set her eyes on him; that, wherever he might wander, or whatever his fate might be, he might never find his way to Arlington. If Betsy turned *that* desire into a prayer, it was not set to the same key as her young mistress, as she had once said of her own petitions and those of Mrs. Dorothy. For as Betsy framed this wish, and uttered it aloud, according to her fashion, over the kitchen fire, another wish, in direct contradiction to it, was finding its way up to heaven in a long, earnest, almost piteously-pleading prayer, in the room above.

We shall see later which of the two found best acceptance in the ears of Him whose 'compassions fail not'—Betsy's emphatic wish, or Charity's fervent prayer.

CHAPTER XXII.

ONLY three months later, and in that same dear old bedroom of Mrs. Dorothy's, which so many, many events had rendered a place of almost holy interest and love to Charity, a scene was passing which was to set the seal of sacredness firmly and fixedly upon it for ever.

On that same bed where Charity had sobbed forth so many of her passionate, childish sorrows—where she had leant her head to listen to the story of dear Aunt Dorothy's life, and to as much of the story of her own as she or any one else knew—on that same bed that dear Aunt Dorothy now lay dying. Charity repeated the word to herself many times—'dying!' The doctors said so—Aunt Dorothy said so—they all said so. It must be true. Charity knew that it was true, yet she could not realise it, and there was nothing in that scene to help her to do so.

Mrs. Dorothy lay on her pillows as peacefully as though she were but resting from the fatigues of the day, about to take a quiet sleep, from which she would be up again to-morrow. There was no suffering in her face—no indication, even, of a passing pain. But those who knew said that gradually the action of that holy, loving heart, was growing weaker; that slowly, but steadily and very surely, the flame of life was waning fainter: they even said that the end was near, and might be at any moment. Yet, all through the day, one and another came gently into the room and up to the bedside, and there was always strength in the hand for a soft pressure of farewell, and in the voice for a loving word of parting and encouragement, as each and all afterwards gratefully remembered. Even the little boys from the Rectory, as they passed the house on their way back from the Grammar-school, and stole noiselessly into the kitchen by the back-door to ask of Betsy, in whispered voices, how 'Aunt Dorothy' was now, were led by her upstairs into the chamber—a room of death as unlike most rooms of death, as the life of her who lay within had been unlike most lives. Aunt Dorothy knew them all—she called them all by name—had a smile and an appropriate word for each, as one by one the little fellows drew reverently near her bed; then one by one passed from the room, with a strange solemnity upon their childish faces, and treading as though they feared to lay their foot upon the floor, lest even that faint sound should chase away the angels, the rustling of whose wings they fancied they could feel in the air.

Thus hour after hour passed in that long day, and there was no change until the evening, when Mr.

Saville's face told that the end was drawing nearer. For some time he had been watching carefully that dear pulse; and the others, they watched his face, and seeing in its changes the changes that he felt in the hand he held so tenderly, they knew without a word when the great change was drawing closer. All knelt around the bed, while he, still never leaving go the hand in his, commended the soul of that dear one into the hands of Almighty God, as into the hands of its faithful Creator and most merciful Saviour. The faces of most amongst the anxious watchers were hidden from sight—perhaps to hide the tears which all had been restraining until now, but which the first sound of an outspoken word caused to flow.

But Charity knelt upright, and never took her eyes off her aunt's face. How could she, when each look, for all she knew, might be the last in life! The dying gaze her own young mother had fixed upon those same features long years ago, was not more intense than was the gaze of Charity now; her whole soul was in it. She alone, perhaps, marked the earnest expression that passed over the dying face as the prayer was offered, that 'whatsoever defilements the soul might have contracted in the midst of this miserable and naughty world, through the lusts of the flesh or the wiles of Satan, might be completely purged and done away by the washing of the blood of the Immaculate Lamb, that was slain to take away the sins of the world, so that it might be presented pure and without spot before God.' Charity felt, that in that moment Briersley and Roland Helstone were not forgotten. The thought of Edward Saville rose vividly within her own heart, and with all her soul she joined in the concluding words of that solemn prayer.

Scarcely had the sound of the last Amen died out in the quiet room, when Mrs. Dorothy uttered the word 'Charity,' and they saw from the look upon her face that sight was failing. Mr. Saville took Charity's hand and placed it in her godmother's. She herself closed the other upon it, and said,—

'Charity, my treasure, my joy! I am going now to where I shall see it all, and soon we shall both see it together. The time is short at longest. Mine has been a long life, and I feel that now. Soon we shall both know and see all. I do see all now!'

And, indeed, she seemed to do so; for as her eyes closed, such an expression of unearthly rapture fell upon the aged face, that Betsy always afterwards asserted that she knew heaven had opened to her mistress's vision before the soul had fully passed away from earth—an opinion which no one who had seen her die was ever heard to contradict.

A week later, and the dear body was laid in the quiet churchyard, on just such an autumn day as seemed of all days most to accord with Charity's feelings. Never before had Charity been present at a funeral service, and as she followed the remains of her one earthly stay her feelings were beyond tears—almost beyond feeling; it seemed to her as though her heart was too full to be able to feel all that it held: and, almost mechanically, Charity's step kept pace with the other mourners by her side, whilst her very heart seemed beating to the same measured tread, and to have no power to beat to any other movement. Some amidst the many who followed likewise —for all the village had come forth to pay that last token of respect to one known and beloved by all—some amongst them whispered to each other that 'Miss Charity was strangely calm;' others said that 'it was no good sign to see such quiet grief: if the feeling did not make its way out, we all knew how much sorer it pressed within.' Even Betsy felt uncomfortable as she glanced from under her own dark hood, through her own fast-falling tears, at Charity's calm face and steady walk, and said to herself that 'she would rather have seen her sobbing; it was not natural to the child to look like that—there would be an outburst at the grave, she feared.'

But no; for ere they reached the grave a sound fell on Charity's ear, and found its answer in her heart, which was indeed as the rising of the Sun of Righteousness with healing in His wings,—'I am the Resurrection and the Life.' Those words met Charity's desolation when it reached the churchyard-gate, and changed it into life and hope. Once inside the quiet pew, where so often she had knelt by Aunt Dorothy's side, she hid her head and wept soft, soothing tears. Then, standing by the grave, she calmly, happily, thankfully saw the earthly frame, which had so often shivered and shaken under the many shocks of this world's sufferings, lowered for its last, long, quiet sleep, knowing that it would be but a sleep—a sinless, sorrowless sleep; and that at the general resurrection in the last day that corruptible should put on incorruption, and that mortal put on immortality, and death be swallowed up in victory. Charity also heard a voice from heaven, saying unto her, 'Write, Blessed are the dead which die in the Lord from henceforth: Even so, saith the Spirit, for they rest from their labours.'

She and Betsy returned to the dear, desolate home together. They neither of them spoke along the road. But when they had come within the cottage, and Betsy had closed the door, Charity threw her arms around the faithful creature's neck and sobbed like a child.

Just then the bells of Arlington Church broke forth into a peal of joyous ringing. They had been ringing thus all day, at intervals, between the tolling for Aunt Dorothy's funeral. A gay wedding had taken place that morning at St. George's, Hanover Square, and Lord Huntley had sent down word the day before that the bells of Arlington Church should ring all day. There was some thought of letting him know that it was the day fixed for Mrs. Dorothy's funeral, when he himself would have been the first to say his order must not be carried out. But Charity had not wished him to be told. Nor to her that day had there been anything of discord in the changing sounds that fell upon her ears from time to time. The tolling bell sobbed out her earthly mourning for the dear friend whose loss she wept, while her soul joined in the thankful chorus of joyful sound, which seemed to her to be ringing forth in triumphant honour of all that soul had gained in heaven.

That night, when Charity at length laid her weary, aching head upon the pillow, her last thought was not of desolation or of loneliness. Mrs. Dorothy was gone, but such a life as hers had left its record behind it. Through faith and patience—much faith, and long patience—she had inherited the promises. Her work was done, and she rested from her labours. Charity's work remained yet, and it was 'to follow.'

Next morning, when she came down to the home which was now, alas! her own, and only her own, her face was not sad, or her step heavy. For within her heart were the words she had been repeating to herself before she left her room—words which must now be carried out lovingly, patiently, perseveringly throughout her daily life:—

'Then pass, ye mourners, cheerly on,
Through prayer, unto the tomb;
Still, as ye watch life's falling leaf,
Gathering from every loss and grief
Hope of new spring and endless home.

Then cheerly to your work again,
With hearts new braced and set
To run, untired, love's blessed race,
As meet for those *who, face to face,*
Over the grave their Lord have met.'

It was found that Charity was left so well provided for as to be almost rich. She herself had never imagined how comfortable an income Mrs. Dorothy possessed, for even she had never known how much good she did, nor to how many. Benevolent and liberal as Mrs. Dorothy Helstone had been known to be, it was only after her death that the extent of her liberality came to be at all known. Fresh stories of her bounty discovered themselves day by day; one pensioner after another, who had lived upon her purse for years, came to be known, during the next few weeks. Charity no longer wondered how Aunt Dorothy could have managed to spend the income which had now passed into her own hands—feeble hands, indeed, they seemed to be to carry on so good a work; but Charity knew whose strength was to be made perfect in weakness, and never doubted but that God's blessing would be all she needed. Only she did wish sometimes that Aunt Dorothy had lived just a few years longer—just till she was a little older, and better able to walk by herself.

But even this wish had soon altogether ceased, for Mrs. Dorothy had not been sleeping in the churchyard three short months when an event happened which more than told Charity why the good and tender Master, whom her dear aunt served, had removed His faithful servant at that time.

It was evening—Charity's usual time for visiting her godmother's grave, and she had gone to pay her daily visit there; thinking as she did so, that soon she must give up the practice of coming at the same hour when first the dear remains had been laid there, for the evenings were growing too short for her to be out so late. Even now, it was so dark that she almost regretted having declined Betsy's offer to accompany her: for, amongst other remains of childhood, Charity still retained her old dread of the dark; and to this hour, when the objects that met her sight assumed the dim, indistinct outline of twilight, there was always a painful struggle between common sense and imagination before her mind could look upon them as the trees or stones her reason told her they were, rather than as the ghostly creatures her fancy made her feel they might be. Therefore she hastened her steps, as she perceived how very rapidly the night was closing in, and hurried to the churchyard, and to the dear grave, where she would stay but a minute this evening, and which she would not have visited at all but for that extreme unwillingness which all feel to omit for the first time any token of love or loyalty which has been long and regularly rendered.

But Charity's visit to the grave was not to be paid that evening, for as she drew near she perceived that some one was there before her. The tall figure of a man stood between her and the white stone which marked the resting-place of her mother and her godmother, where, till now, she had never seen a living soul; and, startled at the sudden and most unexpected sight, Charity turned and fled. How she reached home she never knew, for her knees were trembling beneath her, and her heart beating violently; and when she came into the kitchen, Betsy, who was never known to let fall anything, frightened at her ghastly appearance, dropped the cup and saucer she was about to place upon the table, as she exclaimed,—

'The Lord have mercy on us, Miss Charity! what *is* the matter now?'

'Oh, nothing, Betsy,' replied Charity, with a faint attempt at a smile, and such pale cheeks and lips that Betsy went to the dresser to pour out some cold water for her young mistress. 'Oh, nothing, Betsy; only I've been so startled.'

'So I see,' said Betsy. 'And who's dared to startle you? I felt uneasy like at your being out so late, though I did think you were as safe outside your house as inside of it in this place, where all know and love you, like as if you were their own. Who's dared to frighten you, my lamb?'

'No one, Betsy; it's my own fault for being so silly: I'm so easily frightened, you know. It seems strange, considering how brave I am about some things, but other things take away my very breath with terror; and when I came to our dear grave to-night, Betsy, I was so startled at seeing a man there!'

'Well,' exclaimed Betsy, 'no doubt it was one of our own working-men—one of them as loved our dear one so well, and had gone to pay his respects to her grave after his day's work!'

'Oh, no, Betsy!' interrupted Charity, 'it was no working-man; it was a gentleman—at least, it was some one dressed in black. I can't say more, for I scarcely caught sight of him before I ran away, being as foolish as I am.'

'Then it was Mr. Saville himself, Miss,' replied Betsy; 'for there 's no other dresses like that on week-days in the whole place. Oh, Miss Charity! they will laugh at you for being afraid of Mr. Saville!'

'Betsy,' said Charity, 'it wasn't Mr. Saville; it was a tall, tall man—some one I 'm sure I never saw before.'

Betsy went to shut and lock the front-door.

'Miss Charity,' she said, on her return, 'it 's my belief you're just mistaken. You 're short-sighted, you know, Miss; and perhaps you were a bit frightened before you got into the churchyard, and I dare say you didn't quite know what you did see: for you know, Miss, it couldn't have been any one but some of our own people—unless, indeed, it was the clerk.'

'No,' Charity said, 'it wasn't the clerk, and it wasn't Mr. Saville.' And having said this, she said very little more on the subject; but all the evening she felt ill and uncomfortable,—'the effects of the shock she had given herself by her own imaginings,' Betsy kept saying, continually, in plain words to herself in the kitchen, and in a rather more modified form to her young mistress in the parlour.

But people are not to be scolded out of their belief, any more than they can be scolded into belief, and when Charity lay down to rest that night she knew very well, that though she was very unfortunately short-sighted, and at times very foolishly imaginative, the tall figure she had seen at her godmother's grave that evening had been neither the creation of her short sight or of her imagination. And Betsy, in spite of the last reasonable words of good advice she had given her mistress, looked carefully to every bolt and bar before she went up to bed, and after lying awake for hours, turning over Charity's strange story in her mind, at length fell asleep with the half-muttered ejaculation,—'The Lord of mercy grant it isn't *he!*'

Early the next morning Betsy appeared within the parlour, where Charity sat quietly reading the morning psalms before breakfast, her face almost as pale now as Charity's had been the night before, and said,—

'Miss Charity, my dear!'

'Well, Betsy, what?' said Charity, at once catching the look of Betsy's face.

'I think, my dear, that what you said last night was true, Miss, and there might have been a gentleman in the churchyard.'

'Yes, Betsy, I know there was. But what makes you say so now? Have you seen him?'

Betsy's knees trembled so violently she could scarcely stand—indeed, she could not stand, and dropped into a seat; but the look upon Charity's face was such, that it would have put words into any one's mouth.

'Yes, Miss, I have! When I went for the milk—Miss—he was coming out of Mrs. Bryce's—he slept there last night, it seems—and he's gone now to the Rectory.'

'Betsy!' said Charity; 'oh, dear Betsy!' and she put both her little trembling hands into her old nurse's; 'was it my father?'

'The dear Lord have mercy upon you, my lamb!' exclaimed the old woman. 'How should I tell? You know, my precious, I never set my eyes on your father.'

'No, Betsy; but you've seen others,' said Charity, imploringly. 'Was there anything to remind you? Was he like——?'

'So like, my dear,' said Betsy, who had learnt now for herself the lesson Mrs. Dorothy used to try so hard to teach her, that the whole truth was the only thing for Charity: 'so like, my darling, that when I set my eyes upon him I should have dropped down where I stood, only that Martha Bryce she held me up. She came along home here with me, and never left till I told her I would come in here to you; and then she said you'd take good care of me, and she could see it was a passing faintness; and she went home, thank God, for we don't want no strangers here, my lamb.'

'Then it is my father!' said Charity, 'and God has heard my prayer. Oh, Betsy! Betsy! he will come here!' And she burst into violent, almost hysterical weeping.

'God have mercy on us all, to be sure!' exclaimed the distracted Betsy, her own faintness proving very passing indeed in her concern for her young mistress, whom she laid upon the sofa whilst she went to fetch some of the medicines, which had not been touched since last she had used them for her mistress, on the day that Mr. Morton had talked with her. As she did so, she looked up and down the street, and reflected with satisfaction that she had locked the door after Mrs. Bryce went out.

Betsy need not have made herself so uneasy. Charity soon recovered her composure, and the first visitor that morning was no one more formidable than Mr. Saville. Betsy had left the whole work of the house that day to the girl Phœbe, who came in for two hours every morning to help, and had done nothing herself but watch her mistress and the windows; without appearing, however, to be watching either one or the other. Charity herself had never once looked out of the window, but had spent the morning in going from one room to another, occasionally locking herself into her own room, but soon coming out again, as Betsy knew, lest she should be uneasy about her; and passing the anxious time by moving constantly about—often, as Betsy did not fail to remark, leaning over the large Bible which stood open on Mrs. Dorothy's dressing-table, and reading from it, with her head—it ached dreadfully, Betsy could see—resting on her hands. At length, Betsy came quietly up to her, and said,—

'Mr. Saville is coming down the street, Miss, quite alone.'

'He's coming to tell us, Betsy,' Charity said, receiving the information as composedly as it was given. 'Show him into the parlour.'

Betsy did so; but first she said to him,—

'Miss Charity 's been very poorly this morning, Sir.'

'Indeed!' said Mr. Saville. 'And what has made her so?'

And Betsy told him all that had passed. He could not reprove her, for he felt that this step, like every other in the course of this strange story, had no doubt been ordered by Him who, knowing that Charity's first tears would be best shed on the faithful breast that had cherished her from childhood, had led Betsy's footsteps that morning to Martha Bryce's cottage, just as the tall stranger was standing at the door, being shown the way to the Rectory.

All Mr. Saville had to tell was soon told, when once he found that the news he brought was known to Charity. He had, indeed, nothing to say himself, but merely came to break the tidings to Charity, and support her with his counsel and sympathy, while she read a letter from Mr. Morton.

That letter, though written by the hand of her dear friend in London, came to Charity from God. It told her how Mr. Helstone, whom they had not seen for so many, many years, had come to them, returned from long journeying in foreign lands, broken in health but renewed in soul; a humbled, contrite penitent. He came to seek the wife whom all those years he had thought to be dwelling in her own father's house, to which he had believed her to have returned when she left him. Having discovered the mistake under which he had laboured so long, he had sought information concerning her from Mr. Morton, or, in the absence of that, he sought for comfort for his own remorseful, sorrow-stricken soul. Both of these Mr. Morton hoped he had found; the hand of our good God, he said, was so manifestly upon the whole matter, that he had no fears but that Charity would receive in rich abundance all the strength and grace she would require under such exciting circumstances, but they hoped she would soon write, as they should be very anxious to hear.

Charity did write soon, and we think we can scarcely close this chapter of her life better than by imagining ourselves in Mr. Morton's study a fortnight later, when, calling his wife to him, he said,—'Listen to this, my dear, and see if God does not, indeed, answer prayer in a way which startles our own souls; because our faith, however strong, being mingled with the workings of our poor weak flesh, we wonder when we find within our hands the very blessings which we had importuned our God to give us. Listen to this letter of Charity's. "I would have written before," she says, "to you and dear Mrs. Morton, but at first I had no strength to do so, no power for anything, but just being with my father and listening to him. I could not, it seemed, even pray. But I am sure I praised God, although perhaps not just in words; for, somehow, when I tried to put my thanksgivings into a form they would mount up, as it were, above my head, so that I could not quite lay hold of them as I should have wished to do, and arrange them as seemed most fitting: but they were always there, I never lost sight of them; and God must have seen them, too. And, oh, dear Mr. Morton, what cause I have for thankfulness! My father is so good to me—so loving and so tender. At times he is very sad, and when I look most like my mother he will turn away his head, and lean against the mantelpiece, and cry so bitterly it almost breaks my heart to see him: but at other times we are happy—very quiet: we both have had so much to make us so; but happy—more really happy, I think, than I have ever been before; so much happier than I ever expected to be after dear Aunt Dorothy's death. The thing most upon my mind now, and what I want you and Mrs. Morton to pray about for me, is, that I shall perhaps have to go away, all by myself, to see my mother's relations. My father tells me he told you about his having met my dear mother first on board the ship where they were fellow-passengers, and how she left her father for his sake, and how he believed she had returned home when she left him, from the note left for him saying she had gone where she knew she would be welcome. Ah, that was to dear Aunt Dorothy! My father says he had never thought of her going there, but he had told my mother about the mysterious lady who had been such a friend to them when they were in America. He thinks she must have read some of Aunt Dorothy's old letters to him when he was a boy, and if so, I don't wonder she found her way to Arlington. Any one in distress would have felt there was a heart waiting with its welcome there. So it was no chance that brought her (and me) to dear Aunt Dorothy. Not that we any of us ever thought it was, only it makes me happy to think that dear mamma meant me to be Aunt Dorothy's child; and though she had no strength to say the words to Aunt Dorothy in her dying hour, God heard the words in her heart, and whispered them into Aunt Dorothy's. But my father never had any other thought than that she had returned to her own home, and had been received there. He went there, you know, first on his return to England; and as you know, my grandfather will not see him: but now he writes that I am to go to him, only that he is never to hear my name—I mean my father's name: but perhaps if I go he will change. God has given us so much, I feel as if He could and would give us everything we pray for, if only we wait His time."'

CHAPTER XXIII.

FIVE quiet, peaceful years passed away, and there had been as few changes at Ivy Cottage as perhaps it is possible for there to be anywhere in this shifting, changing life. It seemed as though all the exciting events in Charity Helstone's life had been fixed for the first chapters of it, and those chapters over, the rest was to flow on in a quiet, even stream of undisturbed peace. Very soon after her father's return there had been one most remarkable change, which was felt as such, not only by Charity herself, but by the whole village; but since then, until now, there had been no change at all. That remarkable event had been the marriage of old Betsy to the miller, which took place shortly after the marriage of his youngest daughter, who up to that time had kept house for him—just six months after Mr. Helstone's return.

How much the latter event had to do with the miller's obtaining Betsy's consent to the union it is perhaps as well not to inquire. Betsy had never been heard to say one word in the village against her young lady's father; indeed, we doubt whether she could have found one word to say, so gentle, so so kind, so truly Christian and considerate, was Mr. Helstone's conduct to all and everybody. But after her marriage she had confessed to the miller—who, man-like, had betrayed her confidence to his daughter—who, woman-like, had circulated it amongst all the neighbours—that 'she didn't believe as ever she would have made such a fool of herself as to marry at her time of life, or to marry at all; but that she had never felt altogether like herself in the house since Mr. Helstone came into it. Not but what he was the best of gentlemen, but that somehow a tall man about the house, with all that black moustache and beard, made it feel queer like. She was used to Mrs. Dorothy and to Miss Charity, but she wasn't used to any one else in the house, and that had gone a long way towards gaining her consent to the miller's request that she should be the second Mrs. Brown.' To her dying day Betsy never alluded to her marriage without making an apology for it, the more public one being always that the 'miller told her all he wanted was some one to keep the place in order, and have a "bit of conversation" when he came in.'

If these were all his requirements, no one could say but that they must have been gratified to his heart's desire, and beyond. Not a house in the village could compare to Betsy's in order and smartness; and morning, noon, and night, we know the 'bit of conversation' can never have been wanting.

Mr. Helstone and Charity were returning one day from visiting Mrs. Dorothy's grave. A perfect garden that grave was, kept by the loving hand of Charity, who looked upon the dust of her who slept beneath, not in the light of decay, but as sacred seed of everlasting life, and treasured it with holy love. Every day she paid her daily visit there, and to-day her father had gone with her. On their return they met the postman, who gave them a letter: for Charity it was, and told her of her grandfather's death — the old, old grandfather, whom she had visited twice every year since her father's return, but who had never consented to see her father, and who would never allow her to be called by the name of Helstone.

Very painful had those visits been to Charity, for the old man dwelt alone, and seemed to have no relations to care for him, or for whom he cared; whether he had loved his own pretty daughter much or not Charity could never discover, but she could not fancy him loving anything very much, his manner was so cold and stern to every one—almost so even to her, though she was, and he said so himself, the image of her mother.

There was a picture of that dear mother in her grandfather's hall, and Charity would stand for hours gazing at it in admiration of its beauty, never imagining that at the same age her own was quite as perfect: not, perhaps, as reflected to her in her glass, but as seen by others, who watched the varying play of her bright countenance and the dancing light of her blue eyes. An old servant still remained at her grandfather's, who had been her mother's nurse before she accompanied her father in the journey to America, from which he never brought her home, and from her Charity heard more concerning her mother than she could ever gather from her taciturn grandfather himself. From her she learnt that this young mother had been an only child. 'Very pretty indeed, she was, and guileless as a baby all her life,' the old woman would say; 'so simple and docile, too, one might have made anything of her, but there was never anything done to teach her and train her: her mother had died when she was a baby, and master he didn't care for children, and felt just what they said most folks did feel when they wanted a boy and got a girl—he took little notice of her at all, and never seemed to care about giving her much education; till at length he went on business to America. He meant, he said, to put her to school on her return; but, as you know, Miss, he came back without her. People said he ought to have had her back and forgiven her, considering how little he had ever done to make the home pleasant to her, and how natural like it was for a poor, pretty young thing like that, to have her heart stolen away out of her. I dare say, Miss, she made sure her papa would forgive her, and have her and her young husband here very soon: but he would never hear her name mentioned. Many letters came but he put them one and all in the fire, and has never alluded to the subject all these years, till he gave me his orders about your coming, and how you were to be received.'

This much Charity gathered from the old nurse, and now that she knew her grandfather, she did not wonder that her father had won away her mother's heart; nor that her mother, in her sorrow and fear, should have sought Aunt Dorothy, but never ventured back to Burfield Hall.

Now, however, it was discovered that Burfield Hall, and the considerable funded property which would have been her mother's, had been left to her—with one condition only, that her father was never to enjoy any portion of it. Should she die unmarried, it might be left to any one she chose except to him.

Within a very few weeks Burfield Hall was sold, Charity never would have left Arlington, unless some strong duty had called her away, and Burfield would have been an unknown and painful home to her. So the place was parted with, and after much thought and prayer, and many consultations on the subject with her dear friends, Mr. Morton and Mr. Saville, it was decided that Charity, since she could no longer, as one of the richest women in that county, or most other counties, live at Ivy Cottage, should purchase the estate of Huntley Tower, which Lord Huntley had for some time been wishing to sell, could he find a purchaser who would carry on the work he had begun amongst the tenantry. He had now a little family growing up around him, and having lately inherited by his brother's death the other family estate, he wished much to part with this one, which he had never made his place of residence since he left it some years before.

So the matter was settled to the satisfaction of all parties. Ivy Cottage was considered by strangers as a lovely lodge belonging to the Huntley Tower estate; such a 'gem of a cottage,' that they really did not wonder the lady of Huntley Tower spent so many hours there with her books, and work, and writing. To Charity it was *home*. She could not write as well, or read as well, or teach her poor people as well, anywhere else. She delighted to make Huntley Tower as delightful a home to her father as she could; he was the superintendent of everything that went on there, and no house in the neighbourhood was more deservedly praised for its perfect keeping and extensive liberality. But to Charity, Ivy Cottage and the churchyard were the most cherished places in Arlington parish.

Not long after this great change in Charity's life another event happened, which, people said, had its effect upon her, judging from her looks, and that was Edward Saville's death. The news came to his parents in a letter from the captain of his ship, and when Mr. Saville brought that letter to her, Charity knew what tidings he had to tell before he spoke a word. His life had been a wild one, and his death was premature; but they trusted there was hope in his end. Mr. Saville read to her his last words, which the captain had repeated for his parents' comfort—words of penitence and hope. Then he paused, but Charity begged him to continue; and seeing that he could not do so, herself took the letter from his hand and read the closing words, which were,—'And give my love to Charity, and tell her I see now it was well we did not marry. I should not have made her happy: men who have lived as I have rarely find happiness in domestic life—perhaps, they have no right to expect it.'

'Mrs. Charity Helstone,' as in time she came to be called, often gave rise to much speculating wonder amongst strangers. That one so rich, and so singularly beautiful, should pass the whole of a long life in quiet bliss amongst the Huntley Tower turrets, seemed very extraordinary to those who, not knowing anything of the beginning of her life, naturally could not understand the end. But to those who had known the beginning, the end seemed very natural, simple, and beautiful. Charity never married, though she had twice so nearly been on the point of doing so. Her mother's prayer had been heard and her mother's words engraven on her heart,—'What God hath set asunder let not man join together.' The union with Lord Huntley would have been a union of hand, in which the heart would have had no share, and, therefore, God had set her and him asunder. The union with Edward would have been one both of hand and heart, but the soul—the immortal soul, must have been set apart, therefore were they two also set asunder by God. And what God had set asunder Charity had not dared to put together.

She was very rich, and never was more good done with wealth. Alice Rhodes declared to the last, that she had always known her dear Charity would turn out to be a 'fairy princess' at the end, and would point to the Huntley Hospital and the Huntley Almshouses, and the lovely new church at Arlington, to prove the truth of her words. Five days out of the seven in every week, and that at the lowest calculation, the 'bit of conversation' in the miller's comfortable cottage turned on the various good works which 'Miss Charity's' liberal hand and heart led her to effect in Arlington parish, and for the good of the dear Arlington people.

How Mr. Morton and Mr. Saville managed to educate and put out in life so many sons and daughters, with so much advantage to their children and so little difficulty to themselves, would, and did, puzzle many who were not acquainted with the secret, that both these clergymen had a good friend in a maiden lady whose name and nature alike were CHARITY!

CPSIA information can be obtained
at www.ICGtesting.com
Printed in the USA
LVHW101936050422
715402LV00003B/70

9 783752 587975